DR. CUBA

A pulp.

By Christopher Paris

ISBN 979-8-9993812-0-0

Chapters

Chapter 1: All Things Are Born

Dr. Cuba liked the smell of gasoline. It reminded him of his childhood in Ancash, his father, and that battered red bus. He relished the smell of gasoline, but the taste of it was bitter. Nevertheless, he downed the entire glass.

Todas las cosas nacen, he thought to himself. *All things are born.*

The ink from yesterday's newspaper headlines had barely dried. *El Mercurio* had reported on the robbery of a large number of gold bars stolen while en route to an official government warehouse in Argentina, and now its ink-stained workers found themselves setting type for a nearly identical story in the paper's home city of Santiago, Chile. It may have been too early to connect the events, but the editors were more than willing to do so anyway.

ROBAN CASI 2,500 KILOGRAMOS DE LINGOTES DE ORO
¿Es el año 1945 una continuación de esta ola de criminalidad??

Just a month earlier, in March of 1945, Chile was fixated less on the nation's tardy entry into World War II and its inevitable declaration of war against Japan and more on the third-place finish of the country in the Americas Cup. Football had, as always, the ability to nudge war and cataclysm onto the second page.

In the absence of either, the theft of 200 gold bars from the Central Bank would have to do. For this week, anyway.

The robbery defied logic. The gold had been stored in a highly secure vault that had been touted as theft-proof. To enter the vault, one would have first to pass a set of bored and underpaid national police guards, then make way through a main building built of concrete walls reinforced with steel bars, and then into one cage of hardened steel bars, through to a second, inner cage with even more bars, until one reached the vault itself. Each cage was sealed by a metal door of increasingly complex design and security, with the vault door being the state-of-the-art for 1945 Latin America. To blast one's way into the central vault, a variety of explosives would have been necessary, with more and more destructive power needed as one reached the center. One of the building's designers had insisted that thieves would have an easier time penetrating the deepest circle of Dante's Inferno than breaking into that vault.

But there had been no explosives used. There was no sign of any force used at all, not a bent hinge nor a pried lock. Everything looked as pristine after the robbery as it had before. The Inferno appeared entirely unmolested.

And yet, 200 gold bars were missing. There were many other items of value in the very same vault, but these were left untouched. Jewels, currency, and even coins had been left behind. Ingots of platinum, of a value far beyond the stolen gold, had been left in their place. Entire caches of silver were likewise ignored.

Only gold.

The next question was just *how* the thieves moved their prize. The gold weighed nearly 5,500 pounds, demanding both time and equipment to move it from the vault to … well, wherever the thieves called home. A train? There were open tracks in the Central Bank's main warehouse, but these were blocked by a disused engine parked immediately outside of the warehouse. To use a rail car, the thieves would have had to carry the gold from the vault through all the inner buildings, with their respective cages and gates, into the railyard, and then somehow get it past the dead engine.

Even with hauling barrows and railcars, the amount of work would have required hours and working in near silence over many days. Yet somehow, the thieves performed the entire operation within a single night, silently, invisibly, and without bending even one hinge or prying a single lock.

The *Mercurio* reporter, Jose Vargas de la Cruz, had uncovered no possible explanations in his brief, but moderately thorough, investigation. He had interviewed a smattering of the Central Bank's employees—at least those he was able to reach before government officials pushed them into a back room away from the press—and received nearly identical accounts from everyone. None of those whom de la Cruz interviewed had seen anything, heard anything, or suspected anything.

"An inside job," *El Mercurio's* editor muttered, scanning de la Cruz's draft. "No other explanation."

"There were at least 50 or 75 people working the day shift," de la Cruz said, with a slight air of defense. "Then, at least 25 night-shift men took over. All the normal procedures were followed." De la Cruz clearly felt his reporting was being challenged.

"Print it," the editor grumbled, shoving the draft back into de la Cruz's hands. Nothing more. De la Cruz understood his boss wasn't questioning him after all; he was just filling the air with his uninformed opinion before yielding to the clock on the wall, which demanded the day's stories be filed within the half hour.

In New York City, the Homunculus walked the streets with an aura of confidence and, one might say, elegance. It wasn't because he was particularly confident or elegant but simply because he lacked a soul and, therefore, did not care at all for the creatures scurrying around him on Fifth Avenue.

He wore a tailored black suit, a crisp white shirt with perfect cuffs, and a fashionable, even modern, bespoke fedora with a shocking red hatband. Black leather gloves snapped tight on each hand. Again, the ensemble would have led anyone to believe the Homunculus was wealthy when, in fact, he had paid for none of it.

The suit was hand-made by an old seamster who had been tied to an oak post in a dilapidated warehouse on Canal Street, copper wires running from his feet and neck to a rusty car battery. Once the suit was made and the fit checked for perfection, a switch was thrown, and the old tailor's career rapidly ended. The elegant shirt, meanwhile, had been crafted by a Chinese tailor, also near Canal Street, who was spared the indignity of electrocution once the last button was affixed; instead, he was thrown into a fire. The hat was made by a relatively young milliner who studied under one of the more famous fashion houses in the city and had a surprising and unfortunate encounter with the front of a train—but only after finishing that lurid red hat band, of course.

It's best not to discuss the gloves at all.

In the end, the Homunculus had filled his closet with an assortment of fine garments, each with a story to tell and each costing him absolutely nothing.

His choice of clothing was neither the product of his upbringing—if you could call it that—nor any particular sense of fashion. It was purely a necessity. If he was to enmesh himself in the fabric of society as his goals required, he would need to dress the part. In that same closet were other types of clothing for other types of needs: mechanic's overalls, a butcher's apron, even a heavy fur-lined coat for use in the Arctic.

The black suit with red-banded fedora was the appropriate dress for today's objective. The Homunculus rounded the corner and entered an opulent restaurant attached to an equally opulent hotel renowned for business travelers of the highest classes. He removed his hat and gloves.

"The name for your reservation, sir?" the maître d' asked, feigning interest. The Homunculus silently noted how the man's face changed to genuine curiosity—if not concern—when he noticed the forefinger of the Homunculus' left hand. The skin was colored a deep, ruby red. If this was some sort of sailor's tattoo, it was unlike anything the maître d' had seen before. The maître d's face oozed suspicions about this strange patron's social status.

"I'm here as a lunch guest for Mr. Leonard Port," the Homunculus said, ignoring the man's poorly disguised disdain; he was used to it. He also knew the name Leonard Port would cut short any lingering doubts as to whether he belonged in this restaurant or not. Port was one of the wealthiest men in New York City and, while no figure of history nor much public renown, maître'd's in opulent restaurants nevertheless knew who he was. Port likely had his own table in most of the city's expensive spots, as he clearly did here.

"Yes," said the maître d', consulting his reservation book. "I see Mr. Port is expecting one for lunch. May I have your name, sir?"

"Mr. Guest," the Homunculus replied. Ridiculous, of course, and no one would have believed the name was real, but it hardly mattered. It matched what Port had given the restaurant's management.

"Please follow me," the maître d' sniffed.

Now, as they walked, the Homunculus noticed the maître d' examining him a bit more closely. For sure, he noticed the pure white skin, with an unnatural smoothness that gave the appearance of literal ivory; if the Homunculus had pores, they were too small to see. For sure, he noticed the coal black hair, neatly styled and recently trimmed. For sure, he noticed the straightness of the nose, the sternness in the eyes. Those eyes, too, were black. In fact, it likely appeared as if the Homunculus had stepped out of a black-and-white film, as the only dashes of color breaking up his stark, monochrome appearance were the red hat band and that single, ruby finger.

They approached a table in the rear, noticeably away from any windows and far from the kitchen, undoubtedly to give Port some intentional privacy for whatever business he might conduct there. Port himself was already seated, drinking a light white wine while fussing over some papers. He was oblivious as the Homunculus approached with the maître d'.

"Mr. Port," announced the maître d', with exaggerated respect, "your guest, um… Mister Guest … has arrived."

Port acknowledged them with a nod. Leonard Port was younger than one might guess from his wealth; about 40, with a stylish suit, stylish short hair, and thin frame. There was more color in his appearance than the Homunculus. Perhaps having a soul did that to a person.

But few might accuse Port of having a soul. He was ruthless in business, uncaring for his workers, and interested in only two things: the profits from his investments and—only rumors, of course— of an enthusiasm for sexual deviance.

The Homunculus was focused on Port's first interest, not his other.

"Please, have a seat," Port said. "I ordered a German white, given the hour."

A look of relief passed over the maître d's face, and he left the two to their privacy.

The Homunculus sat. "Mosel Sahr," he said, glancing at the

wine's label.

"The Germans may be terrible at world conquest," Port replied, "but they can grow a few good grapes now and then."

Port moved the papers to one side, now giving the Homunculus his full attention. "Pardon all this," he said, indicating the papers, "some unexpected and tiresome last-minute wrangling. A birthmark?" Somewhere during that last comment, Port had turned his attention to the Homunculus' red finger. The question was abrupt, but people of Port's wealth rarely had time for courtesy about such things. He was, no doubt, sizing up the man before him.

"Exactly that," the Homunculus responded. "The maître d' likely assumed I was a brawler from the docks, tattooed and such. I daresay he hesitated to bring me back to you."

"Jeffrey is a prude, but he keeps the riffraff out. It's his job, in fact. But he can't tell the difference between a tattoo and a birthmark, unfortunately."

The Homunculus nodded, even as he thought to himself, *It's neither.*

"Your letter intrigued me," Port said, looking into the Homunculus's black eyes. If he saw anything strange in those eyes, Port didn't telegraph it.

"I surmised as such. If it hadn't, you wouldn't have invited me here."

"Correct," said Port, curt to the point of rudeness. "Tell me—why, exactly, do you need private access to one of my largest warehouses in one of the most remote locations in the city? Why must it be empty? A less cautious man would suspect you have something illegal planned for it."

Port certainly was direct. The Homunculus was unshaken, however. Such behavior had little effect on him, no matter how wealthy or powerful the person in front of him might be. More importantly, what Port thought about anything was irrelevant since, in twenty-four hours, he would be dead.

"You are, if I may be blunt, a wealthy man." The Homunculus matched Port's tone. "There isn't any amount of money I can offer you for the use of the warehouse because you don't need the money. And given my admittedly opaque conditions, I can understand if you are wary of the risks."

"Ha! I'm not worried about risks," Port snorted. "Challenging risks directly is how I make my money."

The Homunculus knew Port would fall for this trap. If he challenged Port as a coward, Port's only possible response was to reject the accusation and open himself up further to the deal. Manhood, and all that. "But as I mentioned in my letter, I have something you need that, I believe, will see your way to agreeing to my terms."

Port answered with a raised eyebrow. "I'm curious. What is it that you think I may need?"

"My contacts include men from all levels of society, from those at the highest levels to those that walk beneath their feet. The birthmarked and the tattooed, if you will. My associates in Chinatown alerted me that you were moving large quantities of opium between locations there in an effort to distract ongoing police investigations." The Homunculus paused. Port appeared shaken.

Excellent.

The Homunculus continued. "I am not interested in how or why you are engaged in this business. I have even less interest in reporting such things to the police, who I view with I daresay more contempt than even you might."

If that was intended to relieve Port, it had not.

"I am also wholly disinterested in bribing you, which is an activity I find repulsive. My offer is quite the opposite, one which stands to work in your favor."

"Get to it," Port grunted. His tone had changed, of course.

"I possess a vault of significant size. The building goes nearly entirely unnoticed due to its proximity to a meat packing plant and further benefits from being built below ground. This ensures it is isolated, relatively soundproof, and maintains a cool temperature all year round."

"In Manhattan? How?"

"Not in Manhattan. The vault is located in New Rochelle. One can drive from Midtown to the vault in well under an hour. If you give me access to your warehouse for two days, I will give you the vault. Forever. You can do whatever you want with it, store whatever you want. It would be suitable for both currency and, well, … products."

"Its size?"

"The vault's interior is just under one thousand square feet."

"And you'd give it to me. Permanently?" Port sounded unwilling to believe the offer.

"It no longer serves a purpose for me. I have not used it since before the War, and for me, it has little value. For someone engaged in your business, however, I think it could have value."

"There must be some other angle here."

"I simply have need of your warehouse. The only requirement is that to keep my activities in the warehouse private, you hand me the keys personally. No one else must be involved."

"A huge vault for a tiny warehouse?" Port asked. "This

makes little sense."

"I am more interested in the location of your warehouse rather than its size. Again, I cannot say why, but it is closer to the ocean than New Rochelle, obviously."

"And when do you propose to begin this transaction with me?" Port asked.

"You can have the vault immediately. I have already drawn up the bill of sale for the price of one dollar." The Homunculus withdrew some papers from his breast pocket. "If you sign it, the transfer is complete."

Port took the papers and examined them. His eyes darted quickly over the pages, but the rest of his body remained still. "There is nothing here about using my warehouse," he said. "According to this, you are merely giving me a vault."

"No. That is to keep our arrangement entirely private. I am trusting you, Mr. Port. I believe that you will honor the arrangement."

Port's face finally relaxed, somewhat. The Homunculus knew what he was calculating. Port assumed that the activities planned for the warehouse were far more nefarious than even his opium smuggling operations, so much so that his monochrome guest was willing to make an extreme offer. And likewise, a vault such as that described would have incredible value to Port for reasons not only limited to his Chinatown business.

"I will sign this," Port agreed, pulling a pen from his vest pocket. "But I will need to see the vault before I agree to open my warehouse to you."

"I assumed as much," the Homunculus said politely. "Take a week. Send men to see the vault or visit it yourself. There are three main locks, and the combinations for all of them are listed in that contract. I am sure you will be satisfied. Then, we can arrange a date for you to bring the keys to your warehouse to me. Again, however, I must insist you come alone. No driver, no bodyguard. Alone."

Port signed the contract. "Done," he grunted. It was also his invitation for the Homunculus to leave.

He did.

Inspector Heiner Thumann disembarked the *SS Kerguelen* with some visible stiffness. The nearly monthlong trip across the Atlantic, from Marseille to Buenos Aires, left him not only stiff from a lack of exercise but creaking and wheezing due to extended exposure to sea air.

Thumann was a giant. Standing at six-foot-four, he seemed even larger due to his penchant for wearing a huge overcoat. His face was buried beneath a bushy beard, mustache, and sideburns; it looked like it belonged on currency from some third-world nation fifty years ago. His hands were the size of melons, huge knots like New York City street pretzels but made of solid bone. When he walked, his colleagues said, China reported earthquakes.

Thumann was fat and unhealthy before he boarded the *Kerguelen*. The long journey and the ship's limited menu may have allowed him to shed a few pounds, but it had not made him fit. With little else to do but read and smoke, Thumann arrived in Argentina in worse shape than when he left.

Thumann was a man of the street, not the ocean. His expertise was in solving murders, conspiracies, major crimes. His main places of work were the pavement under his big, clomping feet and his shoddy wooden desk back in the office. For two decades, he worked the dirty alleys and sidewalks of Berlin. When the Nazis took away the only thing that ever mattered to him, he fled to the UK, where he continued his work in dirty alleys and sidewalks, but now the ones in London. There, he was recommended for hire at the prestigious Scotland Yard; Thumann's reputation and references were enough to overcome the Yard's hesitance about hiring a German at this particular time in history.

Thumann already hated the relatively short trip across the English Channel, one he was occasionally forced to make in service of the Yard. Coming by ship to South America to investigate a rash of crimes linked to similar ones plaguing London? No, he felt this voyage was a mistake. But he had his orders.

Next time, they need to send me by aeroplane, Thumann thought. *Damn Scotland Yard's paltry budget.*

Now that he had disembarked, it felt good to be standing on a surface that was not in constant movement. At the bottom of the gangplank, Thumann lit a cigar and waited. His portly frame filled his waistcoat, and his pants and overcoat were filthy from the trip. He smelled of fish guts and diesel fuel, but his nose had stopped picking up the scents about two weeks ago. Others around him were not so lucky; Thumann stank.

He scanned the port for Gentleman, his assistant. Gentleman should have found Thumann's trunk and bags by now, but he was nowhere to be seen. *This might be a two-cigar wait*, he thought to himself.

It was morning in Buenos Aires, and the air was still cool, filled with voices speaking the sing-song Spanish of the region. Thumann spoke only German and English, so he was already at a loss. He had been promised an adequate interpreter, however, a woman named "Hee-main-ah," but she would not be joining them until Thumann and Gentleman reached Chile, still many days away. Until then, he'd have to muddle along in the languages he knew.

Thumann spotted a small restaurant—if one could call it that—across the dock. It was little more than a flimsy shack with a gas burner in the back but had a few rickety chairs and tables outside, no doubt to serve passengers in circumstances such as Thumann's. He crossed the boardwalk, his heavy shoes waking the Chinese beneath him, and lowered himself into what he imagined to be the least rickety of the chairs. For a moment, he felt it might collapse under his weight.

The proprietor emerged, a thin man with sweaty hair and a dirty apron, muttering something in Spanish. In reply, Thumann simply pointed to the coffee pot visible in the back of the kitchen. The thin man nodded and scurried back inside.

As he waited, Thumann scanned the port for Gentleman while running the facts of the case once more through his head. In just over one year, a series of crimes burst across the map of Western Europe. The earliest was a case from March of 1944, where three banks were robbed in France. A massive amount of gold was taken, with no clues left behind. One month later, a high-ranking businessman in Spain killed himself, but only after having deposited his fortune in a secret safe deposit box, which was promptly emptied upon his death. Investigators suspected foul play: someone had induced him to put his wealth into the box and then commit suicide.

And, then, more: in June of that year, two banks and one warehouse were robbed in Germany, while a train in Portugal was also derailed and left without the contents of its high-value cargo. The crimes continued without any apparent pattern: Switzerland, Italy, even Morocco were added to the map.

Now, it was the end of April 1945, and the crimes continued. Thumann had been paying a bit of attention to the various incidents, but—like so many other police detectives around the world—he had failed to notice them as part of a pattern. That is, until they also began occurring in the UK, on Thumann's patch. A wealthy actress in Scotland was murdered, her private safe found empty at the scene. Four banks were robbed in London, and one more in Wales, until finally, Thumann was personally assigned to oversee the crime wave. Thumann now saw patterns.

In each case, no matter where the crimes occurred, the loot taken was nearly always gold. Jewelry was never stolen, nor were other metals, such as silver or platinum. When documents of value were taken, these were somehow tied to gold deposits or other related interests. Paper currency and bonds were ignored.

In each case, the loot was heavy, suggesting a team of robbers were responsible, but without any clues or evidence left behind. The police were baffled. Moving heavy loads of gold would require men, specifically those with the necessary equipment. Confounding the police, there were never any signs of such things.

And, finally, in each case, there were no witnesses. There *should* have been since there were people at the scene in each case. Night guards, tellers, passersby, train conductors… there were always people present at the time of the crime, but later, everyone insisted they had seen nothing. Heard nothing. They did not have even a passing knowledge of what had happened under their very noses. The lesser press gave the criminal various melodramatic names, like "The Ghost" and "The Invisible Devil."

It was Thumann who began to scour the non-English press for similar crimes, thinking the events might be occurring in countries outside of the ones he'd visited during vacation. Thumann ordered copies of newspapers from Northern Africa, the Middle East, and—eventually—South America. Struggling to understand the printed words, Thumann nevertheless realized the crime wave was a global phenomenon. Similar crimes had occurred in the United States as early as 1943 and were spreading across the Americas with lightning speed. Brazil, Argentina, Mexico, Peru, Colombia, Panama… there seemed to be no country that was safe from this Invisible Devil.

An associate of Thumann from Germany, Dr. Brühl, was the man responsible for organizing a global search for the criminals. Brühl was a retired police chief with an impressive military background who had excellent contacts in the halls of multiple governments. Brühl now worked for the International Criminal Police Commission—known to telegraph operators as "Interpol"—and asked representatives from across Europe to put together a task force to investigate the crimes. It was Brühl who recommended Thumann to head it up, and Scotland Yard agreed.

Thus, Thumann now found himself sipping bitter Argentine coffee from a filthy teacup at a rickety wooden table across from a grimy metal ship while listening to local fish sellers shout offers for the day's catch in Spanish at the top of their lungs.

Thumann knew what he'd find in Chile if he ever got there: an empty safe or warehouse or bank vault, with no sign of forced entry and no sign of anyone having removed the contents. And no witnesses.

Only whispers of one name. A name he heard a few times muttered by informants in Edinburgh, by prostitutes in London, by gamblers in Lisbon. By an opium addict in Berlin and by a 12-year-old street thug in Madrid. Always one name.

"Dr. Cuba."

If The Invisible Devil had a name, it was that.

Chapter 2: The Invisible Devil

Henry Chambers was in over his head. He was no criminal, and the entire affair was just an example of how life can go impossibly wrong when a person makes the smallest bad decision.

Henry's smallest bad decision was to agree to a job that he should have known was illegal from the start. When his old school chum Bill told Henry he could solve all his debt problems in one weekend, Henry should have realized—on the spot—that this would end in disaster. Luck rarely schedules its appearances by checking the calendar, and opportunities don't present themselves to desperate men just when they are at their most desperate.

Henry was desperate. So desperate that his common sense was gagged into silence, much like the man tied up in the boot of Henry's car. Henry had not rejected Bill's offer. All he thought of was his crushing debt, his loving fiancée, his hope for a bright future.

And now there was a man tied up in the boot of his car.

Bill was gone, of course. He had panicked and fled when the ringing of police alarms and screaming whistles filled the air, leaving Henry behind. Henry knew that Bill was always a big talker and never one to rely on when things got difficult. But Henry's desperation made it necessary to partner with Bill. And now he would not have to split his earnings with Bill. *Maybe this is better*, he thought.

But Henry was no criminal. He had barely been able to tie up the struggling old man and had a harder time lifting him into the back of the car. For any common thug, this would have been simple manual labor; for Henry, this was an Olympic struggle, each action was slowed by fear and guilt. His desperation pushed him through it, though.

Without Bill to guide him, Henry could only move forward with the few details of the plan he had. He drove the car to the address given to them earlier, where they had been promised payment upon delivering the old man.

It was a part of London that Henry did not recognize. The building sat at the end of a long, thin alleyway, where brick factories stared down, and rusty iron fire escapes creaked in the wind. A single, half-rotted wooden door suggested an entryway; a thick smudge of red paint near the handle confirmed this was the right place.

The alley was too narrow to turn the car around, so Henry allowed his desperation to again grant him Olympic abilities. He opened the boot, ignoring the groaning pleas of the old man, and carried him around to the front of the car, right up to the door with the red smudge.

Inside, he was met with a long hallway that smelled of mold and rot. At the end of that hallway, a single lightbulb dangled from an electrical cord descending through a hole in the ceiling. Under the bulb was a door. Henry resisted the old man's feeble struggles and continued onward.

Through that door, Henry was finally met by someone else—a grim, scarred man chewing on an unlit cigarette. He, too, smelled of mold and rot. He turned to Henry and spoke the words: "Todas las cosas…."

"… Nassen," Henry countered, having no idea what he was saying. Bill had only told him it was the counterphrase.

The scarred man waved them through. "Put the git down there," he said, pointing to a filthy mattress that lay in a corner of the dim room. "Then go through the next door and get paid."

Henry did as he was told. A slight twinge of guilt rose up as he thought he heard the old man sobbing, but his desperation again came to his aid and pushed him forward. He felt as if he were swimming through a viscous liquid; suddenly, everything was taking effort.

Henry entered the final room and found it empty, save for a single chair. Beyond the chair was a curtain. Behind the curtain... well, he was not sure.

Henry sat.

He looked at the curtain and noticed it had holes in it; around each hole, a slight burn mark appeared. Cigarette burns? He could not see through the holes, so he remained ignorant of what might be on the other side of the curtain.

He heard a rustling; someone was on the other side. Henry assumed this was the leader of the gang, or whatever this group might call itself. Henry assumed he was about to be paid.

The voice on the other side was mechanical. Henry at first thought it was a raspy wax recording until he realized it was actually coming through a radio. Whoever was rustling on the other side of the curtain was not speaking but had been merely tuning the radio.

The electronic voice spoke with a slight accent. Henry was not well-traveled, so could not identify the accent. He thought it sounded a bit like the Italian butcher he knew as a child.

"Henry Chambers," the radio voice said. "You have accomplished your task, even after your friend left you for dead."

Henry was startled but remained silent. What did this voice mean, that Bill left him for dead? Bill had just run off. Was "death" somehow in this scenario? Were the stakes that high?

"You now have two choices," the voice continued. "You can accept your pay and leave without electing to take on any additional work from me. Or you can agree to another task and receive double the payment when that is done."

The work he had already agreed to was lucrative but not overwhelming. It was enough to pay his debts, but he'd still struggle to give his fiancée the life she deserved.

But Henry was not a criminal. Already, this was all too much for him. Scurrying the dark, kidnapping an old man, seeing Bill run off like a terrorized squirrel… no, this was not the life for him.

Finally, his desperation receded, and his common sense returned.

"No, sir," he said nervously. "I don't think I'm cut out for this. I will take my payment and leave, sir."

Silence. Had the radio been cut off?

Suddenly, Henry was not sure he had made the right decision. He heard one more rustle right before he heard the gunshot. The bullet tore through the curtain and then through his neck. Henry fell over, gurgling, and continued to gurgle until dead.

There was now one more hole in the curtain. It smoked.

The radio voice returned. "Burn both bodies," it said. "The coward and the old man."

The man behind the curtain answered, "Yes, Dr. Cuba," and switched off the radio.

———————

The Homunculus stood like a lamppost, letting the midnight rain pour down on him. He wore an overcoat and rain hat but had elected to forego an umbrella. If he did not care about murder, he hardly worried about getting wet.

He was waiting outside Port's warehouse. Port was arriving late in order to assert some kind of dominance in the proceedings. If the Homunculus was right, Port was likely sitting in the car around the corner and had even arrived early. Again, none of this mattered. The Homunculus simply wanted Port to personally put the keys to the warehouse in his hand.

The Homunculus knew that Port had already visited the vault in New Rochelle and been pleased with both its size and secretive location. He knew that Port understood the lopsided benefits of this deal, which allowed him to use his warehouse for 48 hours in exchange for permanent ownership of the vault. The Homunculus also knew that Port would not care one whit what his peculiar business partner might be up to inside the warehouse, a lapse in curiosity he was only moments away from regretting.

Finally, Port appeared, umbrella and all. He turned the corner, his shoes slapping the wet pavement as he approached. He was scarcely visible in the dark night rain until he crossed under a nearby streetlight. The Homunculus withdrew his hands from his overcoat to subtly let Port know he had no weapon. Just in case Port was thinking such things.

"Good evening," Port said, with the same casual and confident demeanor he had had when the Homunculus first met him in the restaurant. "The New Rochelle site will be very useful to me."

"I knew as much. Did you bring the keys?"

"Right here." Port pulled a set of keys from his pocket.

"Please," the Homunculus asked, feigning slight incompetence. "Show me which is which and how to enter the property."

"Of course," Port answered.

The two approached the main door, and Port fumbled a bit with the keys until he found the right one for the front lock. As he did, the Homunculus silently scanned the area to reassure himself that no one else was nearby. The warehouse was truly in a part of town that was nearly empty at this time of night.

"Here," Port said, showing the master key. "This blue one opens the front."

The main door opened onto a small inner room with a few dusty desks and chairs that had not been used in years. Port led the way to another door, marked with a sign reading EMPLOYEES ONLY. "The green key opens this one," Port said.

The warehouse interior was damp, but the roof was solid enough that there were no leaks. The rain could be heard pelting the roof above. Overall, the space was massive and completely empty. The only visible details were three or four dozen support pillars lined in neat rows and some dim moonlight coming through a few glazed overhead skylights.

Port closed the inner door.

"Here is the space," Port said. "Large enough to do whatever you may need to."

"Very good," the Homunculus said, reaching into his overcoat and withdrawing a machete. With a single stroke, he cut off Port's head. It hit the cement floor with an echo. Port's body followed, eventually.

The Homunculus turned the body over so that it would have been face up, had it still had a face. He investigated the pockets and found a small billfold. He withdrew one dollar and carefully replaced the billfold into the body's pocket.

The contract for the sale of the vault was now paid in full.

Finally, the Homunculus began his work.

After weeks of feeling like a bull in steerage, Inspector

Thumann suddenly felt like a movie star. Through a combination of luck and influence from the UK government, Thumann was granted a seat on a LAN Chile test flight between Buenos Aires and Santiago in one of the airline's new Douglas DC-3 aeroplanes. Chile was on track to offer commercial flights between the two cities soon but was still working out the kinks in the flight path.

As a result, Thumann and Gentleman—yes, the Inspector finally found his assistant at the docks of Buenos Aires—were the sole two passengers on the bumpy flight to Chile. Thumann had certainly been given a bit of luck but still had no assurances on how he would get back.

The interior of the plane was new. Not luxurious in the way of European or American commercial flights—the plane was a refit, after all—but nevertheless welcoming and comfortable. The noise from the two prop engines on either side was loud but not so strong as to prevent Thumann from discussing the case with his assistant.

Thumann withdrew his pipe from his breast pocket, happy to have been reunited with it, as much as he was with Gentleman since disembarking the *Kerguelen*. It was a modest pipe, apple-shaped, with a slight bend to the stem. Thumann liked the shape because it allowed some of the smoke to fill his thick mustache, letting the scent of the tobacco linger there long after he finished smoking.

He pinched a thick clump of tobacco from a small, felt pouch and shoved it into the pipe. A brisk match strike later, it was lit, and the interior of the DC-3 filled with a rich scent. Whether the pilots minded was not clear, but Gentleman liked the smell.

"We are to be met by the interpreter and a driver named Mujica," Thumann said, mispronouncing the name as "moo-jee-ka."

"Does the driver speak English?" Gentleman asked, with his proper, practiced RP London accent. He was a young man born in a rough part of the country; still, he benefited from an excellent education that helped him succeed in the stuffier stratosphere of Scotland Yard's administrative offices.

"I'm told he does, but of course we will have Fraulein Ximena to assist." Thumann pronounced it "zuh-meen-ah."

"Santiago is the capital," he continued, "but I believe it's not a very complicated city. Not quite like Berlin or London."

Bernard Gentleman was thirty years old, an office "runner" within Scotland Yard, neither quite a police officer nor yet a bureaucrat. Gentleman's future was unclear, but he seemed to be leaning towards the quiet career of a simple office administrator. Whatever his future plans, his eager demeanor and energetic enthusiasm proved a crucial counterpoint to Thumann's lumbering, wheezing deliberateness during official police work. While Thumann might sit for hours contemplating a single detail of a case, Gentleman was scurrying around finding ten more details to hand to his superior for later consideration. This relationship, now in its fifth year, had worked out well for both men.

Meanwhile, Scotland Yard was more than happy to have someone babysit their German import. Given the hostilities between the nations, many within the UK police force still didn't entirely trust Thumann, despite his claims of having fled Germany in protest of the Nazis. Perhaps, many in the Yard thought, Thumann was just saving his skin and would one day reveal his true colors.

Thumann knew his own superiors in Scotland Yard were milking Gentleman for information about him, at least occasionally, and did not care. He had nothing to hide, and worrying about such things was a distraction from his investigation. Gossip was not part of his work.

"Dr. Cuba," Gentleman blurted, clearly trying to start a line of inquiry. "Do we expect the name to appear again?"

Thumann took a long draw on his pipe and allowed the smoke to escape slowly. "I suspect so," he said, exhaling. "We hardly seem able to avoid it."

"But you still think it's not a real person?" Gentleman asked.

"Hmmph," Thumann grunted. "No. Unlikely."

"A myth, then?"

"Not exactly. Sometimes, in these conspiracy cases, the grand conspirator seeks to maintain control by creating a false persona, usually one of menace. I suspect 'Dr. Cuba' is just a fictional character created by the real leaders of this gang to keep the lower-level troops in line."

"And," Gentleman added, "to instill fear in the community."

"That would be an added benefit," Thumann acknowledged, nodding. "It also throws us off the trail. As long as we are looking for an actual person named 'Cuba,' we aren't looking for the real people responsible for this. The real villains could be Smith or Jones or who-knows-what."

"What is your latest working theory, then, on who may be behind this?" Gentleman asked.

"It hasn't changed since we left London. I suspect we are dealing with a group, a cartel. If I had to guess, I suspect we are getting closer, though. I suspect they aren't tied to Sicily or Moscow, but here, in South America."

"Why do you believe that?"

"Delays between crime events," Thumann replied. "The events that occur in Europe always happen at least one month after a similar event in South America. It is as if the actions are being directed from here and take that long for plans in Europe to be enacted."

"Why would this be?"

"Logistics," Thumann snorted, taking another long puff on his pipe. "It takes time for the orders to arrive in Europe, even by telegraph or radio. Then, it takes considerably more time to arrange the necessary resources to pull off those orders. We can assume that the criminals need men and equipment, even if there still remains no sign of such things at the scene afterward. Such resources require planning, payments, bribes, trucks, shipments, movement of goods. An order directed from this continent would easily take a month or two of organization before being executed on another continent."

"Unless, of course," Gentleman countered, "it was the other way around. Perhaps the orders are coming from Europe and being executed here. Perhaps the name 'Cuba' is intended to make you think the leaders come from a Spanish-speaking country to, as you say, throw us off the trail."

"No, I don't think so, Gentleman," Thumann replied, his nose in the air. "'Cuba' isn't even a Spanish word. It comes from any number of other cultures. Some suggest Taino of the Arawak people in the Caribbean. Others say it arose from the old Czech language. So, this isn't demonstrative of much. I suspect it was selected purely to invoke mystery, and perhaps, menace." It was clear Thumann had spent a little time, at least, reading something.

"That's not much," Gentleman poked.

Thumann was not deterred. "In addition, the timing clearly points to events being directed from this side of the world towards the other. If it were the other way around, we would have seen an opposite timing pattern."

"If there's a pattern at all," Gentleman said, poking even further.

Thumann scowled. "You must find a balance between Devil's Advocate," he scolded, "and the Devil himself, my dear Gentleman."

Gentleman knew it was time to let that thread go.

"What, then, will our move be when we arrive in Santiago?" he asked.

"Review the scene of this last crime, assuming there hasn't been a fresher one since we left the UK. It's impossible that there are no clues, no residue. It's simply a matter that the police, to date, have not found them."

"Sir, why do you think that is?" Gentleman asked.

"The police are as susceptible to this 'Dr. Cuba' nonsense as everyone else." Thumann tamped out his pipe. "Many believe they are fighting some supernatural force and have given up applying the science of detection. The rest are simply, regrettably, incompetent."

"And we are?"

"*We* are Thumann. I am neither superstitious nor incompetent."

Despite his confidence, Inspector Heiner Thumann was wrong. Whether he was superstitious or incompetent was irrelevant; he was simply, and wildly, wrong.

Dr. Cuba was very real.

Cuba's name, however, was a fiction.

Carlos Angel Quispe Castellares was born in Ancash, Peru, as far as he could remember. After the accident, everything became a bit muddled. He remembered his father, his father's red bus, the great green farm, the horses and goats, and his mother's baked empanadas. *Never fried*, Dr. Cuba thought. *We weren't savages.*

All other details in between these things were lost, and Dr. Cuba hardly cared.

What he did remember clearly, however, was poverty. That was something no accident could take from him. If anything, poverty was the cause of the accident. If his family had not been so poor, there would have been no trip to the market that day, and he and his parents would have been spared by the aeroplane that crashed down upon them. Everyone would have lived, and Dr. Cuba's memories would be intact.

But likewise, had the aeroplane not exploded that day in the market, killing everyone except the young Quispe Castellares boy, Dr. Cuba would not exist. That young Quispe Castellares boy dedicated himself to understanding how such things could happen, how such things worked, and how circumstance and chance colluded to destroy life at a whim.

And so, he began reading and studying. Physics to understand the gravity that drove the plane into the ground, chemistry to understand the nature of errors in fuel composition, mathematics to understand angles of impact and fields of debris.

But soon, he found that science was not enough. And so, the young Quispe Castellares man discovered the writings of Crowley, Mathers, Regardie, Waite, and the Golden Dawn. Amateurs and charlatans all, pushing Quispe Castellares to seek more ancient truths; *true* truths. If Crowley peddled theatrics, Quispe Castellares sought the myth behind the theatrics and then the facts behind the myth.

And so, at the age of 35, he discovered the Sunken Gods. These creatures, he learned, were not false myths or invented morality tales. These were real beings who roamed the Earth before man even learned to wear the skin of animals. The Sunken Gods were not yet sunken. They shared the world with the proto-humans, terrorizing them as they saw fit, allowing them to breed only in small, controlled pockets, burning and eating them as they pleased.

But after a million years or more, the Sunken Gods found themselves sunk. What happened was unknown, even to the text found by Quispe Castellares, but the event was horrifying, shattering, and of global scale. The Sunken Gods were no more, and Man was left to evolve without their influence or chicanery, becoming creatures of free will and self-destruction.

After years of further study and after adopting a new name and title, the young Quispe Castellares became the young Dr. Cuba. And so, those around him were not aware of his birthplace, his Peruvian parents, or his father and that red bus and green farm. All that remained was the mysterious doctor who relentlessly sought information and, soon enough, vast wealth.

Even his appearance was lost to the years. Now, if anyone had the poor luck or cursed circumstance to encounter Dr. Cuba in the flesh, they would either not know it or not recognize him from any prior encounter. This was because Dr. Cuba had learned how to change his face to alter his appearance, adapting to different identities as needed.

It helped that his natural visage was largely a blank slate, his frame thin and neutral. These attributes allowed Dr. Cuba to alter his appearance with the simplest of tricks. A fake beard and padded waistcoat on Monday might be replaced with thin trousers and a set of brooding black eyebrows on Tuesday.

These parlor tricks worked surprisingly well in simple situations, but it was Dr. Cuba's strange facial anatomy that granted him an unprecedented ability to hide in plain sight. For reasons no physician ever explained—no surviving physician, that is—Dr. Cuba's facial bones were not uniformly attached. Neither was his skull a single, bony mass. Instead, the bones were a mesh of smaller, scale-like structures, overlapping and interlacing; a sort of calcium chainmail. With force, Dr. Cuba could move his cheekbones, spread his jawbone, even raise or lower his nose. He could, to some extent, even alter the very shape of his head. The process was painful, laborious, and difficult. It made horrible cracking sounds and resulted in Dr. Cuba briefly weeping blood from his eyes and ears.

This meant the Dr. Cuba one might see on the street one morning might very well be a strangely different Dr. Cuba at a nightclub only twelve hours later.

For this reason, Dr. Cuba maintained a personal supply of morphine. As The Work proceeded, he found he had more and more need to alter his appearance, which meant more and more need for something to alleviate the pain.

And so now Dr. Cuba—with morphine coursing through him—appeared as a thin, bookish man sporting circular glasses and a wispy mustache. He attracted no attention at all as he walked along the street, being completely forgettable. On this day, Dr. Cuba was Roberto Bosch, a low-level banker on his way to an important meeting in La Paz, Bolivia. He carried a well-worn, thin leather document case in a pair of gloved hands.

Dr. Cuba—Bosch, rather—reached the Diamante del Mar, an upscale seafood restaurant that, in the evenings, boasted a fine reputation for both its menu and its clientele. But it was early morning when Bosch tapped on the glass of the front door, and the menu was neither prepared nor the clientele waiting for tables.

An elderly man came to the door, waving his hand as if to shoo Bosch away. It was too early, he seemed to mutter.

"I am here to meet la Señora Maria Consuelo Vasquez," Bosch said, as Dr. Cuba affected a weak and high-pitched tone to telegraph submissiveness. "She is expecting me."

The old man muttered again and shuffled his way to the back without acknowledging Bosch. Within a minute, he returned, unlocked the door, and waved Bosch in.

Bosch was led into the back office. The office was opulent, even if the building was somewhat small. Clearly, the owner wanted the kitchen and offices in the back, normally hidden from customer view, to be as sophisticated as the dining area and front façade. Bosch smelled onions and did a counting: two cooks chopping in the kitchen, two teenaged assistants polishing silver. With himself, the old man, and the Señora Vasquez, it meant there were seven people in the building.

"Mr. Bosch," the Señora said, welcoming him into her office. She sat behind a heavy oak desk. Within mere seconds, Bosch—Dr. Cuba—noted the likely position of the Señora's safe: behind a medium-sized portrait of some Spanish lord. That painting hung nearly five millimeters further from the plaster than all the other portraits of Spanish lords adorning the wall, suggesting a bulky metal door behind it. He wasn't here for the safe, but it was nice to know where it was in case the future called for it.

Bosch's voice, unlike that of Dr. Cuba, was shaky and timid. "Thank you for meeting with me, Señora Vasquez," Bosch said, bowing nervously. "I will try not to take up too much of your time, as I am sure you must be very busy preparing for tonight's dinner."

"Muy amable," the Señora said, smiling as Bosch sat across from her. "But my staff is capable of handling things without much effort on my part, thankfully. I always have time to manage financial matters."

"Very good," Bosch said, fiddling with his leather document pouch. "I have the necessary papers here." He withdrew a thin stack of documents and passed them across the desk to the Señora.

"With my signature this morning," the Señora said, "my children should have their futures secured, am I correct?"

"Yes, Señora," Bosch answered, adjusting his eyeglasses. The Señora could not know that this was necessary to ensure the spectacles remained in place over a nose that had a very different shape just a few hours earlier. "The mining rights for your property in Potosi will be transferred to your elder son, Juan Carlo, who—upon reaching the age of 25—will take over all ownership and managerial duties for the mines. He will become a very wealthy man, Señora. I hope you are certain he can withstand such responsibilities."

The Señora sniffed, smiling. "Juan Carlo is the smartest of all our family," she said with pride. "He will do well. For now, he is only fifteen, so we have plenty of time to mature him."

"Very good, Señora," Bosch said, sliding the papers toward the Señora. "If you would just sign where indicated at the bottom."

The Señora did just that, still smiling. "I am so grateful your superiors raised this need for a proper, legal document empowering Juan Carlo. I never would have thought of it on my own."

Of course not, Bosch—Cuba—thought. *That's why I arranged it.*

"Everything is now in order, Señora. I will bring this to the law offices immediately and have it safely stored. Please continue to work with Juan Carlo to prepare him."

"I will, and thank you," the Señora said, standing.

Bosch left, taking Señora Maria Consuelo Vasquez's future with him.

The Homunculus did not need Leonard Port; he only needed his warehouse. The fact that Port was a wealthy, upstanding citizen secretly involved in a massive opium smuggling operation was merely a happy circumstance.

Within two weeks of Port's beheading, the warehouse on 110th Street was filled with equipment. Port's body was sunk in the river, while his head was kept for safekeeping.

You never know when you might need these things, the Homunculus thought.

To the army of contracted movers, split up over ten different moving companies and another ten trucking firms, the contents of the various crates and huge pieces of equipment made no sense. Each piece was meaningless on its own, which is what the Homunculus needed to ensure. While the science behind it all was likely beyond what a truck driver and box carrier might comprehend, he opted not to take any chances. His equipment and materials were split into various different shipments to be reassembled by him once they arrived at the warehouse.

The Homunculus had some help, of course. He maintained a small cadre of seven silent, trusted workers to perform physical labor and operate the equipment when it was operational. There were more such helpers in other cities, but never many. Now, his team of seven worked diligently to set up the equipment in this new space, working—as always—in their typical silence.

Their silence was not unexpected since the Homunculus had cut out their tongues. It was the little things that made everything run smoother.

The fact that Port had, at his fingertips, a fleet of ships experienced in operating in secret was an incredible benefit. It was one the Homunculus had not initially thought of using so soon. Still, as news of the great crime wave affecting Europe, Africa, and the South American continent reached him, the Homunculus suddenly realized he'd need a ship sooner rather than later.

The Homunculus needed to confront this matter in person, and a trip to Monito was overdue. A ship solved both these problems. Port may have been dead, but he still had some use.

Leaving the assembly of his machinery to his silent, scurrying seven, the Homunculus turned his attention to one of Port's most trusted operatives: Captain Wu.

Thus, the Homunculus returned to familiar streets in New York's Chinatown, dressed yet again in his black suit, black gloves, black overcoat, and red-striped hat. Normally, he stalked Mott Street or Canal Street in rougher clothes to look less like a lost businessman or tourist. This time, however, he needed to project wealth and authority when dealing with Wu. Wu needed to be intimidated while simultaneously being given respect.

Captain Wu was an important figure within Port's smuggling operation, managing the fleet of ragtag ships used by Port. A former ship captain, Wu now never left solid ground, but instead arranged the routes and dock dates of fifteen vessels within the operation. If Port had been the King, Wu would have been his Royal Admiral.

Wu was also nothing like the myth of the "inscrutable

celestial," as the White press would have Americans believe all Chinese people were. Rather than a mysterious, quiet, menacing "Chinaman," he was boisterous, jovial, and extroverted. Everyone knew Wu, and while they may not have known what he was up to at any given time, they knew it was something illegal. But his demeanor made it hard to dislike Wu, and even beat cops would go out of their way to greet him warmly on the street, perhaps to win an invitation to one of the restaurants in Wu's quarter or simply to hear one of Wu's terribly obscene jokes.

It was only partly an expression of his nature, of course. Wu used this sunny presentation as a means of hiding the true dark nature of his work and to obscure the full reach of his influence. Certainly, Wu had a few farms in upstate New York filled with the bodies of those who crossed him—or Port—and just as many corpses embedded in concrete or brick walls around the city. But while Wu was regaling folks with a story about two nuns lost in a brothel run by a lisping Jew, a few would stop wondering about those farms and brick walls and just let Wu be Wu.

Not everyone fell for his trick, but enough did to alleviate some of the pressure on Wu.

On the day when the Homunculus approached his headquarters on Canal Street, Wu was still not quite within the sights of the New York Police Department. While he was a murderer and smuggler, for sure, Wu had not yet grown to the power and influence of, say, a Sicilian mobster. And the NYPD had to triage their resources to focus on the real problems. For now, Wu had not yet earned a spot on the police's list of major criminals.

The Homunculus entered the trinket shop and walked past the display cases filled with low-quality Chinese tchotchkes and under the lines of flickering, red-and-gold Chinese lamps hanging overhead. If anyone thought he was a tourist, his disinterest in these souvenirs would quickly force them to rethink things.

"Mr. Wu," he said to the young Chinese man behind the counter. The Homunculus made no effort to hide his intention.

"There is no Wu here," the man said with a heavy accent. He was lying.

The Homunculus withdrew the contract for the warehouse with Port's signature. "I represent Mr. Port. I have urgent private matters with Mr. Wu. I am unarmed."

Surprised by the Homunculus' candor, the young man looked around the shop, verifying that they were alone. No tourists, no shop patrons. All clear.

The man checked the contract. "Please come back," he said.

The Homunculus walked around the glass counter and followed the young man into the back of the shop. The air was filled with the scent of fried peanut oil; someone somewhere was preparing lunch. They passed a number of small offices and storage rooms until the young Chinese man stopped.

"Wait here," he said and moved forward into an office at the end of the hall.

It did not take long.

"Come in," the young man said.

The Homunculus entered the office and was surprised to find Wu sitting behind a desk without any guards or additional security. Wu was smoking a cigar and fiddling with some playing cards.

No, not playing cards. As the Homunculus approached, he saw what they were: Tarot cards.

Wu smiled and belched. "They said to let you in," he rasped. His voice was hoarse, probably from too many years of too many cigars.

The Homunculus remained silent.

"The cards, I mean," Wu said. "They said I should speak to you. I don't do much these days without consulting them. I bought these from an old man in Greenwich Village because I liked the artwork on them." He held up the Three of Cups. "Soon, I got hooked."

"You manage risk differently," the Homunculus said matter-of-factly.

"You're wondering why I don't have bodyguards like Port," Wu said, grinning. "I don't need them."

The Homunculus scanned the room. There were no weapons in sight, but surely Wu had one close by. Under the desk, probably. He might even have been standing over some rudimentary trap-door to a basement pit.

"I'm sure you do not," the Homunculus agreed politely.

"Let me tell you a joke," Wu said. "My jokes are famous, you know!"

The Homunculus raised a gloved hand, but only slightly. It was partly to pause Wu but also to show he had no weapon.

"Unfortunately, I have no sense of humor, Mr. Wu," he said, once again matter-of-factly.

"Everyone has a sense of humor," Wu said.

"I," said the Homunculus, "do not. Some say I was born defective in this manner. I don't understand jokes and certainly never laugh at them. While I can recognize and interpret social cues, I can only mimic them, not express them with any genuineness. You see, I feel nothing. I feign courtesy and manners, but I don't understand their necessity. Some have said I have no soul. Do you think I have no soul, Mr. Wu?"

Wu was taken aback, if only for the briefest moment. By asking Wu a question, the Homunculus had shifted the dynamic between them. The Homunculus was not actually interested in an answer; he was asserting dominance. This was a tactic that would be immediately recognized by a seasoned pirate like Wu. How Wu would react in the next few seconds would determine if the Homunculus would be successful today.

Wu remained silent. His face was suddenly expressionless, his smile and jovial warmth gone. His jokes would not work today.

"Let's allow the cards to decide," he said, shuffling his Tarot deck. He put the deck down on the flimsy wooden desk with a thump. "Please take the top card," he said.

The Homunculus approached and removed his left glove. The red forefinger was now visible. Again, he was asserting dominance by forcing Wu to be curious about that finger. Once again, the Homunculus knew something Wu did not. Wu remained aloof, but his brain was no doubt mulling over this strange mark.

The Homunculus drew the top card and flipped it over.

"The Hanged Man," Wu said.

Both remained silent for a considerable amount of time. The Homunculus knew exactly what the card represented, and so did Wu.

Wu did not discuss the card further. "What does Mr. Port want of me?" he asked. His smile had not returned yet.

"Mr. Port has, as you can see in this contract, given me control of the warehouse on 110th Street."

"I see that," Wu agreed.

"We have moved equipment into the warehouse, but some of it needs to be brought overseas. Mr. Port tells me you have ships that can operate more or less undetected by the authorities and that your ships have hidden holds in case of boarding."

"Of course, Mr. Port knows this," Wu acknowledged. "And perhaps Mr. Port knows you. But *I* do not know you. I would need to hear from Mr. Port to let you board one of my ships."

As expected, the Homunculus thought.

"I will not be boarding. We need only ship one small piece of equipment. A single crate, approximately seven by four by four feet in dimensions. The weight will be roughly 250 pounds, including the crate and packing materials."

"Sounds like a coffin," said Wu. Perhaps Wu was smarter than the Homunculus had guessed.

"Only equipment," the Homunculus countered. "And nothing perishable. It can be stored in your lowest hold and requires no effort from your men. Simply load it and, upon arrival, unload it."

"Where is this box going to?" Wu asked.

"London," the Homunculus answered, lying. "But any port in the United Kingdom will do. Our associates there will arrange pickup and truck the equipment to their final installation site."

Wu fell silent, thinking yet again.

"We have a ship named the *Eustis* that is headed to that part of the world next week. It's a smaller vessel, overdue for decommissioning, likely to sink if anyone sneezes too hard. I can't guarantee the condition of the crate upon arrival."

"We will be sure to package it properly," the Homunculus said. "But any sea voyage is, by its nature, a risk. Mr. Port and I understand that. The contents are not entirely irreplaceable."

"How do I know Mr. Port is authorizing this?" Wu asked. "You come here with only a piece of paper bearing Mr. Port's signature. I have no idea how you obtained that."

"I am also authorized to tell you that Mr. Port has arranged a meeting of the captains in nine days to be held at his office in The Bronx. He will be going over some minor changes in the overall operation, including sources of supply for the opium."

By mentioning the opium out loud, the Homunculus further gained Wu's attention. "You can verify the shipment of the equipment with him then," the Homunculus added, "in person."

"The ship leaves next week. This meeting will happen a few days after that. Your equipment will have left port by then," Wu said.

"True. But if, after the captains' meeting, you do not have Mr. Port's verification, you may radio the captain of the *Eustis* and have the crate thrown overboard. You will have lost nothing."

Wu fell silent one last time. Few knew of his relationship to Port, and fewer still of the opium operation. The signature on the contract did match that of Port; Wu had seen it many times. There seemed to be little reason to doubt this arrangement and little risk to Wu himself.

"Very well," Wu said, standing. "Contact Captain Beavin at our docks on the morning of this coming Monday. I won't tell you where those docks are, as I am sure Mr. Port can tell you himself."

This was Wu's last effort, however minuscule, to add some level of security to the arrangement. The Homunculus was not deterred since finding out where Port's docks were would only require a few more trips around town, a few more interrogations, and possibly a few more beheadings. The information would be easy to obtain.

"Very good, Mr. Wu," the Homunculus said, putting his glove back on. "I'll leave you to your day."

When the Homunculus was gone, Wu again looked down

at his desk and the card staring back at him.

Chapter 3: The Hanged Man

"People are moving behind the scenes," Thumann told Gentleman. "You can feel it. People moving. Things moving. Plans unfolding. Things we see, but things we don't see. A very busy silence."

Gentleman was no intellectual and was not entirely sure what his superior was referring to, so he kept his ignorance to himself.

The two men had settled into a temporary office in Santiago. It was surprisingly well-appointed, with fine wooden desks, cabinets, and shelves for books and notes. It had two working phones and electric fans to push away the Chilean heat. Best of all, it had a discrete liquor cabinet under the desk, which Thumann had already stocked with a few bottles of imported—but cheap—Scotch.

The office was apparently the former headquarters of some political party leader but then abandoned when the party was made illegal overnight. Such things happened all the time in South America and Thumann was simply glad that he could benefit from the poor party goon's misfortune, at least.

"Forces coming together," Thumann continued, sitting back in the heavy leather chair and lighting his pipe. The room filled with the forest Thumann's favorite tobacco, a potent Latakia blend that smelled like the entire Amazon rainforest had been set on fire. "You and I are some of those forces, Gentleman," he mused. "We can only hope no one else has realized that yet."

Despite his air of confidence, these musings meant Thumann was stuck and awaiting a break. When he had clues, he had little time for debating the influence of invisible forces. But clues would come soon enough, as they always did; Thumann was not too worried.

In a few moments, they would be joined by the translator, along with representatives of the Chilean police force. They would be taken to the scene of the most recent robbery in Chile for a full examination of the evidence.

Thumann was, however, frustrated that this was not the most recent robbery on the globe. Since the theft of the gold bars from the Central Bank, there had been at least ten other such thefts on the South American continent itself. Heists in Lima, Caracas, Barranquilla, and more. Back in Europe, a shipment of gold had been diverted to parts unknown before it was able to dock in Croatia, its cargo hold emptied. And so it continued.

Thumann knew he was already many steps behind, and this irritated him. Thank God for Latakia and Scotch.

"Inspector Thumann?" a voice at the door asked. Standing in the doorway were two men and one woman—Zuh-mee-nah, for sure—each with a serious look set on their faces.

Thumann stood. "Yes, I am Inspector Thumann." He strode around the thick desk to greet them.

The man with the most medals on his jacket spoke. "I am Director Mateo Frederico Aves, of the Policía de Investigaciones de Chile, and this is Commander Osvaldo Micco de la Costa of the Carabineros de Chile. The young woman here is Ximena Alejandra Torres Orellana."

They have so many names, Thumann thought to himself. *I'll never remember any of this.*

"La Señorita Ximena will be translating for you as needed, but my compatriot and I do speak English."

Hee-may-nah, Thumann thought. *That's not how I have been pronouncing it. Another thing I'll likely forget.*

Ximena was surprisingly young, perhaps only 25, and had a look that darted between mild fear and mock gravitas. It was clear to Thumann that she was trying her best to be professional but was silently terrified. Thumann knew immediately that this young woman was in over her head.

The two Chilean police representatives were the typical South American officials with important-looking hats and sharp uniforms, but none of which fit particularly well and most likely belonged to each's predecessor. Thumann only hoped they had taken the uniforms before their predecessors died, not after. Both men gave off an air of complete and unyielding bureaucratic incompetence, further lowering Thumann's expectations.

"I am very pleased to meet all of you," Thumann said, hiding his disappointment. "This is my assistant, Mr. Bernard Gentleman. He has my full trust in this case. He will be accompanying me throughout."

Everyone exchanged the necessary handshakes and head-nods. Thumann extinguished his pipe, shoved it into his vest pocket, and announced, "Now let us go see this crime scene."

With that single grunt, Thumann was suddenly in command of this investigation, if only because no one else was authoritative enough to say otherwise.

———————————

Derek Fell understood the routine. He would enter the room, sit in the lone chair, and wait for a voice on the other side of the curtain to address him. If this took minutes, he would be lucky; a month ago, Fell waited two hours to hear that crackling, familiar voice.

Fell also knew, simply from listening well, that the voice belonged to someone on a radio. This explained the need to wait.

Dr. Cuba—if it even was Dr. Cuba on the other side of the radio—would only address someone when he, himself, was situated at the transmitting station. How could he even know if Fell was waiting?

At the thought, Fell laughed at himself. Dr. Cuba knew everything; to think otherwise was foolish. Many in the underground believed Dr. Cuba to be supernatural, a devil with a thousand eyes in a thousand windows on a thousand street corners. Fell was not superstitious and knew what was more likely was that Dr. Cuba's "thousand eyes" were actually his secret horde of informants, street thugs, and criminals, all working for whatever greater plan the Doctor may have. If Dr. Cuba knew Fell was waiting for him on the other side of that curtain, it was because someone told him this.

Fell also understood the curtain and its holes. It did not take a seasoned criminal mastermind to know that those were bullet holes and that if he ever said something wrong or expressed the slightest doubt, a new hole would be created in both the curtain and his forehead. Fell knew a man stood on the other side, operating both the radio and the rifle. Fell was not an idiot.

And so, he waited.

This time, only for 15 minutes. Luck.

"Derek Fell," the voice said, crackling to life. Fell could smell the dust burning off the radio's vacuum tubes. "Report."

"The German inspector has arrived in Santiago, Chile," Fell said, maintaining a respectful but abrupt tone. Dr. Cuba wanted facts, nothing more. "He was not sent to the States as originally planned."

Silence. Dr. Cuba wanted more; Fell realized he was reporting something the Doctor already knew.

"He's accompanied by two national police agents and a

Spanish translator. He has also brought an assistant from Scotland Yard with him. He is months late investigating the job in Santiago, but his reputation suggests he must be taken seriously. This inspector previously solved complex cases in the UK involving both financial crimes and murders. On the outside, he appears incompetent and perhaps even a little buffoonish. He's not. He must be taken seriously."

More silence. Fell summoned up more information still.

"The inspector cannot be bribed, nor can he be easily blackmailed. His wife died in Germany years ago, and he has no children. He drinks, but not enough to weaken his attention. He gambles, but not enough to put him in debt. His politics are traditional European, but he abhors the Nazis and has thrown his lot in with the Allies. His health, however, is poor. He is moderately obese, with a poor heart and lungs."

Silence, but then: "The assistant," the voice said. It was a question, but not framed as one. Fell simply understood the intent.

"A timid office clerk named Gentleman. He seems to be of little concern," Fell said.

"Wrong," the radio said. Fell snapped to attention. Would a new hole be added to that curtain?

"Sir?" he asked.

"Pursue the assistant. That is the path forward. Pursue the assistant."

Fell exhaled, at least knowing he'd survive this encounter. Being given an order meant he would be leaving with this brain intact.

"Yes, sir. I will report back next week."

The radio fell silent.

Dr. Cuba did not set the fire that burned the Bolivian villa of the Señora Maria Consuelo Vasquez to the ground, with her and her staff still inside.

Of course not. Dr. Cuba had a vast army of people to do that for him, each paid handsomely with cash derived from some of the sale of just a tiny portion of the gold he now amassed.

It was not as if Dr. Cuba could not do such things; he had no delicate constitution nor fear of proximity to a crime scene. It was simply that he was far too busy coordinating other aspects of his empire—all while preparing The Work—and needed to rely on his army of brutes and spies. He was, after all, just one man.

And now Señora Maria Consuelo Vasquez was very much dead, even if the press had not yet learned of it. That would come soon, so Dr. Cuba had to act quickly.

Within a makeshift, temporary headquarters in La Paz, Dr. Cuba turned off the radio, the thick metal switch making a loud snap as he did. The radio's tubes dimmed. Derek Fell had proved useful; Inspector Thumann was now in Santiago, where he needed to be, and not wandering the streets of Chicago or San Francisco, where Dr. Cuba might have a harder time tracking him. Two well-placed telegrams and a cheap bribe had altered Thumann's course. *Cheap investments*, he thought.

But Fell had only confirmed facts about Thumann that Dr. Cuba already knew from his contacts within Santiago. What Dr. Cuba had not known, until Fell told him, was that Thumann's ever-present shadow in England—Bernard Gentleman—was now his ever-present shadow in Chile. Given Thumann's well-known reputation for being entirely without sentiment and driven nearly to drink over his obsession with work, his attachment to his weak, sniffling assistant seemed strange. Most in Scotland Yard simply thought Thumann appreciated Gentleman's efficiency at managing mind-numbing minutia.

Dr. Cuba suspected something else. But he needed more information and so expected Derek Fell to deliver it. If not, well, curtains can be replaced.

Moving to another room, one fitted with a mirror and makeup kits set on a flimsy wooden table, Dr. Cuba prepared himself for manipulation. He sat at the table and opened a small cedar box. Inside was a vial of morphine and a clean hypodermic. He prepared his dose and injected it.

He could not wait for the effects to take hold and put the cedar box aside. He adjusted the mirror and saw the weak face of Robert Bosch still staring back at him. He removed the fake beard, mustache, eyebrows, and wig. Then he raised his hands to his face.

Slowly, over the course of the next half-hour, Dr. Cuba shifted and crushed his features. In place of Bosch's weak chin, an even weaker chin emerged, but with a prominent central dimple. In place of Bosch's tall head, a shorter, more roundish shape took form. With crunches and pops, soon his eyebrows were less prominent, making his eyes appear set more forward. His ears were pulled back, his nose shortened.

Blood oozed from his eyes and ears. The morphine was not helping, so Dr. Cuba moved his attention to the passing of seconds. Not on seconds, no: on the space *between* seconds. This was a technique he had learned years ago from some long-since-dead shaman, allowing Dr. Cuba to bypass the pain and let it flow over him as he moved his consciousness to some other plane of being. By applying his focus thus, Dr. Cuba was able to complete the manipulation without the dulling effects of morphine fully in play.

His face arranged, Dr. Cuba then reached into a box with

more traditional elements: fake wigs, beards, and eyebrows. He chose a youthful, thick head of hair, dense but cropped eyebrows, and no facial hair at all.

When done, Robert Bosch was gone, replaced by a young man in his mid-20s. He dabbed away the drops of blood. Bringing his conscious mind back to real-time, he was greeted with a throb of pain pulsing through his skull.

He stood and moved to a large trunk. Opening it, Dr. Cuba saw a small assortment of clothing. He opted for a business suit in the style of the day, which was popular among young professionals in La Paz. Donning this, the conversion was now complete, except for the necessary paperwork. This was South America, so of course, there would be paperwork.

Dr. Cuba exited the room and returned to where the radio sat. He reached into a small drawer beneath the radio and pulled out an envelope. Inside were documents—a national identity card, passport, and assorted contracts and correspondence—left for him by his team of forgers. Each was expertly crafted, as would be expected for the amount of gold Dr. Cuba had paid his team.

He placed the identity card and passport in his breast pocket and the rest inside a small briefcase. As the first effects of the morphine finally settled in, Dr. Cuba—no, Juan Carlo Moreno Vasquez—left the building and hailed a cab.

Todas las cosas nacen.

———————————

The *Eustis* was a simple ship, technically registered to an owner in the Philippines but actually within the control of Leonard Port's smugglers. Its captain was a drunken Welshman named Beavin who, the Homunculus had learned, was wildly uncaring of his crew but fiercely loyal to Port. As a result, Beavin was more than accommodating when he realized that Port, himself, had authorized the cargo now being presented to him.

The Homunculus oversaw the loading of the crate but did not interfere. His role now was simply as an observer, and he did not want to raise any suspicion by appearing anything more than that. He knew Wu did not trust him, but he had a week at sea to wait before Wu found out that Port was dead and, thus, likely to start questioning this entire arrangement. The Homunculus knew that in a week, barring any unusual circumstance, Beavin would receive a radio message exposing the trickery and order the crate to be thrown overboard.

Fortunately, the Homunculus had planned some unusual circumstances. For now, however, he was protected by Wu's instructions to allow the loading of the crate and by Port's signature on the warehouse contract. So, he silently watched as an overhead hoist lifted the crate from the dock, raised it over the main deck, and then lowered it through the cargo hold doors.

Beavin, standing on the main deck, waved the Homunculus to come up.

The Homunculus strode up the plank, hoping no one would notice how much it bent under his unlikely weight. He reached Beavin at the top.

"She's all loaded," Beavin said. He did not sound drunk, but he smelled it.

"Very good," the Homunculus said. "If possible, I'd like to check its position in the hold."

If Wu was carefully suspicious, Beavin was idiotically trusting. "Sure, mate. Follow me." He escorted the Homunculus over the deck to the cargo hold stairway, and the two descended. Some parts of the ship smelled like rotting fish and burnt engine oil, while others like burned fish and rotting engine oil. Suddenly, the Homunculus was not sure the vessel would survive the trip, given its disrepair. *Some things,* he thought, *are best left for Fate.*

The lower deck smelled worse. If the *Eustis* had a cargo, it must have rotted weeks ago. This made no sense until Beavin—sensing his client's thoughts—explained. "We carry rotten fish to keep inspectors from lookin' too closely," Beavin said. "If they board us, they disembark right quick when they get a whiff. The crew is used to it, don't worry none about 'em."

"Very smart," the Homunculus said. Perhaps Beavin was not an idiot after all.

"It's also why so many of my men are single," Beavin laughed. "No woman will go near 'em."

"I see," the Homunculus said. He noticed his crate, placed surprisingly gently in a corner.

"There she is," Beavin said.

"That's a fine spot, yes," the Homunculus noted. "Away from your operations, and it shouldn't give you any trouble."

"It was much lighter than we were told," Beavin said. "You sure you packed it? We thought it was empty."

"Yes," the Homunculus replied. "It's fine."

"Well," Beavin said, rubbing his filthy hands together, "I hope you'll give a report to Mr. Port and Captain Wu about the old *Eustis* here."

"And her captain," the Homunculus added, knowing full well where Beavin was headed with this. He was seeking a promotion.

Such a thing was unlikely to happen, given the fate awaiting the old drunk.

The two went back up the stairs to fresh air on the deck and then back down the plank. It was odd that Beavin followed the Homunculus off the ship, as surely he had other captainly duties to attend to. It was not that he wanted to be sure this stranger left the ship; no, he wanted to give his client a white-glove treatment.

"I'll be on my way," the Homunculus said, shaking Beavin's hand. "I thank you for your kind service today."

"No worries," Beavin said, smiling again while exhaling. Rum, and a lot of it. "We'll be in port in the UK in two weeks. Maybe more if we have to dodge some flagged ships out there."

"I understand. Do your best, Captain."

The Homunculus left Beavin, who returned to the ship and began barking orders at his crew. But the Homunculus did not leave the port.

Instead, he walked through a long set of dockside market stalls, most selling fish but some selling ship hardware and tools. He continued until he felt he was far enough away so that anyone on board the *Eustis* would be sure he had left.

Then, finding a discreet spot on the boardwalk, the Homunculus shed his black overcoat, boots, and hat and quietly slipped into the water. The *Eustis* was far back at port, but the Homunculus began swimming, nevertheless. Within 15 minutes, he reached the *Eustis* without even being short of breath.

He came alongside the ship but on the side opposite the dock so that no one could see him from land. Fortunately, the waters were calm, and there were no significant waves to give him any concern. Treading water, the Homunculus shed his gloves and pressed his hands into the side of the *Eustis*. Then, with uncommon strength, he flexed the fingers on each hand until he quietly crunched the steel of the ship's side. Just ten small dents, enough to create a handhold with which he could pull himself up.

And so, he continued, ascending the side of the *Eustis* by sheer force, creating handholds with each reach, pulling himself ever more upward as if the ship's powerful steel cladding were simply thick-ply cardboard. Upon reaching the deck, he scanned the area for nearby crew and, seeing none, swung himself over the rail. Silently, avoiding detection, he made his way to the cargo hold stairs, downward following the same path Beavin had shown him, and into the rank shadows of the hold itself.

The Homunculus, still undetected, found his crate once again, used those same hands to pry open the lid, and climbed inside. In the darkness of the crate, he felt for the latch that had been already built inside it and slid it into position. Now, the crate would remain shut even after the Homunculus had pried it open.

He then settled himself in position for the trip, stopped his heart from beating, and fell asleep.

Inspector Thumann and his entourage arrived at the Central Bank. Any disappointment he already felt due to the oozing smugness of his incompetent Chilean police handlers was tripled when Thumann realized that he had arrived far, far too late. The crime scene was not only contaminated but it had also been completely wiped clean and restored to its everyday state. Now, Central Bank employees and security guards had resumed their regular duties and had been trampling over every bit of evidence daily... for weeks.

Examining the scene for the usual aspects—fingerprints, discarded cigarette butts, blood—would be useless here. Thumann knew not to waste too much of his time on the basics; instead, he'd have to rely on whatever information he could glean from witnesses.

But, as the official account said, there were no witnesses.

Thumann did not believe this, however. *Horseshit*, he thought.

Thumann and Gentleman found a small, unused office within the bowels of the Central Bank and set up camp there. Thumann had been able to convince the two police officials to give him privacy during his interviews, mainly because his Germanic tone granted him nearly supernatural powers over their weak, bureaucratic mindsets. If he commanded a thing, they did the thing.

Slugs, he thought. *This is how Hitler won power.*

Now, only Thumann, Gentleman, and the nervous translator Ximena remained.

"He's suggesting we start in the main strong-room," Ximena said.

"What?" Thumann asked, snapping his attention back to the present.

"The bank director," Ximena replied. "He says we should start there."

Thumann was distracted. The unintelligible noise of people uttering a language he did not understand had muted his ears to details. By tuning out what people were saying, he was losing crucial information. He would not do that again.

"Right," he said, nodding. "But no."

"I'm sorry?" Ximena asked, confused.

"We won't start in the strong-room. We will start at the rail entry."

Thumann knew the thieves had used the rail system to escape with the gold. He was not exactly sure how, but he knew that was the only way out. He'd start at the end, then, and move backward.

Ximena translated Thumann's request for the bank guards, who shrugged and slumped off towards the railway entry doors. Whether Thumann followed or not, they did not much care.

The rails terminated inside a large room, looping around in a lazy, wide arc that allowed whatever train cars might enter to be loaded and then to continue on, re-entering the track so they could then be connected to an engine left parked outside. Thumann paused, thinking.

"Ask them for a rail map," Thumann told Ximena. "I need to see where these rails go."

Ximena obliged, and one of the guards ran off to fetch the maps.

Thumann began talking directly to the remaining guards, trusting Ximena to translate as he did. "The train engine outside, you say it has been there for some time and wasn't moved?"

"That's correct," one of the guards answered, speaking in Spanish. Ximena dutifully kept pace, translating for Thumann. "It's blocking the way out, so they could not have used the rails to take out the gold."

Thumann could see outside the building, and it did appear that grass and weeds had started to grow around the engine. It did not appear freshly moved.

They must have used that rail, Thumann thought. *But how did they get around the dead engine?*

He knelt, with some difficulty, given his paunch and poor knees. His waistcoat strained at the buttons. Thumann ran his hands along the rails. They were well-rusted, except for the upper surfaces of each rail, which were shiny; typical for railroad tracks.

Wait. That's not right.

"When was the last time these tracks were used?" he asked.

"A year or more, Señor," someone answered, through Ximena.

No. The tops of the rails indicated they had been used more recently than that. If they had not been used for a year, the rails would be uniformly corroded. Something *did* pass over these rails, polishing them as it did so.

Thumann stood again, grunting as he did. He followed the rails outside, towards the dead engine sitting frozen outside the bank. About ten feet before the engine, the shiny strip of exposed iron stopped. Thumann then walked to the front of the dead engine and examined the tracks heading away from the bank. Completely rusted.

Whatever had traveled along these rails recently only went from the interior—where the gold had been stored—to the outside, just before the dead engine blocked any further travel.

"The thieves used something else to transport the gold once it was outside," he said, not particularly to anyone. Ximena translated anyway.

Thumann looked for tracks or tire impressions, knowing that the effort was futile. So much time had taken place since the robbery that any such evidence would be long gone. If he could somehow have gotten to Chile faster, maybe he'd have more clues.

Thumann returned to the inside of the bank, continuing his backward path. Now he followed that shiny strip atop the rails inward, towards the gold. The rails fed through the bank, moving deeper and deeper into the secure inner vaults through a series of pass-throughs. Each of these had an iron grate that could be raised or lowered to allow a rail car to pass. The guards helpfully raised them, one by one, allowing Thumann to continue inward. He stumbled somewhat, walking along the uneven cross-planks that ran between the rails. His shabby detective's shoes were used to such things, but his aging ankles had begun to protest. Gentleman paced close behind, ready to pick Thumann up should he fall.

Finally, Thumann and the others reached the inner vault where the gold had been stored. As expected, there were ingots of platinum and silver sitting nearby, equally ready to be taken but left unbothered.

Why only the gold? Thumann thought.

Equally as expected, there were simply no overt clues. As he had moved from the outer rooms to the inner vault, the environment was increasingly cleaner. The gold vault itself was pristine, which should have made spotting traditional evidence much easier. But there were no signs of any forced entry.

"Has this room been cleaned since the theft?" Thumann asked.

"No, Señor," one of the guards answered. "Except for some transfers in and out since the robbery, it is exactly how it was."

The air in the vault was warm, and there was little ventilation. Despite this, the air was dry, no doubt to keep the silver from oxidizing. Any gold or platinum—both chemically inert— would not need such protection, but the room housed a large cache of easily tarnished silver. While technically inert as well, silver would darken with any minute amounts of sulfur that happened to be in the air.

The metals were stored in wooden crates, some of which had open tops. Each crate had paperwork attached to the side detailing the metal's foundry, lot numbers, and transfer information.

Thumann ran his hand over some platinum ingots. Unlike gold, this metal was not formed into large bars but much smaller rectangular forms. He had never touched anything of such value before.

Absentmindedly, he continued to run his hand over the silver. This, too, was formed into ingots slightly larger than the platinum.

Hold on, Thumann thought. The silver felt … odd.

He repeated the activity with another set of silver pieces next to the first. And then a third. Some felt different than others.

"How long has this case of silver been here?" Thumann asked.

One of the bank employees scurried over to check the papers attached to the side of the crate. "These have been here for about eighteen weeks," he said.

Before the robbery, Thumann thought. "And these?" he asked, pointing to another crate of silver ingots.

"Just two weeks," the bankman said.

After the robbery.

Thumann paused. Gentleman watched with intense interest; a revelation was forthcoming. Thumann withdrew his pipe from his waistcoat pocket and fumbled for his matches.

"Call your local hospital or clinic," Thumann demanded suddenly. "We need everyone who was working immediately before the robbery to get blood tests."

Dr. Cuba, now having assumed the appearance of Señora Maria Consuelo Vasquez's son, Juan Carlo, entered the red brick building that served as the main office for D y F Castro Abogados, one of the oldest and most prestigious law firms in Bolivia. If everything went well today, he would be nearing the end of the preparation and nearly ready to begin The Work itself.

After introducing himself, the young-looking Juan Carlo was escorted to meet one of the many lawyers in the firm, an equally young attorney named Juarez. Dr. Cuba had previously sought out Juarez due to his age and the fact that the young attorney had never met the Señora. This point was crucial, and so Dr. Cuba arranged the meeting with Juarez rather than one of the older attorneys of the firm who usually handled the Señora's matters personally.

The matter at hand, of course, was the handing over of mineral rights for the family mine in Potosi to the young heir, as stipulated in the documents Dr. Cuba had arranged only a few weeks prior. But—predictably—young attorney Juarez was confused.

"I beg your pardon, Señor, but there seems to be an error," he said.

"Oh?" Juan Carlo replied with a slight wince. The morphine was already wearing off.

"Yes, sir. The paperwork states that Juan Carlo is only fifteen years old. This can't be right."

Juan Carlo sniffed. "Oh, yes, I'd forgotten. There was an error in the document. As you can see, I am 25. In fact, only as of yesterday."

"Curious," Juarez said, his eyes still on the documents in his hand. Papers were all these people cared about, so Dr. Cuba would give him more.

"Please review these records," he said, withdrawing the documents from his briefcase. "My birth certificate, university records, other forms of evidence. I knew when I saw the error about my age in the transfer documents that I'd need to show some proof." The forgers had again earned their gold.

Juarez was relieved for a brief second, then shifted to overwhelmed as he looked at the thick documents Juan Carlo was handing him. He coughed slightly. "I'll... I'll have to have someone look these over," he sputtered.

"I can wait," Juan Carlo said with authority. He sat, ensuring that Juarez knew he expected this to be brief.

Juarez left, allowing Juan Carlo to dab a slight drop of blood from his left ear. When Juarez returned, however, he was not alone. Alongside him was a senior attorney, Domenico Castro. This complicated matters; Castro had previously dealt with the Señora himself and likely had met Juan Carlo as a child. When he entered, Castro fixed his gaze directly on the young man seated in Juarez's office, not on any papers.

Juan Carlo stood.

"This is one of our founders," Juarez started.

"Yes," Juan Carlo interrupted. "Señor Domenico. We met once or twice at my mother's house." He extended a gloved hand to Castro, whose face suddenly switched to confusion. Castro took his hand, however, telegraphing that this disaster may yet be turned around.

Castro did nothing to hide his confusion, though. "I'm sorry, Señor, but I could have sworn when I met you, you were only a small child. But you say that you and I have met?"

"Yes, sir," Juan Carlo continued. Had he been an actual 25-year-old innocent, pulling this act off may have been more difficult. Thankfully, Dr. Cuba was neither young nor innocent, no matter what his facial bone arrangement suggested. "You met my younger brother, Elio. I was actually there, too, the last time you visited. You must have forgotten."

"Elio," Castro repeated, clearly searching his mind.

"That's right. If I recall, Elio was playing with a wooden car on the office floor that day. My mother brought up the Potosi mines that day, so perhaps that is why there is confusion in the paperwork. I think Elio's age was inserted instead of mine."

None of that was remotely true, but by blaming Castro, however politely, he now put him in a position to defend what now appeared to be incompetence… by the firm's founder. Castro was not likely the type of man to let that remain floating in the air.

Now it was Castro who was sputtering, "Oh, well," he said, adjusting his mustache. "I'm sure it was my assistant."

Juan Carlo raised a hand to interrupt. "No, Señor, your office wasn't involved at all in the transfer paperwork. As you can see, this was done by another firm, represented by one Robert Bosch. I suspect my mother made an error in not having your firm do the work, as I'm sure you would not have made this error."

And with that, Castro's reputation in front of Juarez was salvaged. Castro exhaled with relief. "Yes, that's it, I'm sure," he said. "Well, then, everything appears in order. Señor Juarez, please get the property papers from our safe deposit box in the back, and let's begin signing them over to the young man here."

Juarez nodded and scurried.

Now Castro was confident again. "You're about to become a very influential young man," he said.

Juan Carlo nodded. *And you,* he thought, *are helping awaken the Sunken Gods.*

On the second day at sea, the Homunculus restarted his heart, slid the latch, and exited his crate. The lid creaked noisily as he lifted it and stepped out, but he was not worried. If there was anyone nearby to hear him, they would not live long to say much about it.

But no one was in the cargo hold at the moment that he revived himself. The Homunculus reached back into the crate and withdrew a second black overcoat to replace the one he had left behind at the dock. Despite having been out of the water for two days, his clothes were still damp, but the Homunculus did not care about such things. He was not the sort of man to catch a cold, of course. Technically, he was not a sort of man at all.

Beneath the bedding of the crate was a false bottom. The Homunculus removed this, revealing a meager set of laboratory devices. The crate contained some "equipment," after all.

The Homunculus withdrew each piece of equipment and set them on nearby crates. The sea was calm, so—for now, at least—they would not topple. The devices included bizarre pumps, metal stands, tubes, and glassware, some of which appeared quite fragile.

He then reached back into the coffin-crate and pulled aside a false endpiece. From this space, he retrieved a copper vat, approximately two-and-a-half feet long and one foot in diameter. The Homunculus then closed the lid of the crate and began to assemble the components into—something—on the crate itself. This would apparently become his workbench.

The assembly process took about a half hour. Once complete, the entire device stood steadily enough on a set of metal legs, able to withstand ship movements during even moderate waves. The glass tubes and graduated beakers were hung from a metal arm, arcing over the pump and meters, allowing them to sway as the ship tilted. One of the pumps required electricity, however, which would create a problem since the cargo hold did not have a nearby generator.

"Who are you?" a voice barked. Someone had entered the cargo hold, after all. It was a young, fresh-faced kid whose name—Ducky—was embroidered on his shirt.

"Good," the Homunculus said, waving Ducky over. "I can use your help."

"I ain't helpin' you at all. Yer comin' with me up top to see what the captain wants to do with ya." The young boy was eager to score points, the Homunculus surmised, with his new crew.

"I am not a stowaway if that is what you are thinking," the Homunculus said, approaching the man. "I am a paid passenger."

"Stay back," Ducky said, raising his hands. He had no weapon.

"I need a generator for the equipment. Where can I find one?"

The young man turned to flee, but the Homunculus' hand darted out fast enough to grab his collar. With tremendous force, Ducky was yanked backward and thrown into an iron support beam, breaking his neck. The Homunculus' lips pursed for a moment; he had not meant to kill the kid. After stopping his heart, it took a while for the Homunculus to regain precise control of his muscles.

No matter, the boy would be of use once a generator was found.

The Homunculus dragged Ducky's body towards a hidden corner so that it would not be easily seen if someone else came down. He then searched the section of the hold for a power source to no avail. The *Eustis'* belly, while not large, was nevertheless divided into three sections, and the Homunculus' crate had been stored in the aft section. Stepping over crates and cables, past rats and roaches, the Homunculus made his way to the center hold, where he heard the throbbing hum of some form of machinery.

Luck. In the middle section, the *Eustis* had something stored that required refrigeration. Three large metal refrigeration units stood in the dead center, rusted and abused but rattling away to keep their contents cold. If the refrigerators were running, they had electricity.

The Homunculus circled the machines and found the thick electrical cables that fed into each unit's noisy compressor. He then followed the cables backward, finding them connected to more cables that ran upward into the hold's ceiling. These, for sure, were extensions that ran power from the ship's engines to the cargo hold below. They would do nicely.

The Homunculus disconnected one of the refrigeration units, allowing it to fall silent, even as the other two machines continued to complain angrily. He dragged the extension cable back towards the aft hold, through its doorway, and towards the crate. It would reach.

After another few minutes of tinkering with the cables, the Homunculus was ready. Hoping the three-phase power coming from the engine room's compressors would not blow the delicate laboratory pump, he flipped a switch, and the small machinery came to life. It sputtered like a dog's heartbeat. The Homunculus turned it off.

Everything worked.

It was growing darker in the hold as the limited light coming through various slats and portholes was fading. Sunset. The Homunculus moved back to Ducky's dead body, dragged it over to the machine, and grasped a red rubber tube. One end of the tube was connected to the pump, and—with a quick thrust—the other end was now embedded into the dead seaman's heart. The Homunculus again flipped the switch, and the pump once again sputtered. Now, blood flowed from the dead man through the pump and into the weird equipment sitting atop the coffin-like crate.

It would take about an hour to drain him completely. *Enough time to kill the radio operator*, the Homunculus thought.

Chapter 4: The Rajah's Court

Bernard Gentleman knew he was never going to become a detective at Scotland Yard. His personality was simply not a good fit for the job. He was, and admitted as such, a weakling, both physically and intellectually: thin and puny in stature, with the colorless hair and bland blue eyes of the typical British bureaucrat. Whereas the impressive Inspector Shrake was an athletic specimen and capable of wrestling down the worst street thugs, Gentleman was not. Whereas his beloved mentor, Inspector Thumann, was an intellectual giant, able to extract clues from the most tainted crime scenes, Gentleman was not.

Some saw his name—Gentleman—as a sign of what he would become before he even became it. But Gentleman disputed even this since his surname hinted at some status within British society that he also lacked. He was no "gentleman" of the sort that might be invited to soirees or fancy dinners, and he was not the sort that someone else might surrender a cab for out of respect.

No, Gentleman was simply a working-class Joe with no particular skills other than a keen ability to keep paperwork in order and maintain a moderately organized calendar for whoever may need it. A bureaucrat of the lowest order.

Yet Gentleman, surprisingly for some, was entirely happy with his place in life. He had no special designs on higher office nor any particular need to make a mark on the universe. He did not want to split the atom or rule the world. He just wanted to ensure that his employer's papers were in order.

Working for Inspector Thumann allowed him to do these things while also allowing him a mild sense of excitement. Gentleman would never find himself out of breath chasing down a thief in the street. But he would have occasion—as he did now, in

Santiago—to perform his bureaucratic duties in an exciting locale, a foreign country, or a murder scene. It was just about as much excitement as Gentleman wanted.

He would never admit it openly—Thumann would be unlikely to acknowledge such things anyway—but he thoroughly enjoyed working for his German superior. Before Thumann emigrated to the UK, Gentleman was performing his filing and calendaring in a dingy basement office at Scotland Yard for a superior who did not know his name while working on papers that made no sense to him. He thought he was satisfied, but when he was reassigned to Thumann as his direct assistant, he soon realized that his prior life at Scotland Yard had been unfulfilling.

The joke around the Yard was that Thumann was training Gentleman as his replacement. This joke was aimed as an insult for all involved: it was intended to mark Thumann's impending death due to his obesity, bad diet, and constant smoke and drink, as well as a sarcastic smirk at the fact that Gentleman would never become an inspector under any circumstances even if Thumann did fall over dead. The club of younger, fitter officers, including the handsome Inspector Shrake, always seemed to balance themselves between mocking Thumann and respecting him.

It was Shrake who had invented the nickname "the Flywheel" for Thumann, suggesting he was not only running on pure momentum but might very well run forever. This made Gentleman the "Flywheel's Apprentice." If the nickname was intended to sting Thumann, it did not succeed. He took silent pride in the name and smiled quietly whenever someone called him by it.

Despite his weak appearance and thin frame, Gentleman was entirely up for physical work. His trip to Santiago was not as uncomfortable for him as it clearly was for his gruff superior,

Thumann. As a result, Gentleman found himself helping Thumann—physically—far more than he ever required in England. Thumann was aging, and it was apparent to everyone. He needed more help with his bags, with his coat, opening a jar or bottle, or even, sometimes, lighting a cigar.

Thumann was also losing his patience more often, a common symptom for older police officers. He would bark more loudly and grunt more frequently, displaying annoyance and contempt at minutiae and—some thought—at Gentleman himself.

But Gentleman knew better. He knew that Thumann was frustrated with himself, with his slowing gait, his stiffening limbs, and his increasing weight. If there was a Thumann back in Germany who could run down thugs as quickly as Shrake, that Thumann had disappeared at least twenty years ago. The remaining Thumann was a shadow of his former physical self, and any frustration he had about this fact was likely justified.

But while the aging inspector complained about his slowing wits, both Thumann and Gentleman knew this was not justified. Thumann was as sharp as ever, and his groaning about his "decrepit brainpan" was, to some extent, mere theatrics. Sometimes, Thumann moaned about such things to lower the expectations of those around him or to confuse an opponent. But Gentleman knew he, Thumann, did not believe any of it. Intellectually, Thumann remained a shark, circling and hunting for prey.

In fact, Scotland Yard had adopted another nickname for Thumann; the German Brain.

Gentleman might not have been the brightest man in Scotland Yard, but he was smart enough to fully sense Thumann's trust and respect for him and to return it threefold.

The silent mutual respect between Thumann and

Gentleman helped forge the deep friendship between the two men.

Most of all, however, Gentleman simply liked Thumann's company. He liked the smell of his Latakia pipe tobacco, which smelled as if someone had set an entire forest on fire. He liked the tone of Thumann's voice, its deep rasp and occasional boom. He liked the way Thumann thought, the way he laughed—usually at the end of a successful case—and even his way of walking. Thumann always walked in front of Gentleman, not because he placed Gentleman in a subordinate role that deserved to stay four paces behind a superior, but to protect Gentleman. Once, when drunk, Thumann admitted he walked in front so that "the baddies can take their shot" at him without any risk to Gentleman himself. Thumann had adopted the role of human shield for his trusted assistant.

As a result of this close camaraderie, Gentleman had grown to be an extension of Thumann. He alone knew Thumann's thoughts, his plans, his projections. While he may have always remained a few steps behind—both physically and intellectually—no one in the world knew the investigator better than Gentleman. There were not many things that Thumann knew that Gentleman, eventually, did not also know.

And now, this was a thing that Dr. Cuba knew.

Ximena Alejandra Torres Orellana did not like Thumann's Latakia tobacco or his cigar smoke. It was bitter and made her cough. She thought it rude that the big German ignored her obvious reaction and continued to blow smoke near her anyway. But she kept these things to herself.

It was now a few weeks after their first visit to the Santiago bank vault. Thumann was waiting for the results of the blood tests he had demanded but never explained to anyone why he wanted them. Ximena overheard Thumann grumbling to Gentleman about how long the blood collection and tests were taking. *He doesn't understand our bureaucracy*, she thought. *They won't work fast unless you pay them extra.*

During the wait, Ximena stayed in a hotel with the rest of the team, often translating inane dinner conversations between the German and the bored police officials. She was being paid well, however, and was learning about investigations and police procedures at a rapid pace. Ximena only stifled her annoyances when the conversations turned dull or when the German lit that awful pipe.

Ximena was born in Chile, in the northern region of the Atacama Desert, about fifty miles from the coastal town of Arica. Eventually, her parents moved to Arica for work, and this is where she called home. She was quickly made to join her parents in visiting the local Catholic church in Arica and even joined the tiny, four-girl "choir." Ximena soon learned to enjoy the Mass, marveling over the complex rituals, occasional Latin utterances, and all those strange movements. The church at Arica was tiny and nothing like the cathedrals from around the world that Ximena had seen in books, but her church was hers. It was real; she could enter it, smell it, touch its walls. And even with their tiny budget, earned from meager donations from the few who attended, there were still golden candlesticks, ornate robes, and the statue of a pained Jesus hung, bleeding, on the cross.

But Ximena was doomed. Arica had poor schools, and no one who did not seek success elsewhere ever found it. Jobs were scarce, resources were few, and abuse against the citizenry was rampant. It was not just Ximena; *everyone* in Arica was doomed.

Ximena, somehow, sensed this at an early age. In her

church's few missals, placed in slots in the wooden pews, some of the words were in English. These songbooks had been gifted to the church from some US visitors many years ago, and the words sparked Ximena's curiosity. Already a voracious reader at age six, Ximena was drawn to the idea of people communicating in other languages. She listened to the priest's homily in Spanish, heard the prayers in Latin, and read the missal in English.

Hungry for more, Ximena began reading the few English books in the local library to teach herself the language. She took one English class in primary school, taught by an elderly woman who barely spoke English herself, and excelled. Then, at the age of 14, she sought out tourists or immigrants from the United States or England who might be able to help her further. Eventually, she met a retired American archaeologist named Pettigrew, who agreed to give her regular lessons. His Spanish was abysmal, but it hardly mattered, and soon, Ximena was one of the only young people in all of Arica who could translate—quickly and efficiently—between Spanish and English.

It was then that Ximena realized that a career may await her if she continued her studies. And, so, she did, eventually spreading word through Arica that they now had a translator available to them, should anyone need it.

Ximena was pretty, which also made her sought after by the occasional foreign businessmen who came to Arica to conduct trade and who thus needed translation services. Fortunately, Ximena's father was like a magnet for his daughter, always at her side and always protecting her from any unwanted looks or stray hands. By the time her father died, when Ximena was 20, she knew enough about how to defend herself.

The assignment to assist this strange, fat German detective

from England, however, was nothing for which Ximena was prepared. She now found herself traipsing through a crime scene, standing next to enough platinum and silver to buy a hundred Aricas. And the things she had to translate—phrases about motives and criminal methods and evidence—were new to her.

But Ximena always maintained a professional posture, even as a young girl; much of this was also due to the influence of her beloved father. Now, all of these things came together in her favor. She was nervous, yes, and confused, yes. But she kept these things inside, letting little of it project outwards, and focused only on translating the words as she heard them into words someone else could understand.

Ximena noted that the frail assistant, Gentleman, remained fixed on his boss, the fat German. She knew nothing of their relationship but could tell that it pre-dated this trip to Santiago by many years. And while she had no immediate opinion of Gentleman, she decided it may be best to mirror his fixation on the German to support her own role in this strange situation.

And so, she did. Whereas usually, Ximena might only watch someone's mouth moving—to improve her comprehension of what they were saying—she now began to watch the giant German's posture and movements even when he was silent. This was a man trapped deep in thought, she realized. He was frustrated and confused, unable to come up with an answer to what was clearly an impossible puzzle.

She also realized he lit his pipe or cigar under two circumstances: when frustrated and faced with a brick wall or when relaxing after some minor victory. As the fat German ran his hands over the silver ingots, she watched him pause. Then, he took out his pipe.

Thumann, she knew, had breached a brick wall.

Ximena recalled how, a few days earlier, Thumann had shocked his police escorts and the bank officials by calling for blood tests. "Call your local hospital or clinic," he said. "We need everyone who was working immediately before the robbery to get some blood tests."

Ximena had been intrigued. What could the fat German have found that would have caused him to demand this? Was it something he smelled? Something he felt? What caused that gray bulb in his puffy, bearded head to light up?

During the days of waiting, the German and his entourage continued to look around the dark vaults of the Central Bank for additional clues. The work was interesting, even if she had little to do; more and more, the team worked in silence, requiring less of her with each passing hour. By the third day inside the bank, she was barely translating more than an occasional grunt or bark from the fat German. Most of her translation was for the dull dinners after they returned back to the hotel.

Ximena had seen the bank's staff being escorted out in groups, presumably to be taken to the hospital for their tests. The German had still not revealed to anyone what he was looking for in their blood. If he had admitted it to his assistant, the Señor Gentleman, he had not done it in her earshot. But Gentleman did not appear to be anxious to learn what the German had in mind, leading Ximena to believe he had been told, perhaps late in the evening back in the hotel, or that the Señor Gentleman simply understood his mentor so well, it never needed to be communicated at all.

During those days, Ximena would listen to what the workers were saying as they came back from their lab tests. She chose not to translate these private comments into English for the fat German; he had not asked her to, after all. But Ximena quickly realized that because each worker had no idea why they were being tested, frightening theories were growing.

"Do you think we were exposed to something?" one asked.

"For certain, they think we were all drunk."

"The men in the front office are saying we are possessed and that a priest is coming."

"The German wants to experiment on us. They do that sort of thing!"

As the days passed, things were worsening. The staff were growing increasingly suspicious, some openly belligerent. The Director of the Policía de Investigaciones, Mateo Frederico Aves, had finally had enough. Now, in the hotel and away from the bank's staff, he approached the fat German. He waved Ximena over to translate.

"Detective," he said, pausing as he spoke to allow Ximena to do her work, "we must say something to the staff."

"I'm not ready," the German said gruffly.

"It cannot wait," Aves persisted, "I know these people, and if they continue with their theories, they could create problems. Problems for the bank and for us."

Ximena watched as the German fell silent. There was no way this attentive inspector could not sense the growing tension. The people at the bank were visibly resentful and frightened, and his police escorts were becoming anxious. Their support would disappear if he alienated them entirely, Ximena thought. *Surely, this German has realized this, too*, she thought.

The assistant, Señor Gentleman, spoke to the German, and Ximena translated for the Chilean police representatives.

"Sir," he said, "you have read the results. They are consistent."

Ximena did not understand what the assistant was saying, but it sounded as if he was taking the side of the police and trying to convince his superior to relent.

The German huffed. "Very well, Director," he said. "They used *gas*," the German said. "The silver ingots that were there during the robbery have a layer of oxidation on them that is not present on the silver brought in after the robbery."

"And the gold?" the Director asked.

"The gold and platinum are nearly entirely inert. They don't tarnish as easily. But silver tarnishes easily when exposed to certain chemicals in ordinary air. This is why your grandmothers spend so much time polishing your spoons and forks. The silver that was present after the robbery had a different texture from that present during the robbery. So, something was sprayed in the air that also coated and tarnished the silver prematurely. Whatever gas was used reacted with the exposed silver but then left no other trace. Except in the blood of everyone who was here on the day of the robbery. If a gas coated the silver, then it was also breathed in by the workers."

"Are they sick?" the Director asked.

"No," the fat German said, lighting his pipe. "But they all have the same pollutants in their blood. I can't be certain that the chemical is exactly what it appears to be until we have specialized labs perform additional tests. We will need some additional blood samples and scrapings from the silver. My guess is, however, that we won't know for sure since so much time has passed."

One of the bank guards coughed as the area filled with the German's pipe smoke. Ximena repressed a giggle; the German was exuding his own toxic fumes. The Director pressed further. "If it was a gas," he asked, "then what was its purpose?"

The fat German straightened. "We thought there were no witnesses when, in fact, *everyone* here was a witness."

"That's not possible," the Director said. "No one saw anything."

"No. Everyone saw something. But no one *remembered*," the German said. "The gas made them forget."

The group fell silent. "It's astonishing!" the Director finally declared. "This can't be possible."

"It's worse than that," the German continued, jabbing his pipe in the air to add emphasis. "They not only saw everything, they *assisted*. The gas made them complicit, compliant. This is why the thieves didn't need a team to help them. The team was already working in the bank."

More stunned silence.

"But how did they get the gold out?" the Director asked. "The dead train engine outside blocked the path on the rails."

"That," said the fat German, "is the next question to answer." He shoved the pipe back into his mouth and grunted.

He was frustrated at himself for not having an answer. Ximena did not need to translate that.

Captain Wu was seated in the middle, as he was the center of power for Leonard Port's ship operations. To his left were the captains of the *Carnival*, the *Mercy*, and the *Rugged Opal*. To his right sat the captains of the *Witch*, the *Parliament*, and the *Bloody Nancy*. The rest were captains from ships and boats of various sizes and hold capacities, from simple fishing trawlers to big-bellied haulers.

Wu was called "The Rajah" behind his back. It was intended as a double-edged insult due to the other captains' resentment of his proximity to Port and the power that brought him. Wu was Chinese, and very not Indian, so calling him "The Rajah" not only insulted his nationality, it mocked his authority. One of the captains in attendance had a knife wound in his gut after Wu overheard him using the term.

Wu was curious as to the purpose of the "Captains Meeting," but it was not without precedence. Port had, twice before, summoned his smugglers for a meeting of this sort but never ran them personally. In fact, Port only appeared in person for one of them and typically had other representatives, such as Wu, conduct the meetings. This time, Wu was in the dark, so he expected either Port himself or one of his high-ranking delegates to appear.

They did not appear. When 30 minutes passed, Wu became uncharacteristically nervous. He had been making dirty jokes to the two captains at each side of his seat but slowly fell increasingly quiet. Captain Smick, to his right, desperately wanted to hear what happened to the four sisters in the fish market, but now he was never going to hear the punchline.

Wu stood, and the men's chatter quieted. "Your ships are shit," he roared. The men perked to attention at the taunt. "I understand the *Eustis* barely made it out of port the other day. The *Rugged Opal* should be renamed the *Ragged Opal*, given the condition of its sails and timber on its bulwark. The *Parliament* has been docked for repairs for a year now. You captains are failing Mr. Port and this operation."

"You haven't had a ship in over a decade, Wu," someone shouted. "You've forgotten what it takes to maintain one!"

Wu scowled. His joking nature had long left the room. "Maintaining a ship is the captain's highest duty. How else will you protect your crew and cargo? This fleet has become a laughingstock, and you are all to blame."

"Give us money, then, Wu!" someone else shouted.

"We operate one of the most profitable shipping businesses in all of New York City," Wu countered, banging his fist on the table. "You should all have ships that can outrun the best they throw at us. We should be leaving port inspectors and Coast Guard cutters in our wakes. With the state of some of your ships, I'm surprised we make it more than a mile from the docks. No, you can't blame this on Mr. Port or his money. You earn more than enough. You've become lazy and greedy, all of you."

"Spend a week on the *Filipine*, Wu. You'll see how it really is once you get out of that damned office of yours!" another shouted.

"Who's that, Captain Saldo?" Wu asked, squinting his eyes. "You spend all your profits on poker games and whores, Saldo. That money is meant to keep your engines running, your gunwale free from rot, and your rudder able to turn more than two degrees, you degenerate. Your own crew is watching your ship fall apart while you waste the money given to you for repairs!"

The crowd was grumbling now. They did not like having hard truths shoved at them so publicly. This was not going well, but Wu was just filling time. Unfortunately, the meeting was about to get much, much worse.

One of the guards from the door entered and motioned towards Captain Wu. Wu waved him forward.

The guard leaned in. "There's an orphan at the door. He has a package for you."

"An orphan? For me?" Wu asked. "He used my name?"

"Yes, sir," the guard answered.

"Send him in, but watch him," Wu said.

The guard returned to the door, opened it, and ushered in a filthy, 10-year-old boy. He carried a hatbox and had a look of terror on his face. As he walked, he appeared to wince with each step.

"Ordered yourself a snack, eh, Wu?" someone shouted. The crowd of captains laughed, unsure if the heckler meant the box or the boy but agreeing it was funny either way.

"What's this?" Wu asked. "What are you delivering?"

The boy stopped in the center of the room and put the box on the floor. When he bent over, he winced again, and blood was visible on his filthy shirt. He appeared to have a recent injury in his abdomen.

"Speak, boy!" Wu commanded.

"I... I'm sick," the boy said. "Help me." His voice was weak, fading.

The captains gasped. "He's infected with something," Smick yelled. "This is a trap."

Wu stood. "He's not infected. Open your shirt, boy," Wu said.

The boy opened his shirt, revealing a crude—and fresh—set of scars near his stomach. Had he just had surgery?

"Something's wrong," Smick repeated.

Wu was not to be deterred by a street urchin who likely had appendicitis. "Open the box," he commanded.

The boy bent again, in obvious pain, and opened the box. He then kicked it over with his foot.

Leonard Port's head rolled out.

The captains all stood with a noisy commotion. "A trap!" Smick repeated. The other captains grunted and shouted similar worries. Their eyes darted around the room, and most had grabbed their weapons. They expected assassins.

"No note?" Wu asked the boy.

"No... no sir," the boy said, grimacing and holding his stomach. "They said to tell you that I'm the note."

"What do you mean you're the note?" Wu demanded. "Who are they? What did they tell you?"

"The men... who work for... the man with the red finger," the boy grunted, struggling. "Please help me now," he begged.

Wu pointed to one of his assistants. "Get on the radio to the *Eustis* right now. Tell them to toss that crate overboard... quickly. This is some kind of ..."

At which point, the orphan, his stomach filled with TNT and a complex timing mechanism, exploded. Before the flames engulfed him, Wu and the captains were covered in viscera.

Wu and some of the other captains crawled out of the room, their ears deafened and their clothing still on fire. Wu heard men screaming in agony and then the sound of the roof collapsing behind him. He scrambled into the adjoining room and began rolling his body to put out the flames. Wu knew much of his body was destroyed, but his survival instincts attempted to at least keep him alive.

Wu and two captains had made it out of the main meeting room and continued to crawl through the building, away from the explosion, and towards the front door. They scraped and dragged themselves forward into the building's main foyer. A commotion could be heard outside as people screamed and ran, but Wu could not see much through the filthy windows.

Finally, Wu exited with his two fellow captains, their bodies black and smoking, their clothing fused to their skin. Wu breathed clean air.

"Help me," he rasped weakly.

"The man with the red finger," someone said in a frightened, high-pitched voice. Wu, his eyes damaged from the explosion, tried to see who was speaking.

One eye focused, but only barely. There, outside the building, was a cadre of orphans, each dressed worse than the other. The building was entirely surrounded by terrified children. Each was bleeding from his stomach.

Whether Wu realized what was coming was never really clear because it happened so fast. Each of the children exploded, destroying the entirety of Port's meeting-house, ensuring the absolute destruction of everyone within it. Limbs and organs flew through the air, only to be burned before they could land.

Lacking a living radio operator, the *Eustis* never received the radio message.

Chapter 5: The Flywheel's Apprentice

And, so, Dr. Cuba—still with the face of young Juan Carlo—now owned the Potosi mines. Deep within them lay tons of silver and gold. But the mines were, as of right now, of little importance.

Along with the mines, Juan Carlo gained control of two additional operations previously owned by the late Señora Maria Consuelo Vasquez: the smelter and the refinery. The latter was of the most interest since the gold that spit from its maw was nearly of the purity needed for The Work. Crude rocks from the mines or crushed and impure ore from the smelter were not at all sufficient. But owning them, alongside the refinery, ensured that Dr. Cuba would have a steady flow of feedstock for the refinery, should he need it.

As the small convoy of trucks drove towards the refinery, Dr. Cuba was not sure he *would* need it. The quantity of high-purity gold he now had was nearing the minimum amount he had calculated for The Work. A conclusion was within reach, even though he knew he was racing to reach it before the troublesome Inspector Heiner Thumann.

Now that Thumann was shambling around South America, Dr. Cuba could easily track his every move. But this came at the risk that Thumann might uncover Dr. Cuba's greater plan before he could execute it. Dr. Cuba had run the calculations, and they still favored completion of The Work; he was not worried.

But while he had enough gold, more gold was always better. If his calculations were off, the gold would not be enough to waken the Sunken Gods, and he'd have wasted years of effort. So, Dr. Cuba worked to purify more gold; this took more time, making a collision with Thumann more likely.

There was also the matter of purity. A refinery was necessary, no matter what, to further purify the current stock. The Sunken Gods were not going to accept junk gold; divine blood must not be tainted.

The Potosi refinery complex was a dangerous and dirty place. Dr. Cuba's men wore coveralls to protect their clothes from the dirt and dust filling the air. Dr. Cuba—Juan Carlo—rode with them but without any protective coveralls. He would not be needing these clothes for much longer.

The convoy included a lead truck, with Juan Carlo himself in the passenger seat, along with three small, covered trucks and one tanker for the gas. As they circled down the road towards the refinery complex entrance, the tires of the convoy created a plume of dust behind them.

Juan Carlo did not care if the refinery's employees saw their arrival. If anything, he wanted their attention once he arrived.

The main gate was lightly fenced, only to keep out locals or troublemakers. Two guards greeted the lead truck as it came to a stop.

The driver spoke. "I am bringing the Señor Juan Carlo Moreno Vasquez, the new owner of this operation."

The guard looked incredulous. The driver produced papers.

"May I have your identification, Señor?" the guard asked, looking at the important-looking passenger. Juan Carlo reached into his jacket, withdrew his identification card and passed it to the driver. The driver handed it to the guard.

It was likely that no owner of the refinery ever set foot in the complex, and the guard appeared confused as to what exactly to do next. The truck's driver pressed forward. "Now you open the gate," he said with authority.

The guard yielded quickly, handing back Juan Carlo's identification and the paperwork. He signaled for his partner to open the mesh gate and waved the convoy forward.

As the convoy passed—no, as the tanker passed, specifically—the guards heard a hissing sound and smelled an odd odor. And rapidly, without warning, their minds fell blank. They could not have noticed Juan Carlo, his driver, and the rest of the convoy's occupants putting on gas masks.

The last thing they heard was someone ordering them to close the gate and to let no one pass for the next week. They obeyed.

Their minds empty, they could not do otherwise.

As the convoy moved towards the center of the complex, everyone within the area was affected. Upon breathing the gas, they froze in place, their ability to collect memories seized, and their minds made to await orders.

"The gas truck will need to perform a new circuit through the entire complex every eight hours," Juan Carlo told his driver. "The effects will wear off otherwise. A new tanker will arrive every day to replace the empty one."

The driver nodded and mumbled commands into a bulky radio set at his side. The gas coming from the truck was now more visible, as someone had increased the flow rate. It was now covering a much wider area.

It took 10 minutes for the convoy to traverse the facility towards the main cluster of huge refinery buildings. As workers and guards approached, they were each struck still, with blank stares on their faces. There was never any resistance.

Finally, the lead truck reached a building marked as Refining 1. Juan Carlo motioned his driver to stop there. The convoy pulled to a slow stop, except for the gas truck. This, instead, pulled ahead of the convoy towards the main entrance of Refining 1. A masked operator climbed out of the passenger door as the truck was moving and clambered up to the top of the tank itself. There, he unlatched a large hose, similar to one that might be used by a firetruck and scrambled down to the ground. The hose oozed out of a spool mounted behind the truck's cab like a snake as the operator stretched it to reach a window next to the main door. He placed the nozzle into the window and sprayed the gas into the building. Anyone within would be affected in minutes.

Meanwhile, Juan Carlo exited. With a single motion, he stripped off his false wig, pulling it out from under the straps of the gas mask, which he kept over his nose and mouth. He removed his false eyebrows and placed a set of protective goggles over his eyes. While the face beneath the gas mask was still that of Juan Carlo, the ruse was no longer necessary. With all the witnesses under the influence of his gas, Dr. Cuba could once again act openly.

With the rest of the convoy parked, a dozen loyal operatives—all masked—exited the vehicles and circled around Dr. Cuba, awaiting orders. These came quickly.

"Set the radio tent here," he directed one emissary. "Find the plant supervisors and bring them to me." Other operatives scurried off to obey.

Within a mere ten minutes, a small tent was erected, with a single wooden table and chair placed within it. A radio and generator were brought out and switched on. Dr. Cuba sat, pulling a small red notebook from his breast pocket. The pages were marked with symbols, not words; to any third party, they would appear to be the scrawlings of a madman. He checked his watch, checked his notes, and fell immobile. He was waiting.

In thirteen minutes, at exactly 1:22 PM, Dr. Cuba lifted the radio's transceiver and began speaking.

"Berlin, order Cadre 47 to proceed to phase 3. Lima, order Cadre 89 to begin the lifting operation. Buenos Aires, order Cadre 28 to proceed with operation against the customs agent and Red Plague. Mexico City, continue engagement with the Professor." Dr. Cuba's network was listening.

"London," he continued; this message would be received by the strange room with the curtain. "Continue efforts at Scotland Yard. Order Cadre 6 to proceed to phase 2. Provide updated report on Flywheel's Apprentice within 24 hours."

And so, these strange commands continued for another hour. In the background, Dr. Cuba's operatives busily performed what appeared to be rehearsed duties, unpacking equipment and executing their portions of the plan with precision.

Then, on the radio, a set of clicks. Someone from somewhere was sending the code, requesting permission to transmit a message to Dr. Cuba, rather than merely receiving it. This permission—and the code—was only to be used in rare cases.

Dr. Cuba froze, listening intently to the clicks, verified the code. Not only was the sequence of clicks important, but so, too, were the pauses between them. Any slight deviation would mean the radio network was compromised. From behind the goggles, Dr. Cuba's eyes tightened as he listened.

One gloved hand hovered over a single red button on the face of the radio. Satisfied the incoming code was authentic, Dr. Cuba pressed the button once. A short tone emitted. He waited exactly two seconds and pressed again. Then four seconds, and again. This was the authorization to proceed.

A voice scratched over the air. "This is Halifax. We received a short message over code. Very weak, the transmission source is unknown. Please authorize us to read the message as decoded."

Dr. Cuba again pressed the tone button: one tone, two seconds, one tone, four seconds, one final tone.

The operator on the other end read the message in a deadpan voice. "Cease all operations. Suspend all cadres."

Dr. Cuba stiffened. He was suddenly struck by an unfamiliar feeling: adrenaline. Since his rise to power in the criminal underworld, little could affect him. There were few things he had not seen and fewer things he had not done, leaving him to live in a reality without surprise, without novelty. He always knew what his victims would do, and he was always right. This allowed him great success but left him with an unrelenting weight of boredom. To counter this, he always reminded himself of The Work, of the Sunken Gods below, of their need to rise up, and his role in achieving that.

But this message… no, this was *not* part of that plan. This message was not expected nor predicted. And that, Dr. Cuba thought, was impossible.

Someone knew of his plans, knew of his network, even knew how to get a message directly to him. This changed everything.

Dr. Cuba switched off the radio and then the generators. The area fell silent; only the wind through the dusty complex was left.

Calculations silently flowed through his head. Possibilities, ramifications, alternatives. Numbers, names, places, more names. Events that happened and more that had not.

The radio signal had been weak, indicating the source of the transmission was either far or unsophisticated—or both. This suggested the source was not an immediate threat. The message was only picked up by a single station in Nova Scotia, indicating a limited level of capability. A more immediate threat would have been received by multiple stations at once. A single unknown actor? A new piece on the board?

Dr. Cuba would have to consider this later. Two operatives approached with seven glassy-eyed men. They entered the tent. "The supervisors," one of Dr. Cuba's men said.

Dr. Cuba stood and addressed the seven. "Arrange refining operations to run 24 hours a day, commencing immediately and without stop. All refining shall achieve 99.99% purity. This will require additional processing using the Wohlwill process. Place all pure product in the provided trucks and move it to the warehouse. This pace will continue for exactly one week."

The seven supervisors said nothing and turned to carry out their orders.

Dr. Cuba turned to his operators. "After one week, cease the gas routine and withdraw all of our vehicles. Leave no trace."

A new piece on the board?

The radio operator's neck had snapped with a surprisingly loud pop. *Advanced arthritis*, the Homunculus thought. *That was a kindness.*

With the operator dead, no messages from New York would ever be received, assuming anyone even survived the orphan attack to send it. Better safe than sorry.

The attack on the captains had made headlines but was written off as a war between the Chinese and the Italians. The orphans were reported as victims of the blast rather than the cause of it. One reporter for The New York Times questioned why so many orphans appeared in that area, specifically at that time, but he drew no conclusions. Still far at sea, the Homunculus had no access to newspapers, and — thankfully — neither did the ship's crew. The Homunculus only knew his plan had been successful since all his plans were successful.

The Homunculus had planned to burn down the surgical facility, where the orphans had been prepared for their role, but now thought better of it. *The surgeons proved useful and may be yet again,* he thought. *Cutting men up is easy, sewing them back up again takes some measure of skill.*

For now, he had more immediate concerns. He was aboard a small, barely seaworthy cargo vessel in the Atlantic Ocean, heading east. And this was not the direction the Homunculus wanted to go.

Two men were now strung up in the cargo hold. The radio operator now replaced the first man and was attached to the tubes connected to the strange pump. The first man still hung there, but his corrupted corpse was now a paper-thin shell; he almost looked like a decoration, hung for some macabre party.

Their blood was not enough, of course. The Homunculus would need more of it if he was going to survive the journey. Fortunately, the *Eustis* had more crew members, and the Homunculus knew enough about piloting a ship that the crew would not be needed for much longer anyway. This is why he did not hijack an aeroplane, even though that would have been much faster. With multiple fuel stops, the risks of being intercepted were far too high.

And, of course, an aircraft could not land at tiny Monito, a place he very much needed to visit first.

Before seeking his next donor, the Homunculus had more

technical work to attend to. The blood, in its natural state, was of no use to him. And so, he fiddled more with his delicate laboratory equipment, still perched atop his coffin-like crate, assembling yet one more small device and then connecting this to the pump setup. He then fitted the new device with filament-thin tubes; these would pass the blood through various filters and then across a strange metal membrane that appeared to be pure copper. The wafer of copper was submerged inside a jar, but this jar was empty; one ingredient was missing.

This would not do.

What he needed would be in the engine room, and this meant again leaving the cargo hold. He had managed this once already to reach the radio room, but it was risky. The Homunculus was not yet ready to start a panic aboard the *Eustis* and risk an angry mob throwing him overboard. He needed to thin the ranks first.

———————

Gentleman fetched an unopened pouch of pipe tobacco from the smaller trunk Inspector Thumann had brought with him from England. Thumann was smoking more than usual, indicating he was coming to some grand conclusion, and the pouches were emptying quickly.

"Thank you, dear friend," Thumann said as Gentleman handed him the pouch. The Inspector was feeling sentimental tonight. Thumann opened the pouch, and the room filled with the smell of Latakia and Burley. He shoved a thick pinch into his pipe and lit it with one flick of a long match.

"I think some whiskey is due?" Gentleman asked.

"Whiskey is always due, dear Gentleman," Thumann answered, blowing pipe smoke. "Why do you suggest it this evening?"

"The gas," Gentleman said. "You thought of something that no other investigator had considered. This is cause for whiskey if ever there was one."

Thumann accepted the praise but kept his pride—which was definitely swelling—to himself. He opted instead to downplay his ability, at least in this instance. "Everyone was insisting this could only have been an inside job," he said, searching his desk for the unopened package of sweet cookies he knew he left there somewhere. Tonight's triumph called for these alfajores. "And an inside job was the only way this made sense. So, the question was how an inside job could have been committed either under the noses of so many employees or with that many employees as willing participants. I simply assumed they were unwilling participants."

"That, then," Gentleman said, handing Thumann his cookies, which had been atop the filing cabinet all this time and not on his desk, "led you to ask how so many people could have been made unwilling participants."

"Correct," Thumann said, ripping open the brown bag and grabbing an alfajor. The outsides were covered in powdered sugar, with the inside being a sweet manjar blanco; none of this was good for Thumann's health. Thumann had discovered alfajores from an outside street vendor and was addicted after the first bite.

"A chemical agent was the easiest answer," he continued. "Mass hypnosis would have required too much organization and preparation and would not have the same level of effect on each individual. I also knew that Germany had been working on such a gas but struggled to complete one before the war. I would suspect this Dr. Cuba simply stole the German plans and somehow perfected it, so the victims simply wake up later with no memory of what they did while under its influence."

"Or the Americans," Gentleman offered.

"True," Thumann said, his beard now sprinkled with powdered sugar. "For certain, the Americans have a similar gas in the works."

"Would tracking the source of the gas lead us to Dr. Cuba?" Gentleman asked.

"A long shot, I would guess. What little we know of this Dr. Cuba—whether that's the name of a man or of an organization—is that their operation is highly organized, highly sophisticated. Certainly, the gas was purchased through a set of shell companies or possibly even manufactured by Dr. Cuba using stolen plans. The gas is a salient fact and useful to know, but tracking its manufacture wouldn't likely reveal our enemy."

Gentleman pouted. Now he grabbed an alfajor for himself and bit in. They were good, yes, but did not quite go with the lower-shelf whiskey. "Then, we're still where we started from?" he asked.

"No," Thumann replied. "To administer the gas, Dr. Cuba would need a truck. Maybe more than one. Trucks of that size are easier to see and easier to track. We can alert locations with similar stockpiles of gold to be on the watch for gas trucks nearing or entering their properties. It might give us an edge for the next crime."

Gentleman stood and went to the window. He intended only to stare at the sky and think but was immediately distracted by activity on the street below.

"Inspector," he said, with a tone of alarm.

Thumann jumped to his feet, powdered sugar spilling everywhere. He joined Gentleman at the window and looked out. They were on the third floor and had a clear view of the street: there, four cars had formed a circle around the front door of their building, preventing traffic from passing but also preventing anyone from leaving. They were trapped!

"We've got to get to the roof," Thumann declared. "Hurry."

Gentleman did not have time to question this idea and followed his superior's orders. Privately, he wondered what was on the roof that would get them out of this situation.

Thumann quickly grabbed his overcoat and leather bag as Gentleman grabbed his things. Thumann, meanwhile, reached into his coat pocket and produced a set of thick, brass knuckles that bore a Celtic knot pattern across the front; anyone struck with these would end up with a distinctive, decorative bruise. He then turned to grab the bag of alfajores and scotch and fled, with Gentleman, out of the office and up the stairs. They could hear men entering below, making no effort to hide their aggression.

The building was only six stories, so Thumann and Gentleman had to climb three floors to reach the roof. As they broke out onto the roof, Thumann was already wheezing, but his determination pushed him ahead.

"We need to block this door," Gentleman said, looking around.

Thumann shook his head. "No, we need it. In fact, tear it off."

"Tear off the door?" Gentleman asked, baffled by the suggestion. "That will make it easier for them!"

"Trust me, Gentleman. Help me rip it off these old hinges."

The two yanked and tugged at the door, weakening the old, rusted hinges it was barely attached to. Thumann, despite his poor shape, was powerfully strong. His arms nearly tore the door off without Gentleman's help.

Gentleman was confused but finally grabbed the door as it fell free. Inside the building, the men were clambering up the stairs towards Thumann's office.

"Let's move, fast," Thumann said, his breath labored. "To the edge."

Gentleman, carrying the door, followed Thumann as he raced towards the building's edge. Thumann pointed. "Give me the door," he said.

Gentleman understood. Thumann lay the door across the span between their building and the one across from them. The buildings in this part of town were spaced close enough that the seven-foot-tall door was enough to cover the distance. Thumann had created a bridge to walk across, enabling their escape.

But Gentleman paused, knowing how this ended. This time, Thumann was missing a key fact that would corrupt his plan.

With the door in place, Thumann waved Gentleman to follow him. "Come on, cross this way," he said as he scurried onto the door. The door was made of wood, but since it was intended as a fire door, it was lined with aluminum on both sides. It bent and groaned as the obese Thumann stepped on it, but it held. Thumann seemed entirely unafraid of the distance below him and walked somewhat casually—if cautiously—across. To any casual observer, the scene would have been absurd: it should have been Gentleman crossing this rickety bridge with ease, not his fat superior.

But that was not the case. Gentleman froze on the other side of the makeshift bridge, refusing to cross. Thumann stepped off the door onto the roof of the opposite building and looked back. He waved Gentleman across, shouting, "Come on, man. There are only seconds to spare!"

Sure enough, the men below had found Thumann's office

empty, and had already climbed the stairs to the roof. They were mere seconds from spilling out onto the roof.

Gentleman stood erect, facing Thumann with a face of calm. Thumann looked at him with astonishment. "Come on, man, for God's sake!" he shouted.

Gentleman, with one move of his foot, kicked the door so that it went crashing down to the pavement. He could not cross now if he wanted to, but neither could anyone else.

"What are you doing?" Thumann asked, with a face of shock.

"Fear of heights, sir," he said calmly. "I could never have crossed that."

Thumann was furious with himself. After so many years, he had no idea his assistant had a fear of heights. And now, his ignorance of that fact had doomed Gentleman to capture.

"Go, Inspector!" Gentleman shouted, resigned to his fate. "Don't wait for me, sir! You know I'm good at biding time."

Gentleman was, of course, right. Thumann needed to escape and could not wait any longer. If the men saw him on the opposite roof, they'd block the exit to that building as well. He needed to get down to the street.

"I will, Gentleman. I will not rest!" Thumann shouted.

Gentleman waved.

Thumann, with deep regret, ran towards the stairwell to descend the building. As he ran down the stairs, his brain raced for a plan to save his doomed assistant.

The men came through the stairwell and found only Gentleman on the roof, with no sign of Thumann. They grabbed him roughly, covering his head with a burlap bag and dragging him down the stairs to a waiting car.

Thumann could not have known it, but the men were never intending to capture him in the first place. Gentleman was not a consolation prize; he was the actual target.

As Gentleman was thrown into the back seat of one of the vehicles, he could hear the driver speak into a radio.

"Report to HQ. We have the Flywheel's Apprentice."

Captain Beavin was drunk, as usual. The crew of the *Eustis* had long since stopped worrying about it, as they had a fairly orchestrated—if wholly unofficial—array of countermeasures when their captain was dangerously inebriated or, as was the case increasingly these days, outright unconscious. Lucky Ted would take over the helm when needed, while Dave Thomas would double-check navigation. The ship's mate, Trent, held the voyage together by taking command of the crew, at least until Beavin woke up again, oblivious to whatever might have happened during the prior blackout.

Oddly enough, this system kept the *Eustis* running fairly well and, most importantly, kept the little ship out of the way of any nosy customs agents or security patrol boats.

Meanwhile, Beavin was entirely unaware that his crew had lost two souls in the past week: a younger crewman and the radio operator. But this fact had not gone unnoticed by the others, including first mate Trent, who pulled the crew together on deck to discuss the matter. Only a single engineer, Fitch, remained below to man the *Eustis'* engines.

Trent was a straight arrow, a former military man who retained his sense of professionalism despite his Captain's outrageous drunkenness. Trent might have had a better career for himself, rather than smuggling opium via the decrepit *Eustis*, had he not had his own addiction: young girls. With his face on wanted posters in seventeen different countries, Trent found that remaining at sea not only kept him away from his temptation but also from the law. The rest of the crew knew nothing about this problem facing the first mate.

"Lads," Trent boomed, the crew having assembled. "We're missing two men, as you are well aware. Little Ducky Dudley went missing a few days ago after having been sent to fetch some lamp oil. Most of you didn't know Ducky, so you probably hadn't noticed him gone."

This was true. The *Eustis'* crew was small, but the majority of the men were also self-centered pirates who paid little attention to some new recruit.

"But now we've lost Pilcher, our radio man. This is worrisome, lads."

The crew was aware of Pilcher's disappearance; it's hard not to notice your radio operator is nowhere to be found. But whereas Ducky's disappearance could have been explained as a simple rookie kid falling overboard, two missing men could have caused a panic. Trent was trying to prevent that panic from setting in.

"We'll have to search the ship. I suggest we start with the cargo hold. Three of you get down there but wrap your faces with towels or scarves. It could be we've got ourselves a gas leak or something that got to our men."

A few men scurried to comply. "Bring weapons," Trent reminded them. "In case it's not a leak." The men grabbed pistols.

Trent addressed the remaining crew. "Now, the rest of you check the upper decks. I know we spend a lot of time up here, but maybe there's something we missed. Check for broken railings, too, in case they fell overboard." The crew jumped into action.

Captain Beavin, however, had just woken from his stupor at that moment. Shaking off some latent dizziness, he reached for a bottle and took a swig. "Poseidon's breakfast," he muttered to himself. "Where the hell is my crew?"

Beavin stumbled a bit as he adjusted his coat and threw on his filthy hat. He made his way down the staircase from his quarters to the engine room. He hoped the men were playing poker down there, and he might win back a few dollars.

"You cretins down here?" he shouted, holding himself steady with a hand on the railing. "You'd better not be…"

Captain Beavin never finished his sentence, nor much of anything else, as the blood began gushing from his neck. Was he too drunk to notice his head had been nearly severed off in one stroke?

The Homunculus stood in the shadows under the stairs, holding a machete. Had Beavin made it much further into the engine room, he would have seen the fresh corpse of the engineer, Fitch, already lying dead.

The Homunculus frowned. The cut across Beavin's throat sent his blood spurting everywhere, and now he could not be attached to the machine. No amount of scrambling to cover the wound would help now. No, he'd have to leave Captain Beavin and only use Fitch.

With great strength, the Homunculus tossed Fitch's body over his shoulder and began walking back towards the cargo hold. He reached down to grab a large gasoline can with his free hand.

Chapter 6: The Cult of Crime

Gentleman awoke to black. It took a few minutes for the drug to wear off, but eventually, he realized his head had been covered by a bag, likely burlap. The rough cloth scratched his face and smelled like old, damp rice.

When his faculties had returned, Gentleman instinctively took an inventory of his injuries; there were not many. A bruise on his head, scrapes on his legs, some kind of cut on his arm. His kidnappers had been gentle with him. And that meant they wanted something from him… or something from someone else, with himself as the bargaining chip.

Gentleman lacked hubris and so realized he was never the end goal of this kidnapping. For certain, the gang was after Thumann, with an aim at disrupting, if not destroying, his investigation into Dr. Cuba.

As he remembered the name, a sense of dread flowed through Gentleman. Dr. Cuba's network appeared vast and, Gentleman acknowledged, now had unprecedented wealth due to the enormous quantities of gold stolen by that network. Focused, powerful, and well resourced… this made the Dr. Cuba operation—or, Dr. Cuba the man—a grave threat.

Gentleman was suddenly feeling terror crawl through him.

"Ele despertou," a voice said. A rustle of movement. "Mas ele ainda está confuso e pode não responder bem, Doutor."

Then, light. The sack was removed roughly, and Gentleman regained his vision, albeit slowly. The drug he had been exposed to still made his vision spin and float; he struggled not to vomit.

Four men were in front of him, perhaps more behind. He was in a small room with wooden walls, dank and humid. Underground, for sure. Three of the men stood about ten feet away, and one man sat on a wooden stool directly in front of Gentleman. This man appeared to be the boss… was this Dr. Cuba? Gentleman thought he heard the word "doctor."

The seated man grinned with a wide, face-splitting sneer. He wore tiny glasses, impossibly thick, and had a greasy single lock of hair snaking across his bald head. He wore a white overcoat. No, a doctor's coat.

"Dr. Cuba…" Gentleman managed to whisper. His voice was hoarse, his throat dry.

The seated man laughed. It was a high-pitched laugh, one that might attract bats. He put his hand on Gentleman's leg. "No, dear Mr. Gentleman! I am not Dr. Cuba! I am just a small function within this great organization, just a dowel attached to a rotating cam, pushing against a larger set of gears, driving a still larger machine forward! Or backward? The dowel doesn't know its function, it doesn't know which way the machine moves. Oh, no, no, no, dear sir, I am not Dr. Cuba."

"Name…" Gentleman grunted.

"I am Dr. Vines," the seated man said, smiling broader now. It appeared to the still-dizzy Gentleman that the man's head might split in two if he smiled anymore. "Whereas the great Dr. Cuba is a doctor of many and various subjects, I am just a poor physician, the lowest form of doctor. I am here to help you wake up, Mr. Gentleman. Both literally and intellectually!"

So, Dr. Cuba is a man! Gentleman thought. He shook his head, trying to shed the last remnants of his stupor. He felt a mosquito bite his arm, but his attention remained fixed on the problem before him.

Dr. Vines did not seem to care about Gentleman's state of mind and continued to talk. "You see, Mr. Gentleman, you've been asleep for many years. For your whole life, in fact! While you have tried to help your fellow man with your, well, diminutive career at Scotland Yard, you were unknowingly working towards their demise. Tell me, Mr. Gentleman," Dr. Vines said, putting his hands on both of Gentleman's legs in a gesture that might have looked to any observer as one of friendship but which was most assuredly intended to assert dominance. "What were you working against while you scurried through the filing rooms and hallways of the Yard?"

"Crime," Gentleman rasped, his voice returning to a low squawk.

Vines seemed pleased, slapping Gentleman on the thighs. "Exactly, sir! You were fighting *Crime*! For the average thinking man, Crime is the enemy of social order! Crime is something that must be stamped out in order to preserve peace! And you, in your small and astonishingly incompetent way, were trying to contribute to this great pursuit of peace by defeating the enemy you call Crime!"

Gentleman was not at all sure where this was going.

"You could not have known, of course," Vines continued, pulling even closer to Gentleman. "Of course not. Your education, your upbringing, your religions and regulations and parliaments and traffic laws could have produced no other result. You are the perfect example of the everyday man created by the everyday system, a system which itself was created by other everyman. A snake swallowing its own tail, a fish nibbling at its own fins. You can't be held accountable for becoming exactly what the everysystem designed you to be! You can be pitied, yes, and you should. You can be mocked, even. Perhaps forgiven? But you can also be awakened. And that, Mr. Gentleman, is what I intend to do.

This is the greatest gift I can give any fellow man."

Gentleman, now fully coherent and no longer spinning, grunted with rude dismissal. "I doubt,..." he began, pausing to swallow and regain some moisture in his throat, "... I doubt you can teach me anything, sir."

Vines feigned insult. "You injure me, Mr. Gentleman. But, again, this can be forgiven. And should be. Does the dog know that learning to sit will help him win food? Does the horse know that allowing a man to ride his back will give him purpose? Does the small child know that learning the alphabet could lead him toward great professional success and power? Of course not. You cannot understand the greatness that awaits you once you embrace Crime as the only solution to the sickness that is society. Only afterward will you thank me for awakening you. Only after!"

Gentleman chose to ignore this strange rant. More lucid now, he spoke. "I know I am here as a pawn to get to Inspector Thumann. Or to reveal his investigation. But I will not reveal anything to you. You may kill me now if that will be the inevitable result. Let us not waste time."

"No, no, no, no, no," Vines tsk-tsked, "you still have so much to live for, Mr. Gentleman! Killing you serves no one at all, no, no one at all. You must be made to understand the nature of Crime, sir. The most obvious explanation, and I hesitate to say this lest I insult your intelligence, is that without Crime, Law has no purpose. Your entire career requires Crime to justify it. You and those working on the side of Law would simply disappear if Crime were to vanish. But... no, no." Vines did not like this argument. It appeared beneath him.

"But that is too pedestrian. Even a schoolboy could deduce that relationship, and it has no practical meaning in the real world.

Because Crime exists, as does the Law. The concepts are opposites. These are things we all know. No, dear sir, there is more to Crime than you can know."

Gentleman settled in, deciding to use the time spent by Vines and his soliloquy to examine possible means of escape. He was struggling to come up with any, however.

"Instead," Vines continued, still smiling broadly, "one must understand the vast *other* difference between these two apparent opposites. This is where true revelation emerges. You see, dear sir, Crime and Law may be opposites on the surface, as any schoolboy learns, but in reality, they are organisms. And like a great whale compared to an amoeba, one is very much larger than the other."

Gentleman felt himself being drawn into the conversation despite his struggle to remain aloof. He remained silent, however.

"Law may purport to fight against Crime, but what so few within Law understand is that Law is, itself, Crime. The shallowest example I can give you is that of bribes. Your Scotland Yard officers rely on information provided to them by 'snitches,' as they are called, paid for with bribes. A simple view is that the lesser crime of bribery is justified if it leads to the defeat of a greater crime, perhaps a bank robbery or a murder. But, think, sir, if in such cases whether Crime is truly defeated, or merely temporarily transferred. A jungle snake moves from the river to the grass to a tree, but it remains a snake. Crime does not care if it exists one day in the form of a murder, the next as blackmail, and later as a simple bribe paid to a snitch by a policeman. It remains Crime."

Gentleman found himself nodding in agreement. Was he nodding? But wait, he couldn't be… but Vines was making sense, after all.

"Even your laws are built from Crime. Powerful lobbyists

pay off politicians through cash or favors to have laws steered in their favor. What Law remains is the product not of good governance but of Crime itself. Crime creates Law as an illusion so that it may survive, changing its form and color at will. Law is just the reproductive process used by Crime to expand its reach."

Yes, thought Gentleman. *He is right!*

"And now you begin to see, Mr. Gentleman, the truth. Crime is eternal, and Law just a skin it wears until it comes time to shed it. Crime is a natural force, an immutable and universal rule. Crime is the only real Law, one might say."

I understand! Gentleman's brain shouted. *It's perfectly clear!*

"But Crime must be led by Man," Vines persisted. "Crime without Man is chaos, and chaos serves no one unless tamed by Man. And, tell me, Mr. Gentleman, who tames Chaos? Who is the God of Crime?"

Gentleman frantically searched his brain for the name. His eyes darted left and right, his lips moving but not yet finding the words. His heart raced.

"Tell me, Mister Gentleman! Say the name! *Say it!*" Vines shouted.

Gentleman found the name. It was there all along.

"*Dr. Cuba!*" he screamed. "*Dr. Cuba!*"

Mr. Vines smiled his broadest smile yet as he removed the hypodermic from Gentleman's arm.

Jeffrey Ladder and his best friend, "Hot Pepper" Dagliss, were usually a boisterous, noisy duo, either joking at each other's expense or arguing over who cheated during the last round of poker. As they crept into the cargo hold of the *Eustis*, they were quite the opposite. Both were outright panicked, shaking in the wet boots, pressing on with flickering flashlights to guide them. The damn flickering was making things worse, as it gave the entire cargo hold the atmosphere of a carnival fright house.

Both men were suddenly regretting their decision to volunteer for this part of the ship search.

"Mebbe we should get more guys down here?" Dagliss asked in a low whisper. "Tear up some floorboards up top so we can see better?"

"Shut up, idiot," Ladder snorted. "Keep going." He sounded confident but was shaking more than his friend.

The two continued on, stepping into a row of large crates that reached nearly to the ceiling of the hold. These were marked "TEXTILES," and probably did contain fabrics or clothing, but given the nature of the *Eustis*' work, such things were never certain. The crates were so high that it would be impossible for anyone to be crouched atop them, waiting to ambush the men, so Ladder and Dagliss moved quickly down the aisle, turned left, into a far more disorderly part of the hold.

Here, wooden pallets contained various engine parts and other heavy metal objects, strapped down with thick straps or chains to prevent damage during the sea journey. Some of these items belonged to the ship, replacement parts and such, while others were just "window dressing" to throw off any inspectors who may board the ship and want to look around. Dagliss recognized one old anchor that had been on the ship for over a decade and which was not even of the proper type used by the *Eustis*, but no inspector ever noticed.

Here, though, things were in such disarray that there were many opportunities for a stowaway to hide in wait, ready to jump the men. Dagliss decided to be proactive.

"If yer in here, we'll find ya!" he shouted.

Ladder nudged him annoyingly, although after he did so, he realized that maybe Dagliss had the right idea. Maybe being noisy might flush out the stowaway.

The yellow, nervous jitter of their flashlights shone only about six feet in front of them, and only a smattering of sunlight broke through a few creases of the cargo hold's ceiling. The oppressive smell of mold and damp would be overwhelming to most, but Ladder and Dagliss were seasoned seamen, so barely noticed it. They did notice a growing stink of carcass, however.

"Jesus," Jeffrey choked. "What the hell is that?"

"Smells like something died down here," Dagliss answered. "Let's go get a few more guys."

As Dagliss' flashlight beam crossed over the back wall, both men froze. Dagliss slowly aimed his light more carefully. There, strung up from chains, upside down, was the dead body of Pilcher, the radio operator. His face was gaunt, sunken, his eyes nearly caved in. His color was greenish-white, no trace of pink at all. And he smelled like rotting meat.

"Good lord!" Dagliss grunted, unable to remain quiet. "Murder!"

"What happened to him?" Ladder asked, trying to examine Pilcher's body while simultaneously resisting his urge to flee the scene entirely. "He looks… drained. There's no blood."

"We gotta go tell the Captain," Dagliss urged.

"He won't be of much help," a voice said from the darkness. The voice was deep, smooth, like a church organ. Ladder and Dagliss froze, their eyes wide. They knew immediately the stowaway was near, but where?

"Where are you?" Ladder shouted, flailing his flashlight around to no effect. "We've got guns, so come out!"

There was a rustle of fabric, probably the stowaway's clothing, suggesting he was on the move. But in the black, neither man could see much of anything.

Ladder turned another corner, but before Dagliss could follow. In that split second, Dagliss disappeared. It took a full 30 seconds for Ladder to notice.

"Hot Pepper! Where are you?" he shouted, panicked. "Where did you go, man?" Ladder began to run, but in the dark, he was not even sure what direction he was headed. Rats scurried at his feet as the sound of his heavy stamping boots echoed through the cargo hold.

Dagliss, for his part, was silent. A cold hand had him grasped tight by the neck while something—a knife? ... a pointed fingernail?—stuck into his jugular. If he moved, he would be dead. Dagliss felt breath on his ear. The deep voice whispered, "Look." Another hand grasped his and forced Dagliss to raise his flashlight. There, hanging from another set of chains, was the upside-down dead body of Captain Beavin. He, too, appeared sunken and drained.

Dagliss gasped in terror. "As I said, he's of much use to you," the voice whispered right before Dagliss' neck was snapped. He fell limp in the arms of his shadowy assailant.

The Homunculus would now have to take the entire crew. This was a bit earlier than he would have liked, but circumstances often drove events, and timing was not always entirely predictable in environments like the *Eustis*. Now, in the dark cargo hold, he stalked Ladder, calculating the best way to kill that man without losing his blood prematurely.

But Ladder had, through dumb luck, found his way to the stairway and scurried, ratlike himself, to the upper deck. "Vampire!" he screamed, to anyone who would listen. "Vampire! Murder! Vampire!"

The Homunculus stood straight. There would be no more killing for the time being. He dragged the body of Hot Pepper Dagliss over to his machine, stabbed it with his tubes, and began the process of draining its blood.

"Vampire," he mumbled to himself. "How quaint."

"We go to Lima," the fat German Inspector had announced, and with that, just a day later, Ximena found herself on an aeroplane flying above the coastal highway of Chile, northbound to the capital of Perú.

The Inspector, oddly without his assistant, had returned from a short disappearance a noticeably different man. He was suddenly abrupt, curt, and impatient. Whatever happened made him appear desperate, incautious. Ximena wondered if it had something to do with Gentleman's disappearance. *For sure*, she thought, *he sent Gentleman on some parallel goose chase.*

The flight from Santiago to Lima would take at least twelve hours, with a few stops along the way to refuel. The German had ordered the captain to arrange a fresh replacement pilot at the first refueling stop so they could immediately take off again. The entire journey was spasmodic; the fat German obviously wanted to be in Lima as soon as he could. Ximena mused that if time travel existed, he would have arrived in Lima two months ago.

She knew why they were traveling to Peru; the latest known gold heist had taken place there, and it appeared the German wanted to investigate the crime scene while it was still relatively fresh. Whereas the Santiago robbery had sat for months before he could visit it, the Lima heist had only occurred two weeks ago, leaving the German with more opportunities for clues.

Ximena had never left her country of Chile. It was only a few years ago that she had even left her hometown. She certainly had never been on the sixth floor of a building, never mind on an aeroplane flying thousands of feet above the ground. She did not like this at all and was now fighting the dueling sensations of terror and nausea.

The Inspector was not helping matters, sucking away at cigars and filling the rickety plane's interior with his smoke. Worse, he was eating alfajores by the dozen, as if they did not have such things in Europe. The entire front of his suit was covered in powdered sugar.

"Could you please?..." Ximena asked, screwing her face into one of obvious displeasure.

The German took a moment to realize what was bothering his young translator. After a few beats, he connected the dots and moved to put out his cigar. "I'm sorry, miss," he said. It was the first time he had shown any concern at all for Ximena; until that point, she had just been a machine translating Spanish for him. "I'm distracted," he admitted.

"Where is Mister Gentleman?" Ximena asked, hoping she was not crossing any professional lines with the question. Just in case, she added: "He usually helps me understand what is going on."

Inspector Thumann stiffened visibly. "Kidnapped!" he boomed, not caring who heard him. "Dear Gentleman was taken by a group of organized thugs, no doubt sent by this 'Dr. Cuba' gang."

Ximena gasped, and her face fell into horror. "Why … why would they kidnap him?"

"To get to me," the Inspector blurted, unaware that he was never Dr. Cuba's target; at least, not yesterday. "I am sure they think by kidnapping my assistant they will rattle me, and I will be forced to drop this investigation."

Ximena's focus on the conversation led her to forget her nausea. Now, she had more to worry about. What had happened to Gentleman? Would they kill him? If that was not enough, would they come for anyone else associated with this investigation? Would they kidnap her next?

The Inspector knew exactly what Ximena was thinking. "Don't worry, dear girl," he said with surprising concern and warmth. "I will protect you to my death. No one else will suffer because of my laziness."

Ximena sat stunned. *Did he just vow to protect me with his life?* she asked herself. *A few days ago, it seemed he hadn't even known I was a person.*

Had she misjudged this man?

Ximena was also not sure why the German had blamed himself for Gentleman's capture. What "laziness" was he referring to? Despite his obese frame and gross smoking habits, the Inspector seemed highly intelligent and dedicated to his work. Ximena could not imagine any laziness from him, at least not during work hours.

She thought to keep the conversation going but to take it in a different direction. "What do you think Dr. Cuba is doing with all the gold?" The way she said the name clearly telegraphed that she believed it was a real man.

The Inspector tugged at his mustache, displaying his

frustration. Whatever answer he was about to give would be a guess, so he decided to answer more truthfully. "I have no idea, miss," he said. "Clearly, they are collecting this gold for some other use. The quantity they are stealing could have an effect on world gold prices, at least eventually… if they keep this up. Otherwise, I suppose they just want to be rich."

The Inspector insisted on referring to Dr. Cuba as "them," Ximena noticed.

"What about religion?" Ximena asked timidly. She was again testing the limits of her professional relationship with the German.

The Inspector scrunched his face. "Religion? What does that have to do with anything?" he asked.

Ximena stopped talking. The nausea returned. She gulped.

"Please," the Inspector continued, his tone more measured. "Continue. Explain what you mean, miss."

Ximena choked slightly, unsure if it was for fear or the nausea. The plane was hitting rough air, much like the conversation. This was the first time she had been asked to give her insight into the case before them.

"The Inkas," she said timidly. "They offered gold to the gods."

The Inspector froze. Ximena was sure she had gone too far and was now set to be fired as soon as they landed.

More silence. More turbulence. More nausea.

Then: "Religion?" the German asked, as if lightning had struck. "Religion." The second time was a statement.

He was lost now, no longer even aware that Ximena—or anyone—was present. His brain was rattling away behind that bushy beard and mop of gray hair.

"Religion."

_____

Dr. Cuba liked the smell of gasoline. It reminded him of his childhood in Ancash, his father, and that battered red bus. He relished the smell of gasoline, but the taste of it was bitter. Nevertheless, he downed the entire glass.

Todas las cosas nacen, he thought to himself. *All things are born.*

He was now deep underground. Dr. Cuba had a small number of such safehouses located around the world, used in circumstances that required complete isolation and the highest level of security. This particular bunker was located near Uyuni, Bolivia, beneath the vast salt flats. A single metal door, seven inches thick, lay beneath the salt at a location known only to Dr. Cuba himself. The door and stairway below it were wide enough to accommodate a single horse, which Dr. Cuba would ride into the flats, to the door, and down. Because of the heat and mirror mirage effects of the salt flats, even someone watching him from a distance with binoculars would never know the exact location of the door once it was closed again.

Beneath was an underground stable for the horse, with food and water and another stairway heading further into the earth's dry deep. A series of metal doors protected the inner room at the bottom of this second stairway: Dr. Cuba's safe room.

The safe room was well-lit, powered by generators, and included a vast array of radio and laboratory equipment. Once inside, Dr. Cuba would flip a few switches, and three tubes would extend upward, breaking the brittle salt layer above and reaching the air. One tube brought fresh air into the small complex's air handling system, another provided exhaust for the generators, and the third included a series of antennas for the radios.

For the moment, the radios were silent, switched off. The noise of the generators—located in a separate compartment—was entirely dampened by the thick walls and surrounding dense brine.

In the center of the room lay a single, deep red cushion. Here, Dr. Cuba would sit, legs crossed, in a meditative position. And so here was Dr. Cuba now, in such a position, sitting in complete silence with eyes closed, his throat making a nearly sub-aural trilling sound.

In this state, Dr. Cuba's mind simultaneously emptied and filled. Perhaps it breathed, taking in numbers and data and facts and evidence, only to exhale and leave a silent emptiness behind. In and out, and so it went.

For ten hours.

The problem at hand, the one being worked inside his breathing brain at this particular time, was this new piece on the board. Who had sent the radio message? It was clearly aimed at Dr. Cuba himself. This fact revealed much: the sender not only knew who Dr. Cuba was but how to contact him and the nature of his plans. All of this, however, could have been gleaned from intercepted radio transmissions between the Dr. Cuba operatives around the world.

What could not have been discovered was what code to use to ensure it was recognized by Dr. Cuba's operative in Halifax. This, then, suggested the sender was someone within the organization itself.

But, within the ten hours of brain-breathing, Dr. Cuba found no facts to back this up. He knew the names and data of every single operative in his entire global operation. He knew their families, their past histories, their weaknesses, their obsessions. These things, in fact, were how Dr. Cuba controlled them. But none of the facts related to any of his operatives fell in such an order, in such a strict set of circumstances, that it would make them in any way likely to have sent the message.

Therefore, this was not an insider. This was an outsider with intimate knowledge of Dr. Cuba's organization and its operations.

This was troubling.

The trilling continued. Now, Dr. Cuba's mind shifted to breathing in new information and data: what law enforcement agency, anywhere in the world, could have pieced together so much about his activities to be able to send that message? It did not take hours for Dr. Cuba to find his answer: none. The world's police were simply too many steps behind, too disorganized, too disconnected, to piece together an organization as large as Dr. Cuba's.

As his meditation ended and his eyes reopened, Dr. Cuba felt something he had not for a very long time: frustration. The unfamiliarity with this feeling almost made it pleasant—nearly—but he quickly snapped away the sensations and resumed his regular duties.

He flipped a series of switches on the various radios and waited for the tubes to heat, using the time to inject a new dose of morphine into his arm. He would need its effect soon enough.

"Berlin, order Cadre 47 proceed to phase 4. Mexico City, terminate the Professor and purge the research files. Poland, continue to phase 2 with the courier."

And so, it went. New orders, updated orders, shutting down operations and launching new ones. Despite whatever frustration and concern Dr. Cuba might have, the organization would continue to operate.

If The Work was successful, of course, there would be no

need to continue such things. The entire world would be changed by the awakening of the Sunken Gods. Cities would fall, nations would be drowned, skyscrapers would be turned into flotsam as the Earth was remade to suit the cruel King God Skyx and his Queen, the stern Macapax. The howling Aan would again destroy the creatures of the air, and the shuddering Fog'h would torment those on the land.

Order would be restored, and Man would be returned to his rightful place as food and kindling.

But until that time, and in the event that The Work did not succeed, the organization would continue to operate normally. For as careful as Dr. Cuba was, he knew the high likelihood of failure. There was a reason that no mortal human had ever tried such a thing.

His transmissions complete, Dr. Cuba switched off the radios and flipped another switch to retract the antenna tube from the surface. He then moved to a small adjoining room, which served as an underground kitchen, and began preparing baked empanadas.

We're not savages, he thought.

———————

Ximena knew the stories of Mamaqilla, the Inka goddess of the moon and mother of Manco Qhapaq and Mama Uqllu, who created the vast Incan Empire. She remembered the surrounding mythology, how Mamaqilla shed tears of pure silver whenever she or the Inka people were in danger, thus creating the vast silver deposits found throughout the Empire.

Mamaqilla was also the sister and wife of the sun god Inti, the father of the Incas born on the Island of the Sun in Lake Titicaca. Whereas the tears of Mamaqilla fell upon the earth as silver, the sweat of her brother-husband Inti filled the world with gold.

And so, Ximena's mind raced to help her German Inspector, Heiner Thumann, by trying to piece together some explanation for the mysterious Dr. Cuba's obsession with gold. She did so with the only knowledge she had available to her: the mythology of the gods of the ancient people of Chile and the western coast of South America. Perhaps if Ximena had been born in South Africa or Denmark or Canada, she might come to entirely different conclusions.

Ximena was not foolish, however. She knew she was grasping for straws from a tiny set that Fate had set before her. She was Chilena, yes. She was poor, yes. She was religious, yes. She had been placed before the fat German almost by accident... yes. But Ximena also knew that sometimes—just sometimes—coincidence could be shaped to produce a result. If she had never met the American archaeologist Pettigrew, she would never have learned English, and she would never have been able to forge a career for herself—a poor girl from arid Arica—as an international translator now working on the greatest criminal investigation of the world.

Ximena also had a hunch, a feeling. Something was connected here. She knew it was unlikely this man, Dr. Cuba, if he even was a man, came from the region. He was unlikely to be familiar with Inka legend. And even if he was, stealing gold was not in any way an act relevant to the ancient culture. There was no evidence, for example, that Dr. Cuba was building some vast golden temple to Inti.

But as her Inspector had noted, Dr. Cuba was not recirculating his gold. He was not converting it to currency or using it to purchase anything. The loss of the gold in such quantities was causing chaos in financial markets, yes, and perhaps this was his aim. Perhaps Dr. Cuba was nothing more than a bringer of chaos, and the thrill of watching the world's governments panic in light of his deeds was all he craved.

Ximena did not believe this, though. She blamed her Catholic upbringing for pushing her towards this line of thinking, yes, but did not dismiss it; she truly believed there was a religious component to Dr. Cuba's operations. Not just chaos, but chaos for a higher purpose.

But what was it? Like Mamaqilla, tears formed in Ximena's eyes, a result of her own fear and frustration. She was no longer just a translator helping an odd, fat German understand Spanish; she now felt part of the team tasked with solving this mystery. The kidnapping of Mr. Gentleman, kind Mr. Gentleman, further inspired her to do whatever she could to contribute to this team, even if it meant breaking normal professional boundaries and going beyond her role.

What was it?

Ximena ran through the stories she had learned over and over in her mind. She recalled how the Inka culture used gold as a means of worship for Inti and the other gods. She remembered how the ancient Inka leaders would adorn themselves in costumes made of hammered-thin sheets of gold to both attract the gods and imitate their likeness. And, of course, she thought about the great Inka complex built in the Peruvian mountains, called Machu Picchu and Huayna Picchu, where the Incas held ceremonies worshipping Inti in the clouds at high altitudes so they could be physically closer to the son.

Wait…

Altitude. Height.

Something was connecting.

Ximena grasped it. While she was searching for a reason why Dr. Cuba might be stealing the gold, she accidentally stumbled upon how Dr. Cuba was moving it. She suddenly knew how Dr. Cuba was able to get the gold out of the Santiago vaults and past the dead engine.

The Homunculus was left alone on the *Eustis* or, at least, the last living thing on board. Saying he was the last living soul on board would not be, technically, accurate.

In prior decades, men would have explained away the events on the *Eustis* as the result of a plague, rat infestation, or food poisoning. Even if vampires had existed, local officials would have found some other explanation for them; anything to avoid the realities of horror. Anything to keep the dock wives from chattering on endlessly. In this case, the *Eustis* would simply disappear and not even need some tortured explanation in a report no one would ever read anyway. As a smuggling ship, its secret operations were key to its success, and now that made its disappearance off the face of the earth that much easier.

The Homunculus, freed of the need for stealth, now prowled the deck of the *Eustis* without any concern. He headed for the wheelhouse, where he could alter course. In the Eustis' belly, the entire crew were strung up, draining, filling his vat.

The Homunculus turned the wheel and pointed the nose of the *Eustis* south. With his new course set, he locked the wheel in place and went to the radio. He would send another warning to this "Dr. Cuba," this time through a relay station in Brazil.

He did not want his arrival to be entirely a surprise.

Chapter 7: The Dead Engine

"An airship!" Ximena announced. "They brought the gold outside by rail until they reached the dead engine and then loaded it aboard an airship. This is why there are no vehicle tracks outside the Santiago central bank."

Inspector Thumann stroked his bushy beard in silence. He had clearly underestimated this young Chilean girl. She was stepping in nicely to fill the void left by the missing Gentleman. Thumann decided to treat her as he would him.

"Very good, dear miss," he said, nodding. He resisted the urge to light his pipe, as he knew she did not like the smell. "This explains much and opens up new opportunities for inquiry. We can send word back to those bumbling Santiago police officials and have them check for witnesses who might have seen an airship in the area. To haul that much gold, the airship must have been of a significant size."

Ximena resisted the urge to smile; she remained steadfastly professional and without any outward expression of pride.

"At the same time, dear miss, I've deduced that this Dr. Cuba gang is building something. They've not put the gold back on the market, but neither have they done anything else that would suggest they are simply interested in manipulating gold prices for their own benefit. We haven't seen any strange investments that would take advantage of the loss of gold, for example. And throughout the world, all the right people are screaming about this problem and genuinely doing so. You'd expect some of the villains to be faking outrage or remaining entirely silent, but we see none of that. No, I think he's using the gold for a physical purpose. A construct of some sort."

"A temple?" Ximena offered. She still struggled to remove herself from her religious leanings.

"Yes," Thumann said, surprising Ximena. She had not really believed the idea herself. "I do think it's something like that. On the aeroplane, you mentioned this may have a religious aspect to it, and that struck a nerve."

Ximena remained silent and thought for a moment, hesitant to reveal what she knew of the Inkas. Then, realizing that poor Gentleman still remained in the hands of these villains, she threw her nervousness aside. She told the giant German of Inti and Mamaqilla, of the use of gold in Incan worship, of the stories of Inti's sweat and Mamaqilla's tears.

Thumann listened to every word, absorbing all. His eyes focused on Ximena. This was a level of respect she had not often received from men, much less older men. Much less older, *foreign* men.

Thumann reached into his pocket and fiddled with his pipe and tobacco pouch but withdrew neither. Ximena noticed.

"Certainly, this Dr. Cuba operates like a cult," he continued. "There are always some overlaps between highly-developed criminal organizations and religious cults. The Italian Mafia relies greatly on a twisted vision of Sicilian Catholicism. The Russian gangs show similar traits, as do crime bosses in Nigeria and Upper Volta. In the United States, we see con men forming entire religions to cover up financial fraud and tax evasion. And, better still for the criminals, inculcating one's followers into believing their service is a 'holy mission' certainly ensures obedience."

Ximena nodded, gently placing her hand in the Inspector's pocket, pulling out his pipe and tobacco, and offering it to him.

Thumann stopped abruptly, taken aback by her kind gesture. He raised his bushy eyebrows in a way to ask, silently, "May I?" Ximena smiled and nodded.

He asked permission, she thought.

Thumann greedily shoved a fat pinch of tobacco into his pipe and lit it. He seemed relieved. "Maybe there is a link between this Dr. Cuba and your stories of … of who, now?"

"Inti and Mamaqilla," Ximena said.

"In-tee and mama-kee-ya," Thumann repeated, getting his mouth comfortable with the names. "But if not directly those figures, perhaps some other similar ones. This has been useful, dear miss. Very useful, indeed."

As he exhaled a puff of grey smoke, Thumann held a finger up to make a point. He was now taking on the role of teacher. "And so, we are here in Peru. We have another crime scene in front of us, and we must remain focused. Let's keep these new theories in mind, dear girl, as they may help us know what questions to ask here, right now, today."

And, yes, they *were* in Peru. Specifically, outside the Central Reserve Bank on dusty Jiron Santa Rosa in Lima, dodging noisy cars along a surprisingly skinny main thoroughfare. Much of this investigation would be similar to the one Thumann had left behind in Santiago: overstuffed national police officials would arrive, treat him with fake courtesy while barely able to conceal their disdain and annoyance; bank officials offering only the barest minimum of assistance, each terrified of losing their jobs should anything suggest they were somehow at fault for the security breach; and, finally, a complete lack of witnesses.

In the case of Lima's Central Reserve Bank, however, the heist itself was entirely different. The gold was not stolen directly from the bank itself, which would have been a much more difficult operation. Unlike the bank in Santiago, the Lima bank did not have rail cars at all. Instead, the Lima bank's layout would have required the gold to be brought in by armed truck via a main street, led through a special secure gate, and then taken further underground to vaults by way of heavy-duty elevators. The number of armed guards and police surrounding such an operation would have been three times that of Santiago, not to mention the hundreds of passersby outside, walking along Jr. Santa Rosa during their typical day of work and shopping.

Standing outside the bank, Thumann caught himself looking up instinctively. The idea of an airship had resonated with him. His attention snapped back as he was approached by the bank officials, with the obligatory Peruvian National Police official in tow. Thumann, shoving his pipe back in his pocket, agreed to a perfunctory walk-through of the bank but then insisted on seeing where the heist had taken place. For this, Thumann and Ximena were unceremoniously tossed into the back of a noisy, fume-spitting, covered military truck alongside the bank officials and police and driven a few miles into central Lima.

They stopped in the roundabout of Plaza Bolognesi, in the district of Brena, where, the officials said, trucks carrying gold intended for the Central Reserve Bank had been stopped at gunpoint. Thumann stepped down from the dirty truck and raised a hand to help Ximena down; Thumann, in a fatherly gesture, ensured that Ximena's below-the-knee skirt remained below-the-knee while also making sure she did not get dirt on herself as she gingerly stepped down. The gesture was certainly noticed by Ximena; their relationship had certainly changed in the past 24 hours.

With Ximena's help as translator, Thumann learned from the officials that two armored trucks had been forced to stop when three large gasoline trucks bearing the Shell Oil logo drove in front of them, blocking traffic. The movement of the three tanker trucks was sudden and clearly coordinated. The officials reported that seven armed men then emerged from the trucks, with another four or five breaking out from buildings near the roundabout to encircle the armored trucks. The drivers and their security men barely had time to radio for help when the attackers used some type of explosive to break through the cabin doors, remove the men, and shoot them on the spot.

"So, there were witnesses?" Thumann asked, waiting for Ximena to translate.

"No, none," one of the PNP officials replied.

"Then how do you know what happened?" Thumann countered.

"We have pieced together the events from the evidence," the official replied. "There was blood on the street where the men were shot. Tire tracks, and the like. And there is a photo."

"A photo?" Thumann asked with surprise.

"A tourist was taking a photo of his mother and daughter near the ovalo," the official said, referring to the Plaza Bolognesi roundabout. "The photo showed the three Shell Oil tanker trucks in the background. Blurry, but unmistakable."

"Did you interview the man and his family?" Thumann asked.

"They insist they don't remember anything. They did not even remember posing for the photograph."

The gas, Thumann thought. *They used the Shell tanker trucks to emit the gas for the entire plaza.*

"And afterward?"

"We assume the thieves loaded the gold into the tankers somehow and drove off," the official said.

Two tankers to spew the gas, one more fitted to store the gold? Or did they have another truck that wasn't captured in the photograph? Thumann thought to himself.

Thumann turned to Ximena. "No need for an airship this time."

The Shell Oil trucks were the only remaining evidence. "What do the trucks in the photo tell you, dear girl?" Thumann asked Ximena.

Ximena looked at the photo again. "There are two... no, three possibilities."

"And what are they?" This would be a lesson.

"That Dr. Cuba stole three trucks from Shell, or that Dr. Cuba dressed up three trucks to look like Shell Oil trucks, or that Shell Oil is part of the conspiracy." Ximena looked up to find Thumann pointing a finger in the air.

"Exactly. So, our next stop is Shell Oil." Thumann boomed.

Ximena asked the officials where the Shell depot was.

"Callao," they said in unison.

Dr. Cuba exited his salt flat bunker by horse, coming up the broad stairway, pausing only to shut the steel door behind him. The door was made to appear identical to the surrounding salt bed, and any seam would be covered by the light wind soon enough. It was now entirely invisible and only accessible due to Dr. Cuba's incredible powers of memory; he could locate it even in pitch-black darkness if needed.

Dr. Cuba then rode his horse to a small outpost in Carpas, about midway from the bunker to the larger town of Uyuni. In Carpas, a small single-engine aeroplane awaited him on a short, dirt runway. From here, the aeroplane carried Dr. Cuba back to Potosi.

But Dr. Cuba—now bearing the face of an older, wide-jawed man named Fitzgerald Wallace—was not heading to Potosi to visit his gold refinery. Instead, he was headed to an abandoned aircraft hangar about 12 kilometers from the town, in an area marked off for munitions testing. The hangar and surrounding empty complex would rarely see anyone sneaking on the grounds, and if they did, they were promptly shot dead.

Upon landing, Dr. Cuba walked across the empty field toward the hangar door. There, he was greeted by an operative named Killeen, an American who may not have recognized the face of his organization's leader but understood it to be him, nevertheless. "Doctor?" Killeen asked.

Dr. Cuba nodded curtly. "I've come to see the *Cassowary*," he said.

As Killeen opened the door for his superior, Dr. Cuba's eyes adjusted to the change in light. Inside was a large rigid zeppelin, the outer form encased in dull, tarnished metal. The shape was not that of a traditional cigar-shaped dirigible, like the Hindenburg, but instead much flatter and wider. Despite being given the name *Cassowary*, the outside was entirely unmarked.

The *Cassowary* sat on a set of squat legs extending from a base structure that included a few gun ports and several visible hoists. The hoists were designed to draw up cargo into the belly of the ship. The ship was strapped down to the floor with large chains.

Dr. Cuba stepped up to a set of mobile stairs to access the entryway to the lower structure. Once inside, he climbed various rusted stairways and railings to climb higher into the squat body of the ship itself. Inside, visible iron ribs held the pancake-shape in place, with large gasbags lining the upper ceiling. These, when filled with helium, would provide lift; for now, they were only half-full, ready to be topped off at launch time. Below the gasbags was a vast, open area with thick wooden floorboards used to store cargo.

Dr. Cuba ascended to the flooring deck and paced over to the central area, where a set of large crates sat, strapped to the deck with thick woven straps. Dr. Cuba indicated to one of the ship's crewmen to unstrap one of the crates and open it. He did so, revealing, of course, gold.

This particular haul was from a more recent heist, a theft of approximately 50 gold bars taken from the private residence of a corrupt government official in Costa Rica. It was not a large amount by any means, but it nevertheless raised Dr. Cuba's overall inventory of Inti's sweat.

Dr. Cuba examined one bar and, satisfied that it was of the right grade, placed it back. "Deliver this to Potosi for additional processing," he said. The standard purity of 99.5% would not be sufficient to awaken foul King God Skyx and his grim Queen, Macapax.

Dr. Cuba then strode back to the stairwell, descended down to the substructure and hoist house, and then out of the *Cassowary* and into the hangar. He headed towards a small office that had, within it, a radio desk and a wooden wardrobe. Here, Dr. Cuba could issue his international commands but instead simply needed to change clothes. He may have altered his face to look like Fitzgerald Wallace, but now he needed the appropriate wardrobe.

As he fitted himself in a suit more befitting of the elder Fitzgerald Wallace, an assistant walked in. "Sir," the man said fearfully, "a coded message." He handed Dr. Cuba a slip of paper. His hands trembled.

Dr. Cuba dabbed some blood from his face—he would need more morphine soon—and took the paper. It read:

X 2 X 9 10 X 7 red Ω

Dr. Cuba crumpled the paper and threw it in an ashtray. Using a match, he then set it on fire as he told the operative, "Listen carefully to what I am about to say and send this message exactly: Y 7 black. Do you have it?"

"Y 7 black," the nervous man repeated.

"Send it via the normal channel at 17.475 megacycles."

The operative started to leave, knowing if he failed in this simple task, his life would end. But Dr. Cuba was not finished.

"After you've sent it, bring me a glass of gasoline."

_____

The port of Callao was both a busy and dangerous place. Here, ships carrying all sorts of goods, from textiles to fish, arrived each day to unload and set back off. The area was filled with petty thieves, smugglers, Peruvian gangsters and every other sort of criminal. The police had long since handed off control of Callao to local politicians, who were part of the corrupt machine, an arrangement the police entered into willingly since it meant fewer of their men would get killed.

The Shell depot, however, was a fenced-off area with its own private guards, and once inside the gates, it became an island of relative security. Thumann and the others drove their official military vehicle right through those gates, avoiding the seedy port itself. Thumann again helped Ximena down from the rusty truck, and the two followed their escorts into the principal office of the depot management.

With Ximena's help translating yet again, Thumann grilled the depot's senior manager. "Have you had any of your tanker trucks stolen in, say, the last month or so?"

The manager shook his head. "No, Señor."

Thumann scowled. This scratched off one of the three possibilities.

"A year ago," the manager offered. "It was a year ago."

Thumann's bushy eyebrows rose sharply. "You had three trucks stolen a year ago?"

"That's right, Señor, maybe 13 or 14 months. It was a while ago. We never found them."

Thumann produced the photo from Plaza Bolognesi. "Are these the trucks?"

The man squinted but nodded. "It appears so, Señor."

A year! Thumann thought. *This plot had been underway for more than a year??*

Thumann knew he had to do his due diligence and ask questions that would have predictable answers and lead nowhere. But he asked anyway.

"Were there any witnesses?"

"Yes," the manager said.

Again, Thumann's eyebrows rose. There were never witnesses at a Dr. Cuba heist. Never. What was this, then?

"Excuse me, sir," Thumann said, waiting for Ximena to translate. "You said there were witnesses?

"Yes, Señor. The maintenance man, Carlito."

Thumann looked at Ximena. Now, it was the old German

who was trying to restrain his emotions and remain professional. Inside, he was nearly giddy.

"Can we talk to Carlito?" he asked.

The manager nodded and moved to a machine behind his desk; it was a public addressing system. He picked up the mouthpiece and announced for Carlito to come to the main office; the message echoed over the entire depot outside.

The manager offered Thumann and the others to follow him into a dirty conference room; it smelled of wet carpet and stale cigarette smoke. Thumann instinctively lit his own pipe, and Ximena was suddenly grateful; at least Thumann's tobacco smoke was fresh and hid the foul odor of the filthy carpet. The manager suggested they sit, but Thumann remained standing. Thumann's official escorts sat, appearing lazy and uninterested, while Ximena remained standing at the old German's side.

It took twenty minutes to locate Carlito and bring him to the office. Thumann heard the depot manager shouting at Carlito and asked Ximena to translate.

"He's berating him for being late," Ximena whispered. "But this man, Carlito, says he works inside the trucks, cleaning the tanks, so he cannot hear the announcements."

Thumann puffed his pipe.

Wait.

"Carlito, ven aqui, por favor," Thumann said in Spanish. Ximena's eyebrows rose up now. She had never heard her German even try to speak Spanish before!

Carlito approached. He was a tiny man, perhaps no more than 5 feet tall, and hunched over so that he appeared even smaller. He was rail thin, about 50 years old at least, with cragged skin and filthy, matted gray hair. He seemed nervous as he addressed

Thumann, clearly caught entirely off-guard by this entire interrogation. "Yes, Señor?" he mumbled meekly.

Thumann nodded to Ximena, indicating she should translate now. The German had probably exceeded his Spanish vocabulary. "Carlito, what kind of work do you do here?"

The manager poked Carlito, indicating he should answer. "I clean the tanks," Carlito answered in a weak voice. Ximena translated.

"The tanks of what?" Thumann asked.

"The trucks. The inside of the tanks on the trucks. They have to be cleaned of the residue and grit that settles inside them."

Thumann paused. "But tell me, Carlito. How do you breathe while you're cleaning inside those tanks? The gas fumes would kill you."

"No, Señor, we use masks. We have to use masks that are attached to oxygen tanks whenever we are inside working."

Thumann looked at Ximena, smiling. They instantly knew what this meant; any gas used by Dr. Cuba during the theft of the trucks would not have affected Carlito, who was breathing his own purified air at the time.

"Tell me," Thumann continued. "Back when the three tankers were stolen, what did you see that day?"

Carlito suddenly understood why he was being questioned; with the police officials—and this strange German—surrounding him, he was suddenly nervous. "You're not a suspect," Thumann offered, trying to calm Carlito. "But you may be the only witness of a crucial case."

Carlito calmed down a bit. Carlito babbled rapidly in the accent of the Peruvian highland, making it slightly difficult for Ximena to keep up. She resorted to paraphrasing.

"He says he was working inside a truck. The truck was parked in the maintenance area next to a row of others. All the other trucks were finished, and his was the last truck being cleaned. He could not hear anything outside but climbed out to take a short break. When he put his head outside, he saw men stealing three of the other trucks."

"What did the men look like? What were they wearing?" Thumann asked.

"Overalls, uniforms from the depot itself. Shell uniforms. But he says he didn't recognize any of them and knew they were imposters immediately."

"What happened next?" Thumann asked anxiously.

"He watched as they got into the trucks and drove off. But he says he saw two strange things."

"What were they?" Thuman asked.

"He says that the other Shell employees were all standing around, frozen in place. They didn't do anything. They looked like they were sleepwalking."

"The gas," Thuman said to Ximena.

"And then he said he saw something very odd," Ximena continued. "He says he saw one man changing his face."

Thumann paused. "What does that mean, changing his face? Is that a local idiom?"

Ximena continued to talk to the man in Spanish, trying to understand. She turned back to Thumann. "No, he means he literally changed his face. He insists he saw the man use his hands to alter his face. His nose, his jaw, everything, as if he was molding clay."

Thumann snorted. "The gas must have leaked into his mask, he was hallucinating."

Ximena continued to probe Carlito but came away with the same story. "Inspector, he insists this is what he saw," Ximena said. "He says the other men even called the man by his name... Dr. Cuba!"

Silence. Thumann froze.

Then, he realized there was nothing more he would learn here today. Thumann thanked Carlito and allowed him to return to work. As Thumann and his entourage returned to the military truck and drove out of seedy Callao to ritzy downtown Lima, where Thumann's hotel waited for him, he remained absolutely silent.

Thumann and Ximena parted with their escorts and settled in at the bar of the hotel. Thumann ordered scotch whiskey, and Ximena ordered a cola. Except for placing his drink order, Thumann remained silent still. Ximena allowed him his silence.

Finally, that silence broke. "There's no other evidence that suggests the gas causes hallucinations," Thumann said. "We've met dozens of people who were exposed to the gas, and none reported hallucinations."

"A matter of dosage?" Ximena asked.

"I don't think so. Someone else would have reported it. I think this Carlito saw something. Perhaps he was putting on a mask or taking one off. Through the lenses of his gas mask, he might not have seen things properly. But he heard things properly, for sure."

"The name?" Ximena asked.

"Yes. He heard them call this man 'Dr. Cuba.' Which troubles me."

"Why?" Ximena asked.

Thumann exhaled and sipped his scotch. "Because until now, I have refused to believe that this 'Dr. Cuba' was a single man. I insisted it was the name of the organization. Now, however, this suggests otherwise. Someone referred to an actual person as 'Dr. Cuba.' Combined with your religion theory, this is more and more troubling."

Ximena, inwardly, beamed with pride that her suggestion that religion may play a role was now "her theory." But she did not let that pride show on her face. Her father taught her that pride in oneself was good but to never let pride turn into arrogance. Ximena was not always sure she knew the difference.

Thumann continued. "If this is all being driven by religious fervor, and if we have one man leading it, then this begins to take on the aspects of a cult. A cult of crime, if you will."

"What do we do next?" Ximena asked.

"We have two crucial duties before us. We have to pursue our search for Gentleman, and we must bring in an expert on cults. This is not my area of expertise, but I know someone who can assist us."

"Who?" Ximena asked.

"Madame Blavatksy," Thumann snorted.

Chapter 8: The Mother Moon

Dr. Cuba could not recall precisely when the King God Skyx first called to him. Was it when he was a child? A teen? It was all very unclear, muddy. And it was not through a voice, nor could it be: Skyx was asleep, buried deep in the earth, waiting to be awakened. How could he speak?

And yet, at some point, Dr. Cuba was awakened, even as Skyx slept. He knew what he must do. Awakening the Sunken Gods would purify the world, cleanse humanity, restore the universe. Man was meant for kindling and food and nothing more. The notions of free will and choice and freedom were illusions. Even crime—the great engine of global society that drove history and revolution and progress—was nothing more than a temporary phantom. Dr. Cuba could use these illusions to bring about the true reality. And he would.

And so, he eventually killed his mother. But not before ensuring he kept her recipe for baked empanadas.

In fact, if memory served him properly, he made empanadas on the day of her death. To honor the day of her death, yes... yes, he recalled it now, clearly. He stood over her body and rolled the dough, using manteca, not mantequilla, filling them with meat and olive and boiled egg, and then—to honor his loving mother in the best way possible—baking them, not frying.

I'm not a savage, he thought as he pulled the starter cord of the chainsaw. Then, wearing the face of a man called Jacoby, he began cutting the girl's head in half.

Thumann had resigned himself to abandoning South America. He knew with every fiber of his bones that any further investigations into the many heists on the continent would yield the same results: bloviating officials, mind-numbed witnesses, and seemingly clean crime scenes.

He had learned enough from Santiago and Lima. He now knew that Dr. Cuba had used gas to perform his crimes in broad daylight. He now knew that Dr. Cuba had used some form of airship to escape with the gold. And Thumann now knew that Dr. Cuba had developed a skill for affecting disguises—although believing he could physically manipulate his own face was still a bit too much.

Thumann had also come to believe that Dr. Cuba was, in fact, a man. Indeed, Dr. Cuba had created a cult around himself, which explained the fear many had displayed when his name was even mentioned. This may have been why so many of Dr. Cuba's lower-level operatives were never caught—they may have killed themselves rather than face interrogation—or, if they were captured, never revealed a single iota of information about their leader. For sure, they were too terrified to do so, as Dr. Cuba likely used his campaign of terror against his own operatives as well, no doubt holding their families as collateral.

It had become clear to Thumann that what he was seeing now, with this "Dr. Cuba" and his vast criminal mob, was far worse than the Sicilian Mafia. Far worse than the rogue Russian gangs or Huks of the Philippines. Dr. Cuba's organization was more structured, more disciplined, and more obsessively secretive than anything the International Criminal Police Commission had ever faced.

In fact, Thumann knew that whispers of an international crime ring had dated back to at least 1910, when a French criminal mastermind, called the "Fantôme" by the national press, terrorized the city, and again in Germany ten years later, when the press blamed an unnamed "Doktor" for a wave of crimes in that country. In both cases, the alleged leaders were never apprehended, and police officials moved on to new cases.

But what if the cases were connected? If so, then this "Dr. Cuba" may have been operating as early as 1910, which would put him in his fifties or sixties, at least. The more Thumann recalled the French and German crime waves, the more he saw similarities. Could this all be a coincidence? Were these three villains all part of the same master organization?

Thumann shook his head, angry at himself. He now felt he had fallen into fantasy. He was losing his professional perspective, letting his decades of training fall away, allowing his head to run wild. It was all moot anyway; who cares if these decades-old crimes were related? The larger point was to solve the crimes happening today, right now. Historians could piece together the rest once Dr. Cuba is withering in a jail cell.

Thumann's decision was firm; he would leave South America and head to the United States, where he would meet with Madame Blavatsky, the notorious mystic, psychic, and well-traveled charlatan. Despite her dubious credentials and mild criminal background, if there was a religious connection between the crime wave and the gold, Blavatsky would likely know it.

The question now was, what to do with young Ximena? Thumann had become, in just a few days, as dependent on her as he was on Gentleman. He was secretly frustrated at himself for requiring an assistant at all, but Thumann also yielded to certain realities. First, he was older now, less able to do the physical work sometimes needed in chasing down evidence, and also at risk of overlooking a fact or detail. Yes, as disheartening as it was to admit,

Thumann needed a younger mind at his side. And he admitted—to himself, anyway, if no one else—that he enjoyed acting as a mentor. Someone would have to pick up his role once he passed on.

Ximena's role was as a translator and nothing more. He would not need her in the United States, even though she might be helpful in Miami. But Thumann also could not justify having the poor girl fly all over the world, putting herself in danger, just to help an old man with an increasing sense of loneliness.

Wait—loneliness?

Thumann stopped himself. *Where did that come from?*

He froze in place. It was true. He was lonely. His beloved wife Hilda had died in Germany, and they were childless. When he fled to the UK, Thumann left behind the few long-lost aunts and uncles he had left. Others still had died in the concentration camps. Once in England, he buried himself in his work and, yes, had befriended Gentleman. But now...

Gentleman was gone, and Thumann realized that—for all these years!—he had been using his young apprentice as a filler for the cold gaps inside himself. He had been lonely all this time and only now realized it.

It was a thunderbolt of a revelation and an unwelcome one. He was angry at himself. He was weak, so weak, and so, so stupid!

No, he would *not* invite young Ximena to the United States. He would not let his selfish insecurities endanger a young woman with a bright future ahead of her.

———————

The *Eustis* now approached the Mona Passage, which would take the Homunculus between Hispaniola and Puerto Rico southward, towards the northern coast of South America. While the most direct route, it was also dangerous. The Passage was notorious for rough and unpredictable seas, and the *Eustis* was not the most seaworthy vessel afloat.

Alone in the *Eustis'* wheelhouse, the Homunculus admitted that having a seasoned captain to assist would have been helpful in this instance. But the drunken Captain Beavin—had he been allowed to live—would likely have just made things worse. No, the Homunculus would have to navigate these waters on his own.

The sea was already rising, and the *Eustis* was feeling the strain. It would take the ship about 10 hours to cross the rough waters, so the Homunculus settled in for what would be a difficult and potentially violent night.

He thus allowed his mind to wander. The message to Dr. Cuba had been received, he was certain, and now a meeting was set. He would confront this problem, face to face, in Caracas. The Homunculus had a fair estimation of how things would resolve, given that his mind was closer to that of Dr. Cuba's than any other living soul. Or, well, whatever the equivalent would be.

This match of intellect created its own problems, however. As far ahead as the Homunculus could predict, so, too, could Dr. Cuba. For certain, his South American adversary would suspect a trap, so setting one was pointless. For certain, Dr. Cuba also suspected this would end in an attempt on his life, so trying anything of the sort was also a waste of time. No, this would have to be an intellectual confrontation.

We're not savages, after all, the Homunculus thought.

However, the Homunculus had one significant advantage. He knew Dr. Cuba, but Dr. Cuba did not know him. The South American was approaching this meeting in a position of weakness. He was curious, perhaps desperate. Dr. Cuba knew nothing of the

Homunculus nor even of his existence.

The Homunculus, meanwhile, knew Dr. Cuba's real history, things that Dr. Cuba himself did not know. The question before him, as he attempted to keep the *Eustis* afloat in the rough Mona Passage, was how much he should reveal.

It was irrelevant. All estimates suggested that Dr. Cuba would be unmoved by anything he may have to say, and the only result of the meeting would be the murder of this defective creature.

But what if he could be saved? What if he could be brought into the fold? So much more could be accomplished.

It was something worth trying, so, no... Caracas would not be an assassination. It would be a summit. Assassination could wait.

Ximena had little idea her fat German was having an existential debate about her. Instead, she was filled with renewed enthusiasm to help. Now, she wanted desperately to prove her worth as an essential part of Thumann's investigative team and not just the innocent young translator.

Fate—or something imitating it—was about to provide her the opportunity she sought.

Thumann was already in his room, likely asleep, while Ximena lingered in the bar area of the opulent Gran Hotel Bolívar. She resisted behaving like a simple Chilena from the desert and pretended she was not in complete awe at the obscene decadence of the place.

At the bar, she timidly ordered only water, afraid of what someone might think if she ordered anything costly, like a pisco sour or jugo de maracuyá. Scotland Yard was stingy, Thumann had told her. But Ximena also knew she might be thrown out if she continued to sit and drink free water, so she would not linger too long. As she watched the wealthy bankers and international celebrities—was that Clark Gable passing by?—she tried to remain focused on the case and what she might bring to it.

Shell Oil trucks. An airship laden with gold. A man who could change his face and who worships... Inti?

Nothing connected. Nothing made sense.

"Ximena Alejandra Torres Orellana?" a squeaky voice said, startling Ximena so that she quite physically jumped from her seat. Behind her, a young boy stood holding a piece of paper.

"Que es eso?" Ximena asked.

"Un mensaje para el Señor Tuman, Señorita," the boy said, handing Ximena the note. He pronounced Thumann's name as "too-man," without realizing it was the proper German way to say it. Ximena took the note, but the boy's hand remained hovering, now with palm open.

"Disculpame, niño, no tengo monedas." She had no money to give him. The few bills she had were in her room, hidden under a lamp in case the hotel staff thought of stealing it, and she had not carried any coins with her.

The boy left unhappy as Ximena unfolded the note. It was handwritten in English.

I AM IN A WAREHOUSE ON THE CORNER OF
DON BOSCO AND CHAVEZ IN BRENA. THEY WILL
MOVE ME SOON SO HURRY. DON'T BRING THUMANN.
~ G

It was Gentleman! He was safe, after all!

Ximena's mind raced. It was late, and her German was

sleeping. She knew she should call the police, but the Dr. Cuba organization had its fingers everywhere. How could she know if the policemen who answered her call wouldn't be on their payroll?

"Don't bring Thumann?" she thought to herself. *Why?* She tried to think of a reason that Gentleman would not want Thumann to come to save him and instead rely solely on her. This, too, made no sense.

Against all logic, against all instinct, Ximena made the rapid-fire, poorly-planned decision that any anxious 25-year-old may have made and to push ahead to save Gentleman herself. Whether this was because she wanted to save her new friend or simply impress the fat German, well… these were things she could think about on the taxi ride over.

If he's able to write, he may not be well guarded, she thought. *Maybe I can just open a door and get him out.*

Ximena was not experienced with such things, as she would soon learn. Kidnappings were not simple affairs, and kidnappers rarely left doors unlocked.

Fueled by a dual mixture of adrenaline and naivety, Ximena ran to her room, grabbed her money from under the lamp, and fled back out to the streets. Cabs waited outside, lined up by the doorman. She did not even negotiate a price, simply yelling at the closest car, "Jiron Don Bosco y Jiron Chavez, Breña, rapido!"

The cab driver hardly needed a reason to drive like a maniac, and Ximena was not clear if it was her anxiety that made him do so or if he was simply suicidal. The driver screeched away from the hotel, speeding across pedestrian crossings, driving over curbs, and even down one-way streets the wrong way—twice!—all while whistling an Yma Sumac song with complete calm.

What should have taken about 20 minutes only took half

that, although Ximena was not exactly sure she had not lost half the years of her life during a few of the right-angle turns. The driver, still whistling, pulled the taxi to a stop at the corner and pointed his finger. They were here.

Ximena paid him—he overcharged her, of course—and jumped onto the street. As the taxi left, Ximena was suddenly overwhelmed by the realization of her poor planning.

What am I doing? she asked herself. *What have I done?* Instinctively, she ran her hand to her neck and clutched the rosary beads that hung there.

It was nearly midnight, and she stood alone in the dark outside an empty warehouse. She had no weapons and would not know how to use them if she had. She was wearing the same shoes she would typically wear to church. The full moon hung over her, providing some light.

Mamaqilla, she thought. *She is here, too.*

But as filled with terror as Ximena was in that moment, she realized that poor Gentleman must be far more frightened. Was he tied up? Beaten? How had he written that note? She pushed on.

"Protégeme, Diosito," she whispered to herself. Then, one more prayer, this time in her native Aymara: "Nayar jark'aqapxita, Mamaqilla."

Ximena found the warehouse's main entrance. Locked.

What would her fat German do? *He'd find another way in,* she thought. Ximena scurried around the corner to one side of the building but was met only with a stone wall; no doors. She raced back to the corner and turned left to the other side. Luck: here was a fence she could climb to at least gain access to the yard inside. Climbing fences was something she had done since she was little, and the razor wire on top was not much of a threat either. This was a child's game.

Ximena removed her shoes, pulled the laces up straight, and put them between her teeth, freeing her hands. Her shoes now dangling from her mouth, Ximena scampered up the chain-link fence with ease, reaching the top in mere seconds. Then—as she had done a million times as a small girl in Arica—she shoved one hand inside a shoe as she held herself steady with the other hand. Then, she pressed the shoe down on the razor wire far enough that she could easily swing her leg over without being cut. Once both legs were over, she dropped the shoe to the ground and scampered down. The razor wire snapped back into shape, but she was already on the ground and had not even torn her skirt.

God let me misbehave as a child so I would know how to do this, now, she thought. *Gracias, Diosito.*

Putting her shoes back on, Ximena scanned the warehouse courtyard. The place was entirely dark, except for a single light coming from a window near to her right. It seemed to make sense to start there; Ximena was not skilled enough in police work to realize this would exactly be where the trap was.

Ximena walked slowly across the courtyard, stepping quietly so her shoes did not ring against the pavement. She reached the building with the lit window and found a door. The light was coming from a second-story room, so she'd need to find a stairway. The door, metal and rusted, creaked noisily as she opened it. For sure, she had lost any element of surprise.

Inside the door, Ximena saw a series of empty, unlit offices but a stairway nearby to the left. She slowly crept towards the stairs, trying to listen for any sounds in the room above. She heard nothing but her own breathing.

Ximena slowly crept up the stairs, trying to keep the wood

from creaking under her weight. The girl weighed nearly nothing, and this now proved to be a benefit.

Finally peering over the topmost stair, she gasped. In the center of the room was Gentleman; he was tied up in a chair positioned under a single hanging lamp. It was at this exact moment Ximena realized everything had been too easy.

She had walked, foolishly, into a trap.

And yet, no one else was nearby. Just Gentleman, in the center of the room.

She dashed up onto the second floor and rushed to Gentleman, trying to find the knots that held him in place. "Mister Gentleman," she whispered. "Are you alright?"

"Mmmfamafmaf," Gentleman mumbled.

He's drugged, Ximena thought. *This makes everything more difficult.*

Ximena struggled to undo the knots, which were clearly tied by someone strong. Bit by bit, she loosened the knots, breaking individual roper fibers with her teeth at times. Her actions were desperate, uncoordinated, chaotic.

As a result, Ximena did not notice the two men emerge from the shadows with weapons pointed right at her. It was only when, in the far corner of the room, a small desk light snapped on that Ximena realized the trap had sprung. There, sitting calmly, was a third man at a radio set. He turned to her.

"We intend to give him to you," the man said. Ximena's face was frozen in terror; she did not know what to do except to remain motionless and listen. "We will even help untie him for you." The man at the radio nodded toward his two armed fellows; one of them approached Ximena with a knife, causing her to gasp audibly. He rolled his eyes and exhaled, pointing at the seated

Gentleman; he intended to free him, not kill her.

Ximena stepped aside.

The man cut Gentleman loose and shook him. Gentleman grunted a bit more.

"Your friend will be confused for another few minutes," the radio man said. "He will be fine after that. You can bring him back to your Hotel Bolívar and the detective Heiner Thumann."

Ximena felt the blood rush from her. She was not a detective but could understand a threat when she heard it. The radio man was letting her know that they—Dr. Cuba's men—knew where she was staying and who she worked for. Of course, she knew this already since the boy had delivered the message to her personally, but hearing it come from the man's icy voice terrorized her anyway. Everything had become real in just the last few seconds.

"With any luck," the man continued, fiddling with his radio dial, "you will be able to return to your family in Arica soon and leave all of this behind you." Now the man was threatening Ximena's family; her fear was slowly being replaced with … what was it? Anger?

The moon shone through an overhead window. For some reason, it gave Ximena strength. She remained silent, trying to help Gentleman to his feet. Gentleman was not a large man, but he was still too heavy for her to lift on her own.

The radio man held up a hand, motioning that Ximena should wait. "Give him just a few minutes. He will fully wake up. Let's talk until then, Miss Torres."

Ximena relented as she scanned the room for something—anything—that might help in this situation. She took inventory of her situation. She was on the second floor, and there were windows on two of the outward-facing walls. There was the stairway she came up, the radio man in the corner. A single light over Gentleman's chair and another light over the radio man. The radio was an old unit, with a coiled fabric wire running to the man's headphones. The two men near her held large pistols. They were dressed poorly. One had a knife.

Details, quickly, what other details?

The room was largely empty except for some crates. No markings, no indication of what they held. Wooden floors, wooden walls. Everything creaking, rusty. The moon.

The man continued to talk. Ximena was running out of time.

"We know your Detective Thumann. We have a message for him, and Mister Gentleman is that message. When you return him to Thumann, you will tell your inspector that we can take him any time we want. We can take his friends, his colleagues. And tell him we can take Hilda."

Ximena did not know what the radio man was talking about. Thumann had told her very little about himself and nothing about someone named Hilda.

She continued to inventory: Gentleman sitting, ropes now on the floor, man with a knife. Guns pointed.

No, wait. The knife was on the floor now. The man set it down when he freed Gentleman. He held a gun, but the knife was on the floor.

"Remember, young Miss Torres. Tell Inspector Thumann we can take his Hilda," the radio man repeated, speaking slowly. "He will insist she is already dead, but deep inside, he will know this is not true. He will know and will understand what to do. Tell him we can take Hilda."

The knife on the floor!

A voice on the radio crackled, forcing the radio man to pause. "This is operator 89 calling operator 62 on 17.475 megacycles. Report, operator 62." The radio man scrambled for a moment; his headphones were not plugged in, and the voice came over the external speaker. Now he quickly moved to plug the bulky headphone jack into the radio's front, silencing the speaker. Was Ximena not supposed to hear that?

She used the moment. Lunging downward, she grabbed the knife and raised it. The men smiled and simply pointed their pistols at her head. The radio man, his headphones now plugged in, refocused his attention on Ximena. "Girl, you cannot possibly hope to threaten us," he said.

Ximena moved behind Gentleman. "I don't intend to threaten you. I am threatening *him*." To the shock of the men, Ximena brought the knife to Gentleman's throat. The radio man flinched, raising his hands as if to stop her. The gunmen quivered.

"If I kill him now, you have nothing," Ximena said, her voice cracking but firm. "You won't have a message for Inspector Thumann. And I think you have some other reason for returning him to us. I am taking away that reason."

Ximena's heart pounded. She had no intention of killing Gentleman, and it was likely the men knew this. But if Gentleman was in any way valuable to their plan, could they afford the risk? Ximena affected the meanest scowl her face could muster to telegraph her seriousness.

The men froze, letting Ximena know her gamble paid off for the moment. She pressed the blade into Gentleman's skin; still drugged, he simply grunted.

"You," Ximena said to the closest gunman. "Put your gun

in Gentleman's lap, right here, and walk backward." To her shock, the gunman complied.

They are being too compliant, she thought. Ximena knew very well how she looked to the men: a young, frail Catholic girl with church shoes, holding a knife in a trembling hand. *Why are they complying?*

Then, in an instant, Ximena realized something. The room with the chair and the lamp and the radio man was not the trap; no, *Gentleman* was the trap. A trap for Thumann, and she was just the delivery girl.

Ximena could not see much more than that but hoped she could figure this out later … if she could only get out alive.

The man gently put his pistol on Gentleman's lap, allowing Ximena to reach down and grab it. Now she had a gun as well. The men seemed unthreatened by her shaking, skinny arm holding a gun at them, but instead more concerned she might actually kill Gentleman.

Then, the radio man moved, slowly lowering his headphones. He had received his message. Ximena continued to hold a trembling gun at the men, waving it back and forth from one to another.

"Well, the situation has changed, Miss Torres," the radio man said. "I've now been instructed to deliver Gentleman through other means. Someone up high has changed their mind about you."

Ximena's eyes widened more.

"Kill her," the radio man said.

Whether it was instinct, God's invisible hand, or Mamaqilla's silver light, Ximena was suddenly flooded with one pure, clear thought: survive. Now came the moment that, in retrospect, Ximena knew was inevitable from the moment she saw the knife on the ground. Now came the moment every bit of her religious upbringing would be thrown aside. Now came the moment her ancestors would be ashamed of her.

Uñtapxam, awicha! she thought. *Look away, Abuelita!*

Ximena swiftly moved her arm to the right, pointing the pistol directly at the second gunman, who still held a gun. She fired, shooting him directly in the neck. He fell back, blood gushing from his pierced jugular. Ximena swung her hand back toward the first gunman, who was frozen in shock. As he began to lunge, she fired again. This time, the bullet missed, so Ximena fired again. And again. The man was so close the bullets smashed into his heart and neck, and he, too, dropped.

Her hand no longer shaking, adrenaline steeling her, she now aimed the gun at the radioman. She tried to remember what the movies had taught her: does a pistol have six bullets? Or seven? She had fired four bullets. If the gun was fully loaded when she grabbed it, she may still have shots for the radioman. But she needed to get closer.

Ximena slowly walked towards the radio man, who—stuck in the corner—had nowhere to go. He fiddled with some switches and began speaking desperately into his headset. "This is Operator 62 on 17.475 megacycles, X red eleven, X red eleven. I repeat, X red eleven!"

Ximena now stood directly in front of the man, who looked terrified. She recalled how he mentioned Arica to threaten her, her family, her world, and she fired.

It was anger, after all.

With all three men dead, Ximena froze. There was a silence once the ringing in her ears dissipated. She half expected to hear police sirens coming, as they always do in the movies. There were no sirens, no sounds. Just the wind through the cracked windows above.

There were no tears. She no longer trembled. If a doctor had been present, she would have been diagnosed as being in shock. Ximena, in her moment, did not care. In the new silence, with the smell of gunpowder in the air, she moved to Gentleman. He was waking up, shaking his head.

Gentleman was still groggy and making little sense but could walk on his own power. He was able to mumble. "The logbook," he said, trying to lift his hand to point to the radioman's desk. "For Thumann," he said.

Ximena went to the desk, stepping carefully over the radioman's body, being careful not to look at his face. She picked up the logbook and rushed back to Gentleman. She helped him down the stairs and out towards the gate. Ximena used her last bullets to shoot the lock on the gate, knowing there was no way she could get Gentleman over the razor wire. Her gun empty, she threw it aside, focusing instead on holding tightly to the logbook and to Gentleman's arm.

They stumbled a few blocks in the dark Lima night until Ximena found an intersection with some late-night traffic. A taxi ride later and Gentleman was returned to Thumann at the Gran Hotel Bolívar.

At which point, Ximena fell and sobbed, the weight of what she had done crushing down on her.

There would not be enough prayers to absolve her now.

Chapter 9: The Abyssal Pit

Any joy Thumann might have had at being reunited with Gentleman was overshadowed by his concern for his assistant's medical condition. Gentleman was fading in and out of consciousness, mumbling unintelligibly and wobbling like a drunk at sea. He showed no signs of significant physical injury—a few scrapes and nothing more—but Thumann knew there was more at work here.

Ximena's account of how desperate the operatives appeared in their desire to have Gentleman returned unharmed furthered Thumann's suspicion. Gentleman was being put back on the board... for a reason. They had done something to him. Perhaps the doctors could find out what.

Through his Peruvian National Police contacts, Thumann arranged to have Gentleman rushed to the official police hospital. There, Thumann was told, Gentleman would receive the best of care. The best of care was, unfortunately, lacking.

Thumann and Ximena were rudely placed in an already overcrowded waiting room that spilled out onto a gravel parking lot. Nurses wheeled patients over the gravel, from one building to the next, their gurneys rattling and causing the patients to vibrate like jackhammers. Much of the hospital was open to the outside, and Lima's air was filled with a combination of dust and bus exhaust, all of which wafted freely into the hospital's interior. *This can't be sterile*, Thumann thought.

While waiting, Thumann could finally greet Ximena properly. He stood in front of her and hugged her, bearlike, his ability to contain his emotion exhausted. The poor girl looked like a ragdoll compared to his tall, bulky frame, but she also broke down in the moment. She began sobbing and recounted the full story of what she had been forced to do.

Thumann had enough experience with conservative Catholics to know the trauma Ximena faced was not only psychological but spiritual. And while the next character in their winding tale—the lunatic Madame Blavatsky—was, by her own assertion, "spiritual," she would not be the kind of spiritual healer Ximena needed right now.

Thumann did his best to comfort Ximena but also acknowledged his weaknesses in this area. He was not used to playing the role of father, and that was what was called for here. It did not take long for Thumann to understand the serendipity of the moment. Ximena needed the comfort of a spiritual father, and Thumann was standing in the middle of a country filled to the gill-holes with priests.

As Ximena's sobbing subsided, Thumann excused himself for a minute. He went to the nurse's desk and simply started saying, "Padre… Padre," while moving his hands across his neck to mime a priest's collar and then making the sign of the cross. The nurses, overwhelmed with their workload, understood the request but were in no hurry to fulfill it. Thumann returned to his seat next to Ximena.

He again wrapped Ximena in his big bear arm and stared out the window. The two of them stayed that way for many long minutes until Ximena recalled two crucial details. She reached into her pocket and pulled out the logbook.

"I stole this," she said, meekly. "Mr. Gentleman seemed to think it would be important. Maybe a code book? The radio man was using it."

Thumann pulled his arm from around Ximena and took the book, looking at it carefully. He opened it and smiled broadly. "Not quite a code book, but useful nonetheless, dear miss!" he boomed. "This is fantastic. A list of times and radio frequencies, no doubt used by the Dr. Cuba gang for communications. They likely cycle through different frequencies at different times to make their communications appear random. This logbook helps decipher that routine."

Ximena nodded. "Yes, I heard the man talking about megacycles. That is a radio term, no?"

"Exactly, Miss. Did you overhear the exact number of megacycles? Did the radio operator say it?"

"Seventeen-something," Ximena answered. "Seventeen point 4 something. I don't remember."

"Close enough. And what time did all this happen, the business in the warehouse? As exact as you can remember?"

"I left the hotel at 11:35, I remember seeing the big clock in the lobby. The ride to the warehouse took about ten minutes, maybe 15."

"Let's say you arrived at 11:50, then," Thumann offered.

"Then, it took me about five minutes to enter the warehouse grounds..."

"11:55," Thumann tallied.

"... and another five to find Mister Gentleman."

"So, midnight."

"But then, I'm not sure. When the gunmen showed up, everything got confusing."

"If you had to guess?" Thumann asked.

"Fifteen minutes inside the room with them. The radio operator was the last man I ..." tears formed again in her eyes.

"I understand," Thumann interrupted so Ximena did not have to recount the exact events again. "That would mean he was sending his message at around 12:15 in the morning, at 17.4 megacycles."

Ximena sniffed. "But the frequency is incomplete. It's useless."

"Not at all. These frequencies are typically used in steps of point-zero-zero-five. So, we just need to turn on the radio just after midnight and scan the frequencies from 17.400 through 17.500, stepping through them to find when a message is coming through. It's quite literally five minutes of work! You've done well, Miss. Very well."

"Won't their messages be coded? The radio man was speaking in code, he kept saying 'x' this and 'x' that."

"Yes," Thumann answered. "But the radio spectrum is filled with messages from thousands of parties all over the world. National shortwave broadcasts, individual ham operators. To know what broadcasts were used by the Dr. Cuba gang is a huge step. Now we can focus on those and start to glean the code they use."

"Wait, I remember, he was shouting 'x red eleven,' as if it meant danger!"

Thumann smiled broadly. "That will help decode the cipher they use when communicating. In such cases, every tiny scrap of detail matters."

There was another scrap of detail that Ximena hesitated to bring up but knew she must. "There is something else," she said, straightening herself. Her demeanor changed, and Thumann sensed it.

"What is it, Miss?" he asked, his voice low.

"They had a message for you. A personal message."

Thumann hesitated. "So, they know I am on the case. But that's to be expected, it hasn't been a secret. What did they say?"

"They said they can take your Hilda. They repeated it. They can take your Hilda."

Thumann's heart stopped. His lungs froze, and his limbs shook. He knew the evil of criminals firsthand and had spent a lifetime confronting it. But this… this was something entirely different. Something sadistic and all too personal.

"My Hilda is dead. She died in Germany. They can do nothing to her," Thumann said, monotone.

Ximena spoke slowly and quietly. "They said you'd say that. They said you would know it's not true, though. And that you would know what they can do."

Thumann's fists shook uncontrollably. He stood, not wanting young Ximena to see his emotions in this way. He left her, walking outside and around a corner, out of view. And Thumann began sobbing. A sobbing not entirely of sadness and loss but of equal parts rage and hate. His clenched fists turned purple, and his heart could be felt pounding the gravel below him.

Hilda!

———————————

Father Antonio approached the giant, bearded man standing in the gravel parking lot. The man appeared red-faced, shaken.

"You requested a priest?" Father Antonio asked in English. "Do you speak English?"

Thumann shook off his emotions to the best he could. He straightened himself and wiped his face with his handkerchief. "Yes, Father," he stumbled. "But not for me."

"Are you okay, Señor?" the priest asked.

"I will be fine. It's my associate, Miss Ximena." For the first time, Thumann realized that he may have pronounced her name correctly. "She's been through a trauma."

"What kind of trauma, Señor?" the priest asked. He appeared a genuine man, one ready to help, unlike many of the other hospital employees who seemed disinterested in the greater good of medicine and merely obsessed with checking forms and running around like madmen.

"She is helping a police investigation, but she is not a professional police employee. She's just a girl from Chile, a translator. She was forced to shoot three men last night to save her life and the life of our associate. There was no other option for her. More than that, she helped obtain evidence that may shut down a global campaign of murder and mayhem. The lives she may have saved can't be counted."

Thumann took a breath. The priest was listening intently. "But she is a Catholic, deeply spiritual. She is in pain. See if you can help her. Make her understand that she has done a great good, even if she can't understand that right now. These were evil men, horrible men doing horrible things. She saved a good man and herself. There was no other option."

Thumann sounded uncharacteristically pleading. He did not care.

"I will talk to her. And you, do you need counsel, Señor?"

"No," Thumann said, "I will be fine. But you are better suited to help my young assistant. There, she's sitting there." Thumann pointed to Ximena inside the waiting room. "Go help. She is important to me."

Father Antonio nodded. "With the grace of God, I will try my best, Señor. I wish you peace."

The *Eustis* was halfway through the rough seas of the Mona Passage when the Homunculus decided to park.

More accurately, he maneuvered the battered smuggling ship to the edge of the cliffs of Islote Monito, a bizarre, uninhabited island in the dead center of the seaspace between Hispaniola and Puerto Rico. Islote Monito was technically part of Puerto Rico and one of a trio of islands in the Mona Passage. To the south was the much larger Mona Island, a nature preserve frequented by researchers and thrill seekers. Monito, on the other hand, was entirely inaccessible by boat, as the entire shoreline was comprised of massive, ragged cliffs. Whereas Mona received an influx of people poking and prodding it for secrets, Monito was entirely untouched. If one were to scale those cliffs, they'd find a green but relatively flat geography, measuring only some 34 acres in total area. But Monito was uninhabited specifically because no one *could* scale those cliffs.

Which is what the Homunculus now intended to do. He brought the *Eustis* as close as he could to the rocks, navigating to a small u-shaped formation along the island's northern coast. While the waves crashed and abused the rest of Monito's coastline, the water within the tiny "u" was calm enough to bring a ship of the *Eustis'* size to rest. A larger vessel would have been out of luck, which is precisely why the Homunculus had sought out the *Eustis* in the first place.

With the rickety ship anchored, more or less, the Homunculus could now be more leisurely with his efforts. He patiently walked to the stairway of the Eustis and down to the cargo hold. Finding some rope, he brought this to where his original crate sat, with its broken lab equipment scattered nearby. He began to wrap the rope around his vat of blood-and-gasoline mixture, fashioning a harness. Once satisfied it was secure, the Homunculus hoisted the vat over his shoulder and adjusted the rope so he could walk normally, with his hands free.

Now, he headed up to the main deck and walked to the port side railing to a point where he could reach out and touch the cliffs. And so, ignoring the bobbing of the *Eustis*, he grasped the rocks and, with tremendous strength, began scaling Monito's cliffside. From a distance, this figure, dressed in black, must have appeared like a man-sized insect crawling up a sheer wall. Within only three minutes, the Homunculus swung himself up and over to flat ground, some 200 feet from the sea below. He adjusted his clothes and the slung metal tank and headed for the center of the islet.

Monito was a tiny speck of a thing and relatively flat. It was patched with green grass and moss, with a smattering of seabird guano but little else. From here, one had a 360-degree view of the Mona Passage and a clear view of the larger Mona Island just a few miles to the south.

Monito was the reason the Homunculus chose to steal the *Eustis* and head southward via ship rather than by aeroplane. No aeroplane could land on its tiny surface.

It was early morning when the Homunculus strode towards the center of Monito, towards a rock formation that stood about three meters in height. The rocky bulge was also covered in short grass and appeared entirely unassuming; certainly, no one would suspect what lay beneath. The Homunculus approached a specific area of the formation, finding a notch in the rocks into which he placed his ivory hand. With a slight tug and a grind of rusted metal, the rocks parted, and one portion swung away. Once the initial rusty seal was broken, the notched rock slid easily, counterbalanced by a pivot and counterweights below the surface. This was not a rock outcropping, after all; it was a door.

The morning sun disappeared as he entered the false entrance. Sitting nearby was a gasoline generator, which the Homunculus started. It sputtered and struggled but eventually relented and ran under its own agreement. A few switches flipped, and the interior was lit with a string of yellowing incandescent lightbulbs.

Inside the outcropping was a set of small rooms, in many ways similar to Dr. Cuba's salt bed bunker. But instead of a radio room, there was a small chemical laboratory with metal benches and curious equipment. A rack of glassware, with petri dishes and beakers, hung from the ceiling. In the corner was a filthy cot covered in moldy blankets, with a small nightstand and lamp at its side. A small ladder led down a set of additional rooms, now buried below Monito's surface, which included a small library filled with scientific texts, a table with chess set, and a tiny kitchen with gas burner and rusted metal pots. Chalkboards lined the walls with strange symbols written, perhaps, decades ago. Spiderwebs competed with damp and darkness for dominance in the moldy space.

The Homunculus carried himself down the ladder to the inner rooms and placed his vat on a table. Under the light of a single flickering bulb, he attached this to a set of tubes connected to a larger metal tank that sat in a darkened corner and transferred the contents. *We have enough for at least four of us*, he thought as he finished emptying the small vat into the large tank.

His offloading complete, the Homunculus headed towards a round submarine-like hatch on the floor. The hatch was sealed with a circular wheel; this was secured with a thick, complex combination locking mechanism. The Homunculus entered the combination and turned the wheel. The hatch unsealed, allowing air to rush downward into the chamber below with a brief sucking noise. With the hatch swung upwards, another ladder was revealed. The Homunculus swung his weight into the hatch and climbed down the ladder.

Once down on what would now be, technically, the third level, the Homunculus flipped a wall switch. Unlike the two floors above, the lighting did not utilize decrepit, flickering incandescent bulbs but bright white illumination of some entirely different nature. A low, fizzling hum could be heard from some chamber elsewhere nearby, but this was not the grumble of the gasoline generator; no, this, too, was something entirely different and much more powerful.

The interior of the bottom level was unlike anything seen in even the best university laboratories or those of the best German or American scientific facilities. An entirely circular room, approximately two hundred feet in diameter, lined entirely with stainless steel. The walls were steel, the floors were steel, and the overhead structure—barring the strange lights—was of the same stuff. The room was clearly sterile and sealed off with an airtight hatch to prevent rain or humidity from entering.

The room made no sense when compared to the hermit-like living conditions just one floor up. Here, some sparse tables sat in the center next to round metallic cylinders, each about two feet in diameter and as tall as the room, fitted with gauges and switch panels. Some of the cylinders had lights that blipped on and off, communicating something to whoever might know what the flashes meant. Other metal-and-glass cabinets held laboratory glassware, surgical equipment, balances, and unmarked white containers of unknown powders and liquids. Along the perimeter of the room, spaced evenly across the 360-degree space, were ten strange copper cylinders, thicker and different from those in the center of the room, appearing like upright iron lungs. A single, thick glass porthole was fitted near the top of each, but the interiors were dark, and whatever contents were kept within remained entirely hidden from view. These strange iron lung devices were then connected with electrical cables and hoses that ran along the room's circular edge into dedicated holes that led them toward the fizzing, humming power source.

One would easily mistake the room for a surgical theater, given its bright lighting and overall cleanliness. One would be wrong.

The Homunculus headed for one of the copper iron lungs. Flipping a series of heavy metal latches, the front made a snapping sound, and the Homunculus swung the entire front open. Now, the iron lung appeared more like an upright iron maiden, clearly designed for someone to repose in. In silence, the Homunculus shed his dirty, damp clothes, revealing a body of the same smooth, pore-free porcelain veneer as that of his face and hands. Other than his black hair—and that single red finger—his skin was entirely ivory. On his chest were eight puncture points, as if someone methodically had stabbed the creature repeatedly.

The Homunculus stepped into the copper iron maiden and settled into a standing position. In front of him, on the interior side of the front panel of the cylinder, several thick metal probes extended inward. Not any number: eight such probes. This truly was an iron maiden; if the door shut, anything inside would be impaled by the probes. Nevertheless, the Homunculus flipped a switch near where his hand rested. The thick door swung slowly shut. Inside, the metal probes contacted the puncture points in the

Homunculus' chest, driving themselves into his flesh.

Silence, for a moment, and then the whirring of pumps.

One of the tubes leading into the iron maiden began to flow. A red mixture filled the tube and started feeding into the copper vault.

A reddish mixture of gasoline and human blood.

––––––––––––

Ximena followed Father Antonio to the small chapel inside the police hospital, leaving her fat German alone in the waiting room. She appreciated the effort the Inspector had exerted to recruit a priest for her, and she was thankful to have someone to talk to about her burden.

Once in the chapel, Ximena and Father Antonio prayed, and she felt worse, not better. She ended her prayer sobbing. Father Antonio hugged her, and she shook and shuddered as she poured tears on the poor priest's robe. To his credit, he simply allowed her time to release her emotions without interrupting with unnecessary lectures or prayers.

Finally, she slowed down, and Father Antonio spoke. "Your Inspector friend told me what happened. At least the broad strokes. I understand you were called upon to do terrible things but in the service of a greater good. Would this be a fair characterization of last night?"

"I don't know, Father," Ximena sniffed. "I killed three men. That's all I know."

"Is that all you know, though? Think carefully, Miss."

"Yes, it is," she whispered.

"It is not, though, is it? I understand you saved a man. You also saved yourself. And, perhaps most importantly, you may have saved untold others."

"What?" Ximena asked, confused.

"Your guilt has blinded you to facts before you. Yes, you were forced to do a horrible thing. But you did so in the service of goodness, as a servant to others, and at great sacrifice to yourself. You do a disservice to God by remembering only one bad part of a far greater equation."

"A disservice to God?" Ximena appeared deeply troubled by this.

"There is a grand design, the design of God Almighty. Solomon spoke of this in Ecclesiastes and told us how each thing that happens is established as part of that design. He told us, 'There is an appointed time for everything. A time to give birth, and a time to die; a time to plant, and a time to uproot the plant. A time to weep, and a time to laugh; a time to mourn, and a time to dance.'"

Ximena finished the verse. "A time to kill and a time to heal."

Father Antonio nodded. "You were playing your role in the service of God and your fellow man. If it is true that you have saved untold lives, as your Inspector friend recounted to me, then your sacrifice has been mighty and not in vain. You may not have sinned, Miss. You may have served God."

"May have," Ximena repeated. "We cannot know. I may merely be a murderess."

Father Antonio exhaled. "No, we cannot know. Not in this life."

"How can I know? How can I live not knowing?" she asked.

Father Antonio faced a choice now. He could lie to the girl and make her feel better but at the expense of her personal development. He opted for the more difficult direction. "There will not be a voice, señorita," he began, being careful with each word that would follow. "You won't hear anything. You will pray, and you will sit in silence. You will remain in silence, in fact. God will not answer you."

Ximena looked up in shock. No priest had ever spoken this way.

"I will not lie to you. You have been handed a great burden, señorita. We cannot know for sure if this is part of God's plan or not, and any priest who says otherwise disrespects you."

"But you said ... there was a Grand Design?" Ximena asked.

"I was disrespecting you. It was a reflexive act, a habit. You deserve better. You deserve the truth. We priests have no better insight into God's plan than you or any other layperson. We dress ourselves in robes and speak Latin, but we still know no more than you do. We can only rely on faith. My faith tells me that you were meant to save your friend, and to do that, you had to do something terrible. But my faith is not your facts. You will have to find your own faith in this matter and see where it leads you."

"I don't want to remember myself as a murderess," Ximena said quietly. "I want to forget all of this."

"But you cannot, and that is a fact. This will burden you for as long as you let it. You must find a way to reconcile what has happened. Both what you have done and what was done to you."

"I don't know how to do that," Ximena said., her voice a mere whisper.

"I know a way to start, señorita. Pray to the men. Call them to you. Whether you believe them to be spirits or mere memories, speak to them. God will forgive you, and your eternity is safe. But to secure your present, you need to obtain their forgiveness. Talk to them. Tell them what you feel, let them know your pain. Tell them you had no choice. And, even more importantly, forgive *them*. They were cruel men led to do cruel things, and they, too, require forgiveness. You and those men are connected together forever in a tragedy that must be turned into a blessing. But to free yourself enough to make that transition, you must speak directly to the dead. And this you do through prayer, señorita. Prayer."

Ximena understood only parts of what Father Antonio was saying to her, but she was memorizing all of it. Later, when she was calmer, with distance between this day and its horrors, she would return to his words and understand them more. For now, she let the sound of the priest's voice alleviate a small amount of her guilt and shame.

As for Father Antonio's assertion that by killing Dr. Cuba's men, Ximena may have been serving God, the Homunculus would have agreed.

Franklin D. Roosevelt complicated matters, which, as President of the United States, was both his right and purpose. He was now very much dead as of May 1945, but the problems he created for Dr. Cuba remained. FDR was himself part of a greater plot to slowly inculcate the American public into the idea of the "benevolent dictator," giving way to the eventual rise of an *actual* dictator. Still, FDR complicated that plan, too, by being a bit too benevolent and not sufficiently dictatorial.

Now, it fell to Harry S. Truman, but the forces at work—of which even Dr. Cuba was unaware—were not convinced he was the right man for the job. He was being given tremendous weapons of incomprehensible power but seemed to lack the stomach to use them. The unique brand of American democracy was proving to be a tough beast to kill.

The fact that Dr. Cuba was unaware of greater powers at work should have been impossible, given his fingers had reached through nearly every international border on the world map. And, yet, there were greater powers at work, invisible to him.

Dr. Cuba saw the effects, however, which sometimes scuttled his plans. These forced realignments and repositioning. Such was the case with FDR's "Limitation Order L-208." This order demanded all non-essential gold mines be temporarily made inoperative as the world war continued. Because Dr. Cuba needed pure gold, not rough ore, the mines themselves were of little interest to him; instead, he focused on vaults and national reserves and private stashes of refined gold bars. But there was one mine in particular that Dr. Cuba needed; Limitation Order L-208 stood in the way by not only affecting all mines in general but restricting this particular mine explicitly.

This was the Homestake Mine in Lead, South Dakota. For nearly a year prior, Dr. Cuba had concocted a complex plan to gain access to the mine through bribery and extortion of major mining company shareholders. He would need uninterrupted access to the mine for precisely one month before a particular date, which was fast approaching. Congress wrangled over Limitation Order L-208, but eventually, it began to impact on Homestake, and operations were shut down.

Dr. Cuba realigned and repositioned. He would have to use the Limitation Order for his benefit. His prior plans to take over the mine were now abandoned, written off as an acceptable loss. Perhaps now that the Limitation Order shut down Homestake by force, he would have an easier time gaining access to it for The Work.

Yes, this might be better.

Large equipment waited for installation at Homestake, transported to a remote field some miles away. Dr. Cuba had the large trucks to transport the equipment to the mine and the men to perform the installation. The problem now was having access to the mine to do it. Dr. Cuba had ten days—less than two weeks—to install the equipment and have it ready to receive the injection material. He needed access *today*.

There was much fighting underway to have the Limitation Order revoked now that Germany had surrendered. As a result, all the major players were positioning themselves for the moment when the gold would once again flow from Homestake. Mining companies lobbied and harassed their Congressmen, using every tactic in the book to get them to fast-track L-208's revocation. The miners' labor unions picketed at the mine, demanding a greater share of the profits when operations restarted, threatening to delay that restart should L-208 be lifted. Some major weapons manufacturers continued to press Truman and his administration to leave L-208 as-is, arguing they needed the men and resources for the fight against Japan and that it was still too soon to revoke the Order.

So many parties arguing over so many different interests complicated matters greatly since it added a multitude of potential outcomes, each of which would impact Dr. Cuba's plan significantly. He decided to focus on the immediate: the picketers outside the mine. They presented a physical barrier to entry and had to be removed.

Today.

And, so, Dr. Cuba injected himself with morphine and crushed the bones in his face to take on the appearance of Charles

Idlewyld, a labor union boss from Chicago, Illinois. The real Idlewyld, a mid-level pit bull from the United Mine Workers of America, was tied up in a basement somewhere, waiting to be incorporated into a cement foundation for a new bank being built on South LaSalle Street.

Dr. Cuba now stalked the streets of Chicago, wearing a bulky suit and appropriate padding to make his body look more like that of Idlewyld. His gait was rough, arrogant, forceful; his feet struck the pavement noisily. People would know he was arriving before he entered a room.

And so, Dr. Cuba—Idlewyld, now—did enter a room within the Hampstead Building in a rougher part of Chicago. Here, Idlewyld would have to convince other labor leaders to abandon the picket at Homestake, leaving at least a few months of peace to allow Dr. Cuba to complete The Work.

Idlewyld clomped his way across wooden floorboards to a meeting room, which was already filled with noisy, arguing labor union officials and shop stewards. Everyone smoked cigarettes, pipes, or cigars, and the smoke filled the room as if it were on fire. A red-faced fat man shouted.

"Idlewyld, you finally made it. You're late! What, some street whore slow you down?" The man laughed. The others in the room lowered their voices until it was more or less quiet.

"Let's just say I slowed her down," Idlewyld said. "She won't be walking straight for a few days."

The room broke out in raucous laughter.

Another man, thin and bearing an annoyed expression, did not laugh. "Get on with it, Idlewyld. Why did you call this meeting? This matter was already agreed on, I have no idea why we are wasting time here today."

Idlewyld walked to the front of the conference table. Some of the men sat, others remained standing. "It was decided, now it will be un-decided."

"What the hell does that mean?" the thin man said, scowling. "Goddammit, man, this was all worked out already!"

Another man stood. "Jacoby's right, our men are at Homestake already and making a lot of good noise out there. The entire town of Lead is under our control. The company officials don't dare set foot there. They are going to have to yield to our demands if they ever want to see a piece of dirt at the mine, never mind an ounce of gold!"

The room applauded. Men banged the table in support.

Another man chimed in. "For once, we're winning!"

The thin man scowled some more. "Now is not the time to back down, Idlewyld. I don't know what game you're playing at here, but you need to go back to your cozy office and let the real men run the play now."

More applause, more banging on tables, more hooting and hollering.

Idlewyld stood firm. He banged on the table to get everyone's attention. "Look, men, this is shortsighted. We are holding a mine hostage, and the mine is shut down. All those men are standing around an unused road guarding a front gate that no one is even walking up to, much less trying to get through. We've got... how many men out there?" he asked.

"About ninety!" someone shouted.

"Ninety men!" Idlewyld continued. "Those are ninety men we could be using somewhere else where it matters!"

A few clapped in agreement, but most remained silent.

The thin man—Jacoby—spoke again. "Homestake is the

most lucrative mine this country's ever seen, and you know it, Idlewyld. We need to be in control of those operations the minute… no, the *second* that mine re-opens. If we have to camp out there for forty years, we will!" The room applauded once more.

As Idlewyld prepared to speak again, there was a commotion outside the room, pulling the men's attention away from their conversation. Loud voices, stomping, someone pleading, "What's going on?"

Eight burly Chicago police officers barged into the room, billy clubs brandished, with one senior officer with a shotgun held at the ready. The shotgun wielder spoke, not quite shouting but using a loud enough tone to ensure he had everyone's attention. "You boys stay where you are and don't move. We don't want to be bashing any heads here today, but we came armed just in case any of you feel like getting bashed anyway."

"What is this?" Jacoby demanded. "You're interfering with legitimate union business!"

The lead officer pointed his shotgun at Jacoby; it was an overt display of menace. "That's the one," he said.

Four of the police officers approached Jacoby and grabbed him roughly, pulling his arms behind his back. One of them strapped handcuffs on him.

"What is this??!!" Jacoby shouted. "What are you doing? I've done nothing wrong!! This is illegal interference in protected organizing activities!"

"Take him downstairs, and if he keeps talking, break his jaw," the lead officer said. He turned to the rest of the union organizers, including Idlewyld. "And we're not here to interrupt your little union tea party. You fellas can continue shouting at the sky all you want as soon as we leave. But this fella Jacoby was caught in possession of pornographic materials the likes I haven't seen in all my years as a cop. He won't be organizing anything for a long, long time."

"Hogwash!" one of the union members yelled. "This is labor intimidation! Jacoby never did any such thing!"

The lead officer paused as his colleagues dragged Jacoby, kicking, out of the room. The lead officer turned and looked the loudmouth in the eye. "Oh, yeah?" he said. "Jacoby never did it, you say?"

"That's right, flatfoot, you and your pals are just making this up to stop our protests! This is a violation of the First Amendment!"

The lead cop flipped his shotgun, so it rested on his shoulder and pointed to the ceiling. He positioned himself very close to the loudmouth. "First Amendment, eh?" he said, reaching for something in his pocket. "Tell me how the First Amendment protected *her*, will ya?"

He threw down four photos, all of them falling face down on the table. The images were horrific. A 12-year-old girl. Blood. A nude Jacoby.

"Your man Jacoby denied her the right to free speech when he cut her head in half. So, no, I don't think I need a lecture from you pompous windbags on rights."

The police stormed out, leaving the stunned group of men in utter shock. The photos sat untouched on the table. Finally, someone—the red-faced fat man who greeted Idlewyld earlier—slowly turned the photos over. They were too horrible to see.

Silence stuck in the room as if the air had been replaced by tar. Some of these men were fathers. Of daughters.

Finally, Idlewyld spoke in a low, calm voice. "I believe I'm in charge now until Jacoby gets released. If ever. I think it's best we adjourn for now, given this... incident."

The men mumbled, unsure what to do or say. But Idlewyld was the next in the chain of command, and no one contradicted it. The air had been sucked out of their sails.

As the men filed out of the room, Idlewyld—Dr. Cuba—turned to the red-faced fat man. "Pull the men from the Homestake Mine. For just a few weeks. We need them back at main headquarters in Pierre. We can figure out what to do once we hold new elections for Jacoby's seat."

Invoking bureaucracy in the wake of a crisis was a surefire way to get the delay Dr. Cuba needed. For all their bluster and talk of immediacy, the union would not move an inch without formal elections and endless debates between delegates. Dr. Cuba now had the weeks he needed, and he could start moving his equipment.

Today.

As soon as Dr. Cuba left, he walked to a local safehouse and radioed the cadre outside Lead, South Dakota. "Begin moving equipment and begin installation of the injector array immediately."

Dr. Cuba expected the order to be received without comment.

It was not.

"Sir, coded message received from Brazil. Code verified."

Dr. Cuba paused. His radio operators knew not to bother him with trivia, so this was likely important. Likely another message from the "new piece on the board."

"Read it as encoded," he said, taking out a pencil and paper from his—well, Idlewyld's—heavy coat pocket. He did not risk having the message decoded by the operator and read out loud over any radio signal.

The radio operator read out the message as a series of strange letters, numbers and color references. Dr. Cuba wrote the message on his pad, decoding it line by line as the radio operator spoke.

CEASE ALL OPERATIONS. SUSPEND ALL CADRES.
NO FURTHER WARNINGS.
HOTEL ÁVILA CARACAS SEVEN DAYS.
RED FOREFINGER.

Dr. Cuba now understood the first message was a warning shot to get his attention. This was the real message, the real intent: a meeting in Venezuela in one week.

On its own, this would be troubling enough. Whoever sent the message continued to have access to Dr. Cuba's network and operations. But the signature—"Red Forefinger"—sent a rare feeling of adrenaline shooting up the back of Dr. Cuba's neck, even as it still supported the head of Charles Idlewyld.

Forefinger? That's not right.

With a slow movement, Dr. Cuba examined his own left hand. It appeared normal.

Then, with his opposite hand, Dr. Cuba began picking at the skin of his middle finger on the left hand. The skin gave way. It was false, a thick latex rubber colored to match the rest of his skin perfectly, for when gloves were not practical.

With the false skin removed, Dr. Cuba examined his real left hand and its bright red middle finger. He did not know why he was born with this mark. He was told this was a simple birthmark, although the color was different than the marks of others. His was ruby red, not the typical deep purple or brown. But since he recalled having it since his earliest childhood, there was no other reasonable explanation.

It caused him great strife, of course. Other children bullied him over it. Adults were sure he had painted it specifically to insult them. It provided endless unwanted conflict to the extent that he eventually yielded and began wearing a glove to conceal it. It would only be much later when, through this skill at makeup and disguise, Dr. Cuba would fashion a latex covering for the finger.

Middle finger... not forefinger.

Chapter 10: The Devil's Virus

Thumann felt responsible. Had he not been sleeping when his young translator received the message in the hotel bar, he would have been the one to rescue Gentleman from the Dr. Cuba gang in Lima. He would have been the one to confront Gentleman's captors, and he would have killed them. Not Ximena.

She has no business in this business, he thought to himself. She was too young, too innocent, too inexperienced. *But she has an aptitude*, he admitted. She might still be a valuable part of his team, and abandoning her now, in her deepest moment of grief, might be crueler than letting her press on. Besides, this next part would not be particularly perilous. Blavatsky was crazy, but she was not going to kill them. The biggest threat they might face in the old witch's hut was mosquitoes, not bullets.

So, Thumann reversed his decision and elected to invite Ximena to join him on the trip to the United States after all. He was now more emotionally invested in the welfare of his young translator, even if he had not yet admitted this to himself. Outwardly, he insisted that Ximena was needed to assist the recovering Gentleman. No one was particularly convinced of this story, especially since Gentleman had entirely recovered by all outward appearances. For her part, Ximena quickly agreed, no doubt anxious to visit the States while also distancing herself from the memories of Lima.

It was now a few days since the kidnapping, and the Peruvian police hospital had released Gentleman with more than a little rude abruptness. Thumann did not argue since Gentleman seemed physically healthy, and there was probably little the underfunded, state-run hospital could do for him anyway. Perhaps a trip to the States would help refresh Gentleman as much as it would Ximena.

Using his official contacts, Thumann arranged for Ximena to obtain an emergency passport from the Chilean embassy in Lima. This still took a few days, and the trio used the time not only to physically recover from the past week's activities but also to plan their next steps.

Gentleman had not been present for Ximena's original revelation that religion may play a role in Dr. Cuba's grand scheme and so had not seen how it organically arose from the investigation itself. Learning of the theory, Gentleman refused to be convinced of it, instead asserting to Thumann that a monster like Dr. Cuba could not possibly have a religious motive. Dr. Cuba, Gentleman said, would not put any gods before himself, and the only golden temple he might be building would be for his operatives to worship him.

This was an interesting angle that Thumann did not discard out of hand. Could Dr. Cuba be building a temple to himself? The idea certainly tied together the gold heists and cultish behavior of the Dr. Cuba organization. But it did not explain the seeming desperation in Dr. Cuba's more recent heists. Within the last year, the gold robberies had become more frequent and somewhat—dare Thumann admit it?—sloppy. Thumann would have thought it impossible that Dr. Cuba could have conducted an open-air highway robbery like the one in Lima while tourists were taking photos of the crime as it occurred. No, something was spooling up, and Dr. Cuba was making mistakes.

Thumann insisted that Madame Blavatsky, now residing in a Florida swamp, would be of help. Gentleman was unconvinced, having met the "old crank witch" a few times when Thumann previously engaged her. She was notoriously unreliable, a documented liar, a known perjurer, and was suspected to have killed a few men over poker hands gone wrong.

Thumann only dispelled the latter. "She doesn't play poker," he said to anyone who brought it up. To Gentleman, Thumann insisted that the swamp witch would once again prove valuable.

Ximena, Thumann noticed, was excited to visit the United States, as she had been led to believe stories of its riches and freedoms. Both Thumann and Gentleman suggested she temper her expectations, explaining that the United States was like any other country, just with cleaner roads. Ximena countered that, perhaps, but at least the United States roads had crocodiles. And she intended on seeing a crocodile.

"They're alligators, not crocodiles, and you'll have no problem seeing them. Madame Blavatsky lives in a nest of the damned things," Thumann told her.

Ximena appeared giddy. Her mood had shifted since Gentleman was released from the hospital, and Thumann was not entirely convinced she was not overcompensating. *She's burying her trauma*, he thought. *I recognize that trick all too well.*

"And after Florida?" Gentleman asked. "What happens next?"

Thumann grunted. "My hope is she can point us to where to look next. But, failing that, I suppose we wait. Dr. Cuba will strike again, and we can only hope to investigate that next crime as quickly as it happens and that he leaves more evidence."

Gentleman needled his superior. "Sir, that's not much of a plan."

Thumann ruffled his sideburns with his two meaty hands. "I'm aware, dear Gentleman. I'm aware."

Exactly four hours and forty-two minutes after sealing himself in the copper iron maiden, the Homunculus pressed the switch near his hand, and the heavy door opened. Blood dripped from the eight inner probes, as well as the corresponding punctures in his chest.

The Homunculus padded, nude, across the steel floor of Monito Island's strange underground laboratory towards a glass cabinet filled with surgical equipment. He removed some simple cotton and alcohol, cleaned his chest, and then returned to the iron maiden to clean the spikes within the inner door. This was done more to keep himself and the equipment appearing clean rather than over concern for any infection, which a homunculus was unlikely to pick up. Satisfied, he then swung the door shut, leaving the iron maiden empty.

The Homunculus took his dirty clothes and walked to a squat metal cabinet. Here, he tossed the clothes, leaving them to be cleaned another day. He then turned towards a metal closet and withdrew fresh clothes. Also black.

Heading towards the overhead hatch, the Homunculus made a final scan of the room. It continued to hum with the fizzle of the odd power source. He then shut off the bright lights, climbed the ladder to the second floor, sealed the hatch, and reset the combination locking mechanism. Now, in the dingy library level, lit only by two yellowed bulbs, he withdrew a set of notebooks, appearing very exact in what he was looking for. With these in hand, he headed back up the remaining ladder to the first floor. He placed the books on the lab table, adjusted the lighting, and began reading.

Father-Father must have an idea what you are up to, Brother-Son, he thought. *Perhaps your secrets are here.*

After reading for about an hour, the Homunculus shut the notebooks. The information was not complete, but it would have to do. He still had to make the meeting in Caracas in four days, and the *Eustis* was not the fastest ship at sea. He'd have to leave now.

After shutting down the generator and sealing the stone door once again, the Homunculus left his strange laboratory entirely and headed back to the edge of the cliff overlooking the anchored *Eustis*. It had been slapping into the side of the rocks for many hours but was still seaworthy.

Spiderlike, he climbed down the cliffs onto the *Eustis*' deck. The effort was far less taxing now that he was reinvigorated by the iron maiden and was not hauling a heavy copper vat. Once on deck, he knew he'd have little trouble navigating the remaining trip across the Caribbean Sea, provided the *Eustis* held up, of course.

Using his strength, the Homunculus shoved the *Eustis* from its wedged position in the u-shaped rock formation, freeing it from its anchor point. Trotting down to the engine room, he started the *Eustis*' engines, returned to the wheelhouse, and forced the rickety ship into full reverse. With significant struggle, the *Eustis* finally broke the crashing waves of Monito's rocky coast and reached open water. The Homunculus spun the wheel and brought the ship to a correct course. He would circumnavigate the tiny islet and then point directly southwest to the coast of Venezuela.

Ready yourself, Brother-Son.

One hundred and twenty-five beautiful young women were unloaded from a US naval vessel on the Demerara River in British Guiana. They were gorgeous and endowed with every skin color mankind had developed: Chinese, Portuguese, Spanish, Creole, and pale European. None were older than 25, and most disembarked with enthusiasm and giddiness at the festivities to come. Only a few appeared confused and nervous but pushed ahead, nonetheless.

The girls were escorted, like dairy cows in a milk processing plant, to a military PX at Atkinson Field, located some 25 miles from the British Guiana capital of Georgetown. The airbase was operated by the United States, although the staff were a mix of British, Brazilian, and American military and civilian personnel. The base represented a true melting pot, an apt metaphor since some of them would be quite literally melting in about 24 hours. At the PX, the girls would have time to adjust their clothes, put on makeup, fix their hair, and get ready for the night's party.

The event was the Enlisted Men's Dance, held every other month at Atkinson, which promised a lot of music, dance, cigarettes, and food for any girl who volunteered. Upriver, a host of girls were left on shore, as the Navy typically received double the number of girls it actually needed. The event was known in the region for not only being a fun affair but relatively safe since the base's MPs were known to strictly control the behavior—and roaming hands—of the men.

Once the dance started, the girls would be escorted by the MPs to the base's cinema, where they would meet the men and begin the party. The Navy would have no idea that at least fifty of the girls were under the influence of Dr. Cuba's gas and had very specific orders to carry out at exactly 10:30 PM.

Two days prior, at another dock on the river, the Old Bay Line steamship *State of Maryland* sat idle, having disgorged its supplies for the base as it had every other month prior. Such private industry ships had been expropriated by the US Navy in support of the war and now provided much-needed support services. The *State of Maryland* was a large ship, already ancient by the time it was put into service in British Guiana, but did a sufficient job of hauling food, equipment and medical supplies to Atkinson with the help of some military escort vessels. With its supplies already unloaded, the *State of Maryland* was readying to disembark in the next day or two to begin the cycle once again.

And, once again, the Navy could not have known that the bulk of the crew of the *State of Maryland* had been killed six months prior, their bodies burned in a pit and replaced by Dr. Cuba's men.

Despite the slow pace of the Wohlwill process, the Potosi refinery was on target, producing sufficient quantities of four-nines pure gold to add to the overall inventory. Combined with the prior output of three other refineries controlled by Dr. Cuba, which had been operating for nearly three years already, the target quantity of 225 metric tons of 99.99% pure gold—the minimum amount of gold necessary to awaken the Sunken Gods—was within reach. The problem now was how to transport the gold to its final destination.

The sweat of Inti, the blood of Skyx, was heavy. Gold was difficult to transport for several reasons: not only did its value incur a high risk of theft—as Dr. Cuba knew all too well—but its weight limited the methods of transport. Making matters worse, the introduction of this "new piece on the board" placed some pressure on Dr. Cuba to begin The Work sooner, not later. He had to assume his opponent knew about The Work and was trying to scuttle it. That could not be allowed.

The *Cassowary* had an upper lifting capacity of just ten metric tons. Fortunately, Dr. Cuba had more than one airship. Using his whole fleet of eight ships and accounting for time to load and unload the gold into the injector array, return flights, etc., the transport phase would require at least a month, perhaps more. This did not account for unforeseen problems such as weather, equipment failures, or bottlenecks at the injector site.

This was not fast enough.

While some flights had already begun months ago, they were too few, and the overall pace of the project was stalling. And, so, a secondary plan was hatched to obtain additional aircraft to speed up the process.

Atkinson Field had eleven fully operational Douglas C-54 Skymaster aeroplanes sitting idle. The base was already being dismantled, as it had been built specifically to support the US against German U-boat activities hindering trade and shipping in the region and along the east coast of South America. Atkinson had no role in the remaining fight in the Pacific, so crew and equipment were being returned to the US and Europe for other assignments. The C-54s had been gathered at Atkinson awaiting redeployment in mainland US, with a few planned for the Pacific theater. Each of these could carry another 10 metric tons per flight and was faster than Dr. Cuba's airships. With these "recruited" to serve Dr. Cuba's fleet, The Work would be put back on schedule.

Dr. Cuba himself was already on a flight to Caracas, to meet his strange opponent, and trusted the operation at Atkinson Field to go as planned. After all, his plans typically did.

Corporal Walter Fried was the first to notice something was wrong when, as he was dancing with a pretty 20-year-old Brazilian girl, his nose began to bleed. A few of his fellow enlisted men laughed at Fried, thinking his nerves had gotten to him. "Wally's finally met a girl, and he blows a gasket!" PFC Ted Billington said, laughing loudly. The girl, however, was not laughing and staring blankly at Fried. Just a few minutes prior, her demeanor had been normal, and she was enjoying the dance. As soon as the clock's hands hit 10:30, however, she fell silent. She remained silent, staring, even as Fried's throat closed, and he fell to the ground suffocating. The music continued mockingly as the group around Fried fell silent, watching him struggle on the floor. When blood and tissue burst from his ears, spraying the feet of those around him, all hell broke loose.

"Medic! Medic!" the men shouted. The music stopped. Girls screamed, and men scrambled. Some tried to revive Fried, others scrambled for towels, and still more ran to find a first aid kit. In the chaos, no one noticed the Brazilian girl's nose had begun to bleed, too. It was only when she fell to the ground, followed by PFC Billington, and their ears spurted geysers of red, that the crowd knew this was something altogether different.

It was, of course, too late. Soon, every man who had been within a few feet of any of the girls under Dr. Cuba's influence began feeling their throats close, their tongues swell, and an incredible pressure building in their heads. By the time they realized they were affected, they were already on the ground, writing, bursting from their skulls. The girls fell, screaming, alongside them.

Within eight minutes, the entire cinema and surrounding outside area were littered with dead bodies, each having sprayed blood over the others. Those who tried to flee found they only fell dead in the dirt a few feet outside the exit. Soon, the pacing MPs were affected as the virus moved from dance girl to enlisted man to anyone within sixteen feet of a fallen body.

By the seventeenth minute, nearly half of the people at Atkinson Field were dead. The only unaffected were those not gathered for the event: mechanics working in machine shops, officers gathered in their mess, kitchen and wait staff in the PX, perimeter security walking the far reaches… and Dr. Cuba's men from the *State of Maryland*, each fitted with a biological warfare respirator.

As officers learned of the viral massacre at the dance, their minds had insufficient time to put the pieces together. "What's going on?" one demanded.

"Food poisoning!" someone shouted. "Secure the kitchen staff! Find the spy!"

"Gas! Gas!" another yelled, scrambling to retrieve a manual on what to do during a biological attack.

Finally, when the first bullets were heard, the officers and others realized what was really happening: a full-on attack against Atkinson, with the virus being the first wave and a traditional massacre by conventional weapons being the closing act. Most died under a torrent of bullets before they could do much about it.

Dr. Cuba's men, about 45 in total, stalked the grounds of the airbase, firing at anything that moved. To identify themselves, each had a small yellow flag tied to a short stick that was then taped to their breathing tanks; the men were under orders to kill anyone not wearing breathing gear with a yellow flag, easily visible in the night.

One crew was tasked with taking over the small control tower, which proved a quick job. The tower was a rickety wooden structure, barely guarded, and within just a few minutes, a Dr. Cuba operative had control of all traffic in and out of Atkinson.

The officers were dispatched quickly but put up some resistance with their sidearms. A few of Dr. Cuba's men fell, but the majority simply walked through the officer's mess and sleeping quarters, cutting down the men like wheat. The base was filling with the gray smoke of gunfire and black smoke coming from the kitchen. Everyone in the PX was now dead, too, and oil fryers had spilled and started a fire. The smell of burned potatoes mixed with the smell of burned short-order cooks.

The attackers took more care, however, when on the flight line and nearby fields, where the C-54s sat idle. Most of these were in a straight line, sitting wingtip to wingtip, but some others were scattered in other open areas. Operatives bearing yellow flags, but with a black "X" on them, paced behind comrades bearing automatic machine guns. These were the pilots, and Dr. Cuba's men were under strict orders to protect them at all costs. Once their path to a given aircraft was cleared, the pilots would rush past their gun-toting advance men and gain climb into the plane. Slowly, over the next half hour, the C-54 Skymasters were each powering up, adding a deafening noise to the smoke and chaos.

Dr. Cuba's men faced their most strident resistance from a group of armed vehicles barreling down at them across the runway. These were light vehicles, jeeps and the like, but mounted with intimidating .50 caliber M2 Browning machine guns or some similar type of leadspitter. The drivers and gun operators had, by this point, sussed out what was going on and had taken to defending the Skymasters. It was likely too late to save the base, but maybe they could subvert the overall plan of these invaders.

Now, it was Dr. Cuba's men who started dropping like dead cherries. The men, advancing on foot and forced to stop to reload as they advanced, were no match for the jeeps and their M2s. Worse, the fact that the jeeps were occupying the airstrip meant the C-54s could not take off, effectively crippling the entire plan.

One operative, recruited by Dr. Cuba's gang from the streets of Jamaica, threw himself into the grass along the edge of the airstrip, trying to remain hidden as he sniped at the advancing jeeps. But automatic machine guns are not sniper rifles, and the Jamaican was quickly spotted due to his gun's rapid muzzle flash.

One of the jeep gunners swiveled his M2 on its mount and destroyed the Jamaican, along with about six feet of ground surrounding him.

Dr. Cuba's men were trained to some extent and used to having an easy time with their various missions. This was going sideways quickly, and some panic began to set in. A few of the advancing gunmen scrambled for cover, leaving their pilots exposed; a few of these, then, were obliterated by the mobile M2s. Dr. Cuba had arranged to have only a few extra pilots to account for such losses, but already, the number of pilots was less than the number of C-54s.

Then, suddenly, one final reversal. One of the jeep gunners saw, for a split second, the head of his driver burst right before the jeep spun wildly to the left and then flipped over, killing the gunner. Then, another driver was shot. And another.

The Atkinson control tower had been taken early just for this contingency: two snipers, armed with proper sniper rifles, pecked away at the jeeps on the airstrip with precision. The tower might not have been an imposing-looking thing, but it served as the perfect high ground to take the jeeps out of the game.

Then, slowly, the C-54s began rolling toward the western end of the airstrip. A line of Skymasters formed and started taking off at a bearing of 24 degrees and then turning left once they were well enough over the Atlantic. Based on predetermined flight plans, known only to each pilot, some then adjusted their course to head towards Potosi, and others still to the other refinery locations in North and South America.

By the time the operation was over, eight of the planned eleven C-54s were liberated by Dr. Cuba's men. The remaining operatives at Atkinson would then meet at the State of Maryland, launch, and head to a rally point further south for final extraction. While not a complete success, The Work would continue.

Chapter 11: The Tsarina of Fraud

The journey from Lima to Miami was unexpectedly arduous. Flying Pan Am provided comfortable enough accommodations, but it seemed to Thumann that they were constantly landing to refuel. The plane only stopped twice, once in Panama City and then Kingston, but with agonizing delays in between each flight. They arrived in Miami after nearly 24 hours of travel, and Thumann, Gentleman, and Ximena were properly exhausted.

Knowing they still had quite a bit of driving to reach the swamp outpost that the foul Madame Blavatsky called home, Thumann decided it best that they spend a night in Miami to recuperate. All three of them were struck by how oppressively humid the Miami air was and how ineffective the room fans were in doing anything about it.

By 10 am the next day, the trio was freshly showered and well rested, their bellies full from the fatty hotel breakfast fare. Thumann had already organized a hired car to take them north, into the Everglades, as far as possible by road. There, they would meet an airboat captain who would take them deeper into the alligator-infested swamp. The car ride was pleasant enough, but any comforts ended as they approached "Little Billy" and his airboat launch.

Little Billy chewed tobacco, smoked tobacco, and probably drank tobacco when no one was looking. His skin had adopted the look of the other local residents—meaning, alligators—and his accent was so thick that only Gentleman could understand some of what he said. Billy might have been 35 years old, or he might have been 65 years old; his cragged, sunbaked skin made it hard to tell. If a cannibal were to make a jacket out of Little Billy's skin, a passerby would probably compliment him on the fine quality of the leather. As Thumann and his entourage approached, it was also clear that Little Billy was not a bath enthusiast.

He collected his pay—up front, of course—and rudely tossed their bags onto the back of his airboat, which bore the curious name of the *"Juliet's Beard."* Thumann and the others were not prepared for the deafening, ungodly noise of the damned thing as Little Billy started his gasoline engine and set the giant rear-facing fan rotor into motion. Gentleman covered his ears while Ximena clung to the wooden seat, fearful that she'd be sucked backward and ground into red mist by the spinning fan blades. The screaming fan ensured there would be no conversation on this trip.

The *Beard* was little more than a slab of wood, slightly curved upward at the front, with a giant fan bolted precariously on the back. The fan's diameter was at least 7 feet, and there was no protective frame or screen surrounding it; anyone getting close enough to it would simply be chopped to bits. In the middle of the boat was a set of wooden benches, also held fast to the deck with rusted metal bolts that appeared ready to snap at a moment's notice. Overall, Little Billy displayed very little care for the safety of any passengers who might be foolish enough—or desperate, as in Thumann's case—to buy passage on his contraption.

If it had not been so deafening, the ride on the *Beard* might have otherwise been a thrilling adventure. Little Billy navigated the boat carefully away from the dock of his shack and into what one imagines was "open" swamp water since Billy opened the throttle and set the *Beard* careening at full speed through the tall weeds. Nobody understood just how Billy navigated, but Thumann suspected it was due to equal parts memory, skill, and the dumb luck that God bestows upon drunks and babies.

The front edge of the boat parted the sawgrass with ease, which was a blessing since it would have otherwise sliced into the arms and faces of those sitting near the edge. Closer to Billy's dock, the grass was tall, making it difficult to see, but later in the journey, the grass—which, Thumann would later tell the group, was not "grass" at all—grew shorter, allowing more visibility of the flat, murky horizon. The rapid speed of the boat kept mosquitoes from becoming a nuisance, although getting hit in the face with flies and perpetually-mating "June bugs" was another problem altogether. Ximena wondered what happened when the fan boat struck an alligator, of which there must have been thousands skulking around the greenish swamp water. A few times, she felt a "thump" and wondered if that had answered her question.

And so, they continued, for an hour or more, cutting through the Florida Everglades to, one hoped, their intended destination and not a place where cannibals might turn their skins into fine jackets. Thumann knew they were heading west—no, northwest—purely from the position of the sun versus the *Beard*'s bow, but otherwise had no idea where he was. But he had made this journey before and survived it; he had little fear of disaster during this trip, either. Thumann's white-knuckle grip on his seat, however, seemed to contradict his confidence.

Finally, Little Billy pulled back on the throttle, bringing the *Beard* to half speed as he entered a large patch of much taller sawgrass. The sun was overhead now, burning everything it touched, and the shade of the tall grass was a bit of comfort. Billy made incremental adjustments to his rudder stick, wiggling the boat left and right as if he were looking to maintain his position on some invisible path in the swamp ahead. None of this made any sense, but suddenly, a dock emerged from the swamp. Billy cut his throttle, and the *Beard* floated with its own momentum to a rickety wooden dock. With the fan shut down, Thumann and his group continued to hear a residual roar inside their ears. The *Beard* tapped the dock with a light thump.

"We're here," Little Billy said, spitting tobacco juice over the side. "I'll be back in two hours to getcha."

Thumann strode across the gap between the *Beard*'s deck and the dock and then turned to help Ximena. Gentleman gathered their bags—Thumann's leather case, Ximena's purse and Gentleman's satchel—and tossed them onto the dock before climbing up himself. Gentleman was barely on the rickety pier when Billy began pushing the *Beard*'s bow away from the dock, turning it around 180 degrees and back towards the way he came. The fan noise started again, Thumann and the others were blasted with air, and the *Beard* sped away into the sawgrass. The roar of the fan was slowly absorbed by the plants, leaving them in the hot, chittering, buggy ambiance of the Florida swamp.

Each of the dock's posts was adorned with some sort of strange wicker-and-sawgrass arrangement, not quite a traditional "dream weaver," but something more menacing. Sawdust-stuffed crow carcasses were nailed to a few of the posts, left to stand guard for all eternity or, at least, until the next hurricane tore them from their perch and tossed them into the swamp. Seashells had been hand-placed in spiral designs on the dock, appearing as either a welcome symbol for guests or a warning for devils.

Calling the shack ahead ramshackle would have been a kindness. It was a mix of weathered, wooden slats with corrugated metal panels, architected in the fashion of a paranoid schizophrenic. The few windows the shack had were all broken, covered by tattered curtains hung on the inside. Chickens ran wild, and one bored basset hound lay sleeping near the front door. Above the door was a single sign made of thick, hand-carved wood; it read "THELEMA" in red lettering.

Thumann and the others picked up their respective bags and headed down the dock towards the shack. Gentleman snorted.

"She's as crazy as ever."

Thumann paused at Gentleman's uncharacteristic bluntness, but he could not disagree. "And that's why we need her."

Ximena looked nervous. "This place feels wrong," she whispered. "Everything is wrong."

"*She's* wrong," Gentleman said with increasing irritation. "She made this place in her own image."

"What is 'Thelema'?" Ximena asked.

"The name of Aleister Crowley's abbey in Italy," Thumann answered. "In it, he performed horrific rituals of debauchery and scandal. Murder, as well, some say."

Ximena had no idea who Aleister Crowley was, but she got the general idea. "This is a satanic place, then?" she asked.

Gentleman snorted a compressed laugh, ready to interject. Thumann cut him off before he could speak. "She adopts the image of a bizarre old crone who practices voodoo and worships Baphomet, but it's all an act. All of this,…" Thumann gestured at the area around them, from the dock to the shack, "… is engineered for the rubes. Sightseeing tourists who want a taste of the occult without the risk of getting splashed with chicken blood. She's a fakir."

Ximena's brow creased. "Why are we relying on her, then?" she asked.

Gentleman clapped. "A ripe question, for sure!"

Thumann took notice of Gentleman's unusually aggressive

tone, but he pressed on. "If this Dr. Cuba is a scammer, then Madame Blavatsky will see through his scam. If he's a religious zealot, she will know the particular belief system that he's adopted. She has us covered from both angles. There are few others alive today who would be able to help us in this way."

They reached the door and stood below the red sign. Thumann told Gentleman to knock and ushered Ximena a few yards to the right under the guise of showing her some odd weeds in the shack's overgrown garden. He knelt, pretending to point to the plants. Once out of earshot of Gentleman, Thumann whispered to her. "Something is wrong with Gentleman. Watch him. Stay alert. He hasn't returned to us in the same state as when he left."

Ximena nodded. She, too, had seen a change in Gentleman's behavior.

Thnumann then stood, speaking more loudly now so that Gentleman might overhear: "The Madame uses these plants to protect her from encroaching spirits."

Gentleman, hearing only the latter part of their conversation, snorted again. "And she grows her cannabis there, as well!" he blurted.

Despite Gentleman's knocks, the door remained closed. There was no audible movement inside.

"She's not here?" Ximena asked.

"She's here," Thumann said. "She's watching us."

Thumann pushed open the door, which had been barred only with a rusted latch but without an accompanying lock. The latch fell off its screws and landed on the interior floor with a clank. It was as if Blavatsky would not prohibit strangers from entering her weird shack but at least expected them to exert some effort to do so.

"Blavatsky!" Thumann boomed, his voice absorbed by damp wooden walls and thick hanging carpets covering some of the walls. As they entered, it was as if the sun had been swallowed by those walls and carpets. Now they were sucked into darkness, with only slices of sunlight sneaking through the shack's wooden slats, the gaps between the hastily placed corrugated metal sheets, and those broken windows with their flimsy, dirty curtains. The entry room—was it a living room? a foyer?—smelled of patchouli or something roughly imitating it. There were also remnant odors of damp, mold, and burnt Burley tobacco. To the right of the door was a small wooden shelf with various ominous-looking knick-knacks for sale, such as fake voodoo dolls, occult books, packs of tarot cards, incense sticks, and pendants.

The floor creaked under Thumann's weight, leading Ximena to worry it might collapse under them, sending them all into the swamp below. She glanced at Gentleman, who clearly had been here before with Thumann in years past. Perhaps his sudden overconfidence and familiarity were simply the result of his past experience? Still, his rudeness towards his mentor was uncharacteristic. Maybe he was still reliving the trauma of his kidnapping?

Gentleman found a book on the shelf and held it up to Ximena. "This is Aleister Crowley," he said. Clearly, he knew Ximena did not know who Crowley was, nor anything about an abbey in Italy. "He's a would-be occult philosopher and bad poet, a drug addict who played his hand at Satanism and got himself thrown out of whole countries for his efforts. For a few years, he ran a made-up abbey in Cefalu, in Italy, and he called it 'Thelema.' This Blavatsky crone pretends to have some connection to Crowley just to sell her junk."

A croaking voice boomed back from another room as if a frog had fallen into a tuba. "You left out the part where I stole my heritage from the real Madame Helena Blavatsky, Mister Gentleman."

Thumann hooked his thumb towards the source of the voice in an adjoining room, indicating they should follow it. Thumann moved them through a doorway covered only by a hanging curtain—or was it a dirty tablecloth?—and entered a small salon, with Gentleman and Ximena following behind. The shack's low ceiling made it appear as if Thumann filled the entire room with his size and height. A few feet across, hidden behind a layer of dark and pipe smoke, sat a figure in a thick, matted armchair. This was Blavatsky. She did not stand as her guests entered.

"You were nicer the last time you visited," she growled at Gentleman. "As for you, Heiner, you were thinner."

"Madame Blavatsky," Thumann said, greeting her from across the room and removing his hat. He did not reach across to shake her hand, maintaining his distance. Out of respect? Fear? Or were they simply too familiar?

As their eyes adjusted, the trio began to make out the woman's features. She had wild gray hair, spraying in all directions, with what appeared to be some form of dreadlocks spewing downward on one side. There were beads everywhere: in her hair, around her neck, circling her wrists. Her features suggested she was about 60 years old, but she also had alligator-like skin like Little Billy, so she might have been younger. Older? She smoked a long pipe, ejecting plumes of foul tobacco into the room; this was not Thumann's fancy Latakia; it was something else entirely. It might not have even been tobacco.

Blavatsky was dressed in something like a dress, or at least it took the shape of a dress. It was more as if she had wrapped herself in a series of blankets or black bedsheets. She was buried under layers of cloth, unbothered by the already oven-like conditions of the shack. But most noticeable was Blavatsky's eye patch, covering her right eye and bearing the symbol of a red pentagram.

Ximena crossed herself instinctively. Thumann noticed Blavatsky twitch at the gesture.

"Miss Ximena is an innocent Catholic from Chile," he said, introducing her and simultaneously explaining her reaction. "She's not disrespecting you."

"There is no such thing as an innocent Catholic, Thumann," Blavatsky said, chimneying more smoke. "As for Chilenos, well, they got what they deserved in '83." Ximena scowled, but Thumann was not entirely sure what Blavatsky was talking about.

Thumann put a reassuring hand on Ximena's shoulder. "Don't worry, dear Miss," he said. "She's not a witch. She's not even a Satanist. She's just a philosopher who dabbles in scams to earn her living."

Ximena seemed unimpressed but maintained a professional silence. Gentleman snorted audibly, prompting Thumann to shoot him a scowl.

"I'm a theosophist, to be exact," Blavatsky corrected. "Like my mother, my grandmother, and my great-grandmother before me."

"Madame Blavatsky is the descendent of a renowned Russian occultist, Helena Blavatsky. That Blavatsky traveled the world and studied all forms of occult and spiritual practices. Eventually, she established the religion of theosophy here in

America."

"Theosophy isn't a religion, Thumann, and you know it. It was a spontaneous eruption from the prior belief systems of philosophy, science and, yes, religion. My great-grandmother identified theosophy as an expression of…"

And then, Blavatsky fell silent, abandoning what was likely to be a lecture. Now she stared at Gentleman, examining him. Then, to Ximena's surprise, she reached up and lifted her eye patch. Beneath was a very normal, very sighted, eyeball. Now Blavatsky scanned Gentleman with both eyes.

The eyepatch was fake, a prop for the rubes.

She lifted a wrinkled, fat finger at Gentleman. "This man," she declared, with a sudden deep and serious tone, "is on drugs."

Gentleman remained strangely stoic, but the denunciation hung in the air thicker than the pipe smoke.

Thumann, however, was taken aback. "What?"

Blavatsky did not respond and did not move, keeping her finger pointed at Gentleman, her stare at him unwavering.

"Nonsense!" Thumann retorted. "Even by your standards, Madame, that's an outrageous defamation!"

"Not if it's true, Thumann. Consider it an expert diagnosis." Blavatsky lowered her hand.

Choosing to change the subject, Thumann blurted, "May we sit?" He took a seat on a sofa across from Blavatsky without waiting for permission. Thumann motioned that Ximena and Gentleman should sit, too. Blavatsky nodded at them, sensing the polite young Catholic girl was not going to sit without being told.

Thumann reached into his coat. He pulled out a small box of cigars from his jacket and placed them on the side table next to his chair. "Upmanns," he said, pointing a fat finger at the box.

"Fresh."

Blavatsky smiled. "If they've been stuffed inside your sweaty coat all this time, they are hardly fresh, Thumann. But I'm not fussy, and your gift is accepted. So, tell me: why did you come to my swamp, Thumann? To deliver cigars? What do you need this time?" Blavatsky asked.

"What do you know of the name 'Dr. Cuba'?" he asked.

Blavatsky puffed deeply on her odd, rootlike pipe. More foul smoke polluted the air. "Oh, you're on that case, are you?" she asked.

"Yes. Scotland Yard sent me to South America. We've been investigating a rash of gold heists. Miss Ximena here," he said, aiming an open hand towards his assistant, "has been my Spanish translator."

"Bienvenida al tercer círculo del infierno, niñita," Blavatsky said, in near-perfect Spanish, holding her hand up with thumb and two fingers raised, making the sign of the cross in the air as if blessing Ximena. Her accent indicated she had learned the language in Spain, however, and not Latin America. Ximena shuddered, however, and remained silent.

Thumann pointed a finger at Blavatsky, scolding her. "Stop that nonsense, for heaven's sake. You'll scare her."

Blavatsky laughed, a rumble from a belly deep within that pile of curtains she called clothing, bubbling up to spill out of her smoky mouth. "Of course, Thumann. My apologies, chiquita. I have many professions, but also many hobbies, and terrorizing Catholics is one of the latter. It's all in fun."

Ximena was clearly not amused.

"What do you know about Dr. Cuba, then? You seem to have heard the name at least," Thumann asked.

Blavatsky snorted. "Of course! That name has been floating around the criminal underworld for at least ten years, maybe twenty. Whispers, shadows, secrets… all that silliness. The man has done a fine job of creating mystery over his identity."

"It's a man, then?" Thumann asked.

"What else would he be? A panda?"

"An organization. A code name for a group."

Blavatsky shook her head. Ximena swore she saw bugs fly out. "No, it's definitely a man. He leads a group, yes. A group of criminals. But he's just one man. Too many people have seen him. In the flesh."

"Seen him?" Thumann asked, surprised. "What does he look like?"

"Well, that changes with the account," Blavatsky answered, puffing away. Had Thumann been smoking at the same time, the room would have turned into a gas chamber. "He seems to have the ability to alter his appearance. Master of disguise and all that."

"Someone with a theater background, then. Makeup," Thumann surmised.

"Maybe. The witnesses are all low-level criminals, street thugs, drug addicts, alcoholics. At least the ones that reach my awareness. As you know, Thumann, I don't frequent debutante balls and opera openings."

Thumann nodded in a way that was, somehow, not insulting and respected Blavatsky's odd position in society.

"So their ability to recall detail is not always reliable," she added. "I believe he's an older man, 40 to 60. Thin."

"He's collecting gold," Thumann said.

"Aren't all criminals? I mean, they don't go out to steal used newspapers or fish bones." Again, the weird belly-chortle rose up in Blavatsky and burped out of her.

"Not just stealing gold…," Thumann said, "collecting it. He's not reselling it. Not holding onto it to manipulate world prices. Not converting it to some other form of currency. Just, well, … hoarding it. Doing something with it."

Blavatsky scrunched her eyebrows. The movement reminded her that she had her eye patch flipped upward, and she quickly lowered it back into position. "Hoarding it? That *is* unusual."

Gentleman was still silent. Since Blavatsky's accusation against him, Gentleman appeared to fall into the background, as if he no longer wanted to be seen or hoped to have been forgotten. Whatever he was doing was working, as Thumann and Blavatsky continued their conversation without any interaction with Gentleman. Only Ximena appeared to be watching him.

"How much gold?" Blavatsky asked.

"More than 200 metric tons so far, maybe more. Maybe much, much more," Thumann answered. "We suspect some illegal operations had their gold stolen and might not have reported it. The actual quantity is not known."

"Sweet Jesus, that's a lot of gold," Blavatsky admitted. "Worth nearly $300 million. I thought I made a lot when I tricked that encyclopedia company to pay for my trip to Norway."

Thumann snickered. "You made a lot more when you recruited an entire Wall Streat stock brokerage to join your prayer-by-post club."

"We all have to eat, Thumann," Blavatsky said, laughing. "And stamps are cheap."

"You should have enough money by now to move out of this shack," Thumann poked.

"It's all hidden under the mattress," Blavatsky insisted. "I'm waiting for the right investment. What do you think he's doing with all this gold?"

Thumann nodded towards Ximena. "We have a theory," he said. "We think he may be using the gold to construct something. There's an intersection here between the cultlike status of Dr. Cuba and his followers and the possible use of this gold in construction."

Blavatsky nodded. "A temple? You think he's building a temple out of gold?"

Thumann nodded towards Ximena. "The young miss put us onto this theory. Her ancient people did such things to worship Incan gods. We believe Dr. Cuba comes from this region. He may have held onto these beliefs."

"What would he do with a golden temple to Incan gods in 1945?" Blavatsky asked incredulously. "He would spend more on the construction of the damned place than he'd ever make on selling holy favors to whoever would be stupid enough to follow him."

"Coming from you, Blavatsky, that's quite a condemnation," Thumann said, causing Blavatsky to laugh. "What if he's not building this... this whatever ... to bilk anyone? What if he believes it?" Thumann asked.

Blavatsky stroked her chin. "Oh, that's interesting!" she belted. "I like it. He's a would-be god himself! Maybe a temple for himself! Maybe this criminal mastermind has begun to believe his own lies?"

"Perhaps he's building a statue of himself?" Thumann posited.

"Hah! A new Colossus of Rhodes? An eighth wonder of the world? Imagine...," but Blavatsky cut herself off. Her mouth remained open, hanging in mid-sentence, but silent. Her eyes darted from left to right as if reading something in the air. Her brows centered, fell slack, then scrunched. "Or…"

"Or what, Madame?" Thumann asked. He knew she had fallen upon something. Her demeanor had changed; she was no longer laughing.

"Wait," Blavatsky said, holding her hand in the air. Her pipe stopped spewing smoke. She was thinking.

She stood. The sound of her rustling dress-thing filled the room. Blavatsky's full size was not at all clear, as she now appeared to be a shambling mound of black fabric and gray hair stomping into the next room. The thump of her feet against the creaking floorboard suggested that beneath all those layers of black was a large woman. She might have equaled Thumann in height and perhaps exceeded him in girth.

Thumann stood, prompting the others to follow. They pursued Blavatsky into yet another back room of the foul-smelling shack. Passing through another makeshift curtain doorway, they entered what, presumably, was the library. The room's walls were lined with bookshelves, filled to overflowing, while in front of these were even more piles of books, some on shelves, others in stacks. It was as if a wave of books had flowed up, filled the shelves, and then retreated, leaving a dune of even more books spread out below. There was no order to it, and the entire thing looked like a firetrap ready to ignite. So much paper around a woman with a lit pipe, it would not take much imagination to predict how Blavatsky might end.

The books covered a range of subjects. Poetry, physics, Shakespeare, Greek philosophy, chemistry, hallucinogenic drug recipes. Moreover, they appeared well-worn and used. Anyone believing Madame Blavatsky of the Swamp was just a lunatic would be silenced in a second when they realized she had read *all* of these books, possibly more than once.

Blavatsky stood in the center of the room. She raised an arm, extended a finger, and pointed. Then she moved her arm around wildly, pointing at various spots along the bookshelves, to the pile of books, left and right. Back and forth, circling, circling, until her hand came to rest. "There. Get that," she told Thumann. Her finger pointed at a stack of books near the doorway where they entered. No, not a stack.... She pointed to a *specific* book.

Thumann moved carefully through the room, navigating the stacks of books to retrieve the one Blavatsky had pointed to. He had to pull away about seven or eight books to reach the exact one: *Gods of Prehistory* by Jonathan Allan Godfrey, first edition, 1824.

Blavatsky wiggled her hand, indicating Thumann should give the book to her. "Hurry up, Thumann. Let me see it." She grabbed it, holding the thick book in one arm as she flipped pages with the other.

"Who is this Godfrey?" Thumann asked. "I've never heard of him."

"Nor should you have. He was debunked, treated as a madman in his time," Blavatsky answered while still searching the pages. "He wrote about prehistorical gods, but not in the traditional sense of animism or simple worship of frightening phenomena by scared Neanderthals. Godfrey claimed there were organized religions in existence before societies themselves organized."

Thumann shook his head. "How can a religion organize if there's no society to organize it?"

"Simple," Blavatsky said, holding a page open. "He said the gods organized it themselves."

Thumann resisted the urge to snort anything, letting

Blavatsky's train of thought race down the tracks. It was, after all, why he came to her in the first place.

"The Sunken Gods," she said, pointing to the page. "Godfrey found evidence of a culture that existed as early as three million years BC."

Thumann could not stand it now. "That's impossible! Man didn't exist then. That would have been the age of … of *astro*…. *ostra*…"

"*Australopithecus*," Blavatsky said, finishing his sentence. "Possibly something even earlier. "As I said, pre-society. Pre-human, in fact! Godfrey claimed these gods didn't need men to form their religion. They used the pre-humans as a source of food."

"And you think this Dr. Cuba runs a cult that believes in these prehistoric gods?" Thumann asked.

"The Sunken Gods were believed to have gold for blood, silver for tears, and opals for eyes."

Ximena quietly interjected. "Like Inti and Mamaqilla."

Blavatsky nodded. "The Incas had founded a religion based on something much older. Over millennia, the Sunken Gods' golden blood was reimagined as the sweat of Inti, the Sun God. A nearly insignificant change, given the amount of time that had passed."

"How could Godfrey have learned all this since there would have been no way for these *Australopithecus* creatures to leave any sort of record, spoken or otherwise?" Thumann asked.

"Godfrey traced existing religions, like the Incas, backward. But his research was spotty at best, and the entire story is a murky mess. Later, an assistant came forward and revealed that Godfrey had admitted his information came to him in a dream. Godfrey was drummed out of his academies, his books pulled from publication.

He later turned to heroin, but unlike some of us, the poor sap couldn't handle his dosage, and he killed himself."

Thumann was unaffected by Blavatsky's casual reference to lethal drug use, even if Ximena and Gentleman recoiled somewhat.

"But Godfrey's level of detail was certainly unusual. He claimed the Sunken Gods were led by the God King Skyx and his Queen-Consort Macapax." Blavatsky turned to Ximena. "Macapax became your Incan Mother Moon, Mamaqilla, with her tears of silver. Oh, they had a host of other gods in their court, too, each with names and histories. But Godfrey's contemporaries claimed there'd be no way the old man could possibly know the names of Gods since the creatures of that day could hardly do more than grunt. They certainly couldn't pass down oral history."

"So, he made this up," Thumann said, frowning.

"Unless the drugs gave him a legitimate audience with the gods," Blavatsky countered matter-of-factly. She seemed to believe such a thing was possible.

"Regardless of where he got the information, we know Godfrey got this published," Thumann said, pointing a finger at the book in Blavatsky's arms. "That book exists. So, it's possible Dr. Cuba has a copy, too. Now, let's say Dr. Cuba believes all of this. What would he want to do with his gold, then? Build a statue of God King Skyx?"

"No," Blavatsky answered convincingly. "That's what is so unique here. For years after Godfrey wrote his book, a small and nearly forgotten cult arose based on things they claimed Godfrey said later in his life. They believed the Sunken Gods could be awakened if one could revitalize them."

"Revitalize them? How?"

"By, in essence, giving them a transfusion. Injecting their

sleeping bodies with fresh gold. Restoring their blood. A few people began digging holes in the earth and pouring melted gold in pits to see what would happen."

"And," Thumann surmised, "nothing happened."

"Skyx hasn't eaten us yet!" Blavatsky laughed. "But think about it. Dr. Cuba might have stumbled on all of this and wants to recreate the Godfrey Cult's experiments but on a grander scale."

"So, he wants to melt the gold and pour it into the earth," Thumann summarized. It sounded insane as the words became real in the air.

"Not pour it. *Inject* it. Into the earth and as deep as possible. It's believed the circulatory system of dead Skyx and his brood runs through the entire planet, so your position on the Earth's surface is irrelevant. The problem is getting to the right depth. If you dig deep enough, the story goes, you'll hit a god-vein. Godfrey Cultists in the 1830s and 40s were digging random holes, a few meters deep, in their backyards in Manchester or Leicester. They were called the Mole People. It was a bit embarrassing, frankly, and the only result was a lot of pensioners with twisted ankles."

"So, Dr. Cuba is likely to be preparing to either make a hole or use an existing one," Thumann asserted.

"I suspect someone would have seen him digging towards the center of the Earth," Blavatsky offered. "But he is a stealthy bugger, and you can't just start drilling the deepest hole on Earth without someone noticing."

"So, is there a hole that already exists? One that he could use?" Thumann asked.

"How would I know?" Blavatsky replied.

Thumann arched an eyebrow and pointed all around the room at the hundreds of books on hundreds of subjects. He widened his eyes and wobbled his head as if to say, "… and these?"

"You flatter me, Thumann! That's why I let you visit me," she laughed.

"You let me visit you because I bring you Upmann cigars."

"Nevertheless, even an old witch like me can't know everything. Geology and mining, or whatever they study to dig up dirt, isn't something I know about."

Thumann remembered something. "The Mariana Trench is the deepest known spot in the ocean. Could he be sinking his gold into the ocean?"

"Has to be molten," Blavatsky said, shaking her head. "The gold would solidify as soon as it touched the cold water. That wouldn't work. There's a sinkhole in Russia, he could pour gold into that, but it's likely not deep enough. Sorry, Thumann, I can't help you on this."

Thumann took the book from Blavatsky, looked at it for a few moments, flipped some pages, and set it down. Then he took both of Blavatsky's hands in his, gripped them, and said, "Thank you, Madame. Again, you *have* helped me, and I owe you a debt."

"They're piling up, Thumann," she joked. "But I hear those new Montecristos are good."

"We'll let you be now, Madame. Again, you have been a great help." Thumann turned to leave with Ximena and Gentleman in tow. Blavatsky followed them to the door; as they prepared to wait outside for the return of the *Beard*, Blavatsky stood in the doorway as if frightened to put herself in the sun. She caught Thumann's attention one final time.

"Remember two things, old German," she said, her face serious. "Do what thou wilt shall be the whole of the law, and …," wagging a finger towards Gentleman, "…that man is on drugs."

Chapter 12: The Sultaness of the Ávila

The Hotel Ávila in Caracas was opulent but in an understated way. Sitting only at a squat four stories, the entryway included a magnificent gazing pool with a fountain that worked … sometimes. Round porthole windows suggested a nautical theme, something the ocean breeze and ample palm trees did little to dissuade. Well-dressed doormen greeted luxurious cars as they spit out starlets, politicians, and corrupt aluminum industry executives from around the world.

Dr. Cuba chose to be dropped off outside the grounds so he could approach by foot. For now, the fountain was working, and the air was filled with a lovely white noise and light, sparkling mist. An obscenely expensive Rolls Royce Wraith was met by an army of doormen, ready to receive a single Hollywood director or producer, or some such nonsensical figure, with all the pomp of a royal arrival.

Inside, there seemed to be some sort of celebration afoot, something to do with the end of the War.

Dr. Cuba assumed the meeting would happen in the hotel's bar or restaurant. As he approached the main entrance, he scanned for signs of an ambush. The likelihood that his "new piece on the board" would attempt any such thing was nearly nil, but given that the risk of miscalculation was death, it was worth being alert.

A doorman approached. "May I help you, sir?" he said in English.

"I am here to meet someone at the restaurant," Dr. Cuba said.

"Very good, sir, come this way." The doorman escorted his guest into the hotel lobby. Dr. Cuba was dressed in immaculate business attire, both appropriate for the exact time of year and for the tony city of Caracas. Because Dr. Cuba so perfectly fit the part he was playing, the doorman never thought to question just who this man was, nor why he was walking up the drive on foot rather than sliding up by Rolls Royce.

The doorman handed Dr. Cuba off to the restaurant's maître d', as Dr. Cuba removed his fedora. "Your party?" the maître d' asked.

Dr. Cuba did not answer. He merely removed his gloves and placed his left hand on the maître d's podium, exposing his ruby-red middle finger. The maître d' stiffened.

"This way," he said.

That is precisely how I would have arranged it, Dr. Cuba thought.

Dr. Cuba was escorted through the noisy restaurant, which was filled with the noise of conversations, laughter, rattling plates and music from the patio. On the tables were plates of filet mignon, chateaubriand bouquetiere, and veal cordon bleu. The wines, as near as Dr. Cuba could tell, were predominantly Spanish and French, with a heavy presence of Malbec from Argentina.

Finally, Dr. Cuba arrived at his table at the far end of the room near the open patio and sufficiently away from much of the restaurant's noise. A man of approximately 35 years of age, with pale, porcelain skin and an all-black suit, white shirt and black tie, stood to greet him. He removed his gloves, revealing a ruby-red forefinger.

The stranger extended his hand. "I am afraid to say, my dear Dr. Cuba, the empanadas here are fried. They are… savages."

Dr. Cuba felt another bolt of adrenaline rise up through his spine. *How?* he thought.

The two sat.

"You seem to know much about me," Dr. Cuba said.

"I do, and I will explain just how that is," the stranger said.

"Wine?" A waiter had approached, offering a wine list.

The stranger shook his head. "Neither of us drinks wine, but thank you." The waiter left.

"What do you drink?" Dr. Cuba asked. "Might I at least know that?"

"The same as you, Doctor. Blood and gasoline. Sometimes blended, and less often as separate components. But the proper mixture, when done under the right conditions, is always preferred. As you well know."

Dr. Cuba would no longer allow himself to be surprised. He forced the adrenaline in his system to dampen, to put itself to sleep. He took control of his body's functions, forcing them to obey his will. He would not be intimidated, and he would not let his body's reactions betray him.

"It would seem you and I are related," he said. "I expect you will explain this."

The Homunculus leaned back and crossed his leg. "I am your Father-Brother. You are my Brother-Son. This is our relationship."

Dr. Cuba remained stoic, although in his mind, he was calculating this new data.

"You were created," the Homunculus said matter-of-factly. "Grown. As was I. We are soulless, not born, not raised. Grown, of genetic fabric and chemical strands. You and I are simply different generations of homunculi. I created you. But before, someone created me. For this reason, I am your Father-Brother."

"And I," Dr. Cuba completed, "your Brother-Son. So you say."

"So I say," the Homunculus confirmed.

"What is your name?" Dr. Cuba asked.

"I have none. I have never adopted one, at least permanently. Like you, I assume many different personas as needs require. The need for a permanent name is unnecessary. Although I do quite like 'Dr. Cuba.' I may yet use it myself."

"This is where we differ," Dr. Cuba countered. "I have a name."

"You do. Carlos Angel Quispe Castellares, from the poor town of Ancash, Peru. One who later adopted the criminal name of 'Dr. Cuba,' to use as a means of inciting terror and ensuring loyalty. But which is real? Dr. Cuba or Quispe Castellares?"

Dr. Cuba again remained stoic, refusing to reveal his surprise that anyone other than himself knew his history. "I was born as Carlos Angel Quispe Castellares. I was not 'grown,' as you suggest. Born from a poor mother and father, and yes, in Ancash. I grew up. I only became Dr. Cuba because I willed it so. I made myself into the person you see before you now."

The Homunculus smiled. "So you say," he repeated. "I say differently. Explain, then, this." He held up his hand with the red forefinger.

"A birthmark," Dr. Cuba said. "Nothing more."

"You know that to be untrue. You, like I, have studied medical science. You know this color cannot be naturally produced by skin cells. Birthmarks, vitiligo, cancer… none can produce this color. The carmine beetle, yes. Human genetics, no. So, what is your theory on how we have the exact same mark?"

"Not exact."

"True, but not exact for a specific reason. Humans have ten fingers. This slight difference is a means of identifying us, individually."

Dr. Cuba kept his face from scowling. "You mean to say

there are ten of us? Each with a different marked finger?"

"That is the purpose, at least. We aren't ten right now. But over time, yes, we may be. And we need this to keep us identified."

"Over time?" Dr. Cuba asked. "How much time?"

"Decades," the Homunculus answered. "Centuries, perhaps. For now, our prime generation arose in the late 1800s. The human progenitor that developed our formula, our Father-Father, died in 1890. I am his first-generation representative. In fact, I have his exact appearance, or at least as he appeared at this age."

"Even then, you'd be in your fifties."

"We don't age as the progenitor did. With proper care and sustenance, we can forestall aging. But I assure you, I emerged in 1885, along with two others. Because we were all perfectly identical, the marks on our fingers were used as a way to uniquely identify us."

"There are three of you?"

"Four, counting yourself. You have three brothers. Myself, and two others in Europe. We were the first generation. You are the first of the second generation, So, you see, you are not alone."

"And when did I emerge, per your theory?" Dr. Cuba asked. "When did your progenitor allege to create me?"

"He did not. Again, it was I who created you, in 1928, as the first attempt to replicate our Father-Father's experiment. He was already dead."

"You created me?" Dr. Cuba mused. He did not believe a word of this.

"I did. However, the technology and equipment had changed since our Father-Father created us, and I was forced to modernize the instructions and formulas. This proved difficult, and there were many discards, many defective batches."

Now, Dr. Cuba leaned back and crossed his legs, deliberately mirroring his opponent. "Defective?"

"You were one such defect. You should have been mopped from the floor like the rest. I can't be certain what might have happened, why you were not disposed of with the other defective batches. But you did escape the incinerator, through whatever circumstances, and underwent cellular growth on your own. By 1929, you would have been fully grown, appearing identical to me."

"But I am not identical to you," Dr. Cuba pointed out. "That should be obvious."

"True, now, Brother-Son. But when you first emerged, you were identical to me, per your genetic instructions. With the exception of the red finger, to keep you unique in at least that aspect. But you have uncovered a new ability, one I had not explored. You have learned how to alter your face through brute force manipulations. But a bone, cracked too many times, will not revert to its original shape. So many decades of these alterations have left your base appearance permanently changed. And in another 20 years, you will change even more. But if you look closely, there are still similarities, Brother-Son." The Homunculus pointed at Dr. Cuba's face. "I am still very much in there."

Dr. Cuba paused. There *were* similarities in their appearance, but only in the most superficial ways. The story, as a whole, however, was implausible. But how did this stranger know so much about his operations, his physical abilities?

The Homunculus allowed the silence to sit in the air for a moment before proceeding.

The team of waiters arrived with menus, glasses of water, and fresh flowers for the table. They left in silence, assuming the red fingers of their two mysterious patrons were the mark of some

Masonic temple.

"Let me not waste your time, Brother-Son," the Homunculus said, tapping the small flower vase and watching the wave patterns produced on the surface of the water.

"Please do not," Dr. Cuba replied.

"I know about the empanadas because your progenitor ate them. His mother, who was Scottish, baked them, but for her, they were simply called 'Mutton Pies.' Always baked, never fried. You transposed the story to align with where you happened to end up… in Peru. You remember the smell of petrol because the progenitor's father drove a bus. A red bus, in fact. You remember an aeroplane accident because this happened to our progenitor. I share the same memory. All red-fingered brothers share these, and all of us forever will."

Dr. Cuba was calculating facts, inputs, data… but coming up with no explanation. He continued to listen.

"Again, I do not know how your material avoided cleanup, nor how it found a suitable substrate upon which to grow, but that you ended up emerging in Peru has an explanation. I had been exploring the use of ayahuasca in my experiments and made frequent trips there. Somehow, your base material was transported there."

"Are you saying I am the product of something stuck to your shoe?" Dr. Cuba asked, insulted.

"Something less crude, but it is a theory," the Homunculus admitted. "Regardless, you emerged and, left without someone to raise you, created a history for yourself based on your surroundings and your fragmented genetic memories. I am sure that if I had been left in such conditions, not as a baby per se, but as a collection of cells and carrier materials, I might have grown to invent my own unique story."

"Let us say," Dr. Cuba said, without any emotion, "all of this is true. You ordered me to cease my operations. Why do you care what I do? What is your reasoning for halting my work?"

The Homunculus uncrossed his leg now and leaned in. "You have become a liability, Brother-Son. Your wave of crime has become too overt, too noticeable and, frankly, chaotic. You risk exposing me and any others like us, and I cannot allow that."

"So," Dr. Cuba said indignantly, "you are white knights, born—or, as you say, grown—to protect the world? To save humanity from 'defects' such as I? From demons?"

The Homunculus chuckled. "Dear Brother-Son, your actions, your inclinations, are all part of who you are. They, like your memories, are embedded in you. And by intent. You were created to embrace crime, to exist within it, to grow it. We are not here to save humanity. Far from it! We are here to rule it."

"Then, if you know my plans, you know we share the same goal. Why stop me?"

"Your goal is *not* the same. For some time now, my two Brother-Brothers and I have worked to steer events to our benefit. We brought about the radicalization of key Serbs to form the Black Hand, who went on to recruit Gavrilo Princip into murdering the ridiculous, porcine Archduke of Austria. The first Great War was ours. This second was also orchestrated by one of my Brother-Brothers, operating in Germany, who urged the Nationalsozialistische Deutsche Arbeiterpartei to purge its anti-business leanings while bribing German officials to take specific steps that further weakened the national economy. At the same time, I maneuvered malleable men into positions of speculation, which led to the stock market crash in the US and the resulting world economic crisis. We not only provided the powder keg and match, but the gasoline as well."

Dr. Cuba sensed, from the Homunculus' body language and tone, that he was telling the truth. Or, at least, this creature believed he was.

"With one Brother-Brother in France, another in Germany, myself in the United States, having a fourth in South America would be a great benefit. But you, my Brother-Son, are, as I said, a defect. You continued your predetermined destiny without control, without guidance, and without restraint. Now, everyone has heard whispers of 'Dr. Cuba' and has increased their guard. Everyone is watching you now, hunting you. They say you are manipulating economies, currencies, elections, and revolutions. This, speaking on behalf of those of us who are actually doing those things, cannot stand. You must be stopped. We must return to operate in secret, and you risk exposing us."

Dr. Cuba uncrossed his leg now and sat rigid. "And you would kill me, then?"

The Homunculus stared. "I have done the same calculations and estimates as you. I know there is little chance you will stop without me killing you. But little chance is not zero chance. If we can bring you back to the fold, we may be able to correct you. And the potential benefit of adding a fourth leg to our platform should be explored before it's cut off entirely. But be clear, Brother-Son, cutting you off entirely is likely the endgame here."

Dr. Cuba was not swayed. "I will not be stopped. Whereas you are concerned with mortal matters and simplistic tweaking of events like wars and elections, I am affixed to a far greater purpose. This may be the one thing you do not understand of me."

Now, it was the Homunculus' time to feel uncertainty. "A

greater purpose? And what might that be?"

He doesn't know of The Work, Dr. Cuba thought. *This is good.*

"It seems I now have the advantage over you. But whereas you have spent the past half-hour revealing all to me, I refuse to give you even a glimpse. You will not know my plan because no one will know it. I will simply execute it, and only after you are a victim of it will you recall—for a brief second, at least—that it was I that brought it about."

With that, Dr. Cuba stood and put back on his gloves. "I think we are finished here."

The Homunculus was, for the first time during the meeting, uncertain as to what to do. This was not an outcome he had predicted. Yes, he assumed he would fail in convincing his Brother-Son of the truth and that he would have to kill this creature. But what was this other plan he spoke of? Without knowing it, he could not take rash action.

The Homunculus stood now as Dr. Cuba began to leave. "Cease all operations, Brother-Son. Suspend all cadres. You will not be warned again."

Dr. Cuba did not respond.

———————————

Thumann, Gentleman, and Ximena survived the trip back on Little Billy's fan boat and eventually returned to steaming Miami. This time, they booked two rooms at the Roney Plaza Hotel along the beach; Scotland Yard had given Thumann some leeway with his spending for his investigation, and his frugal accommodations had pinched every penny thus far. Given all they had been through, it was time to spend some of King George's money.

Ximena took one room, while Thumann shared his with

Gentleman. Thumann explained this as a way to save a few of the King's pence, but he was actually using the opportunity to watch Gentleman's movements, mannerisms and attitude. Thumann had also settled into the role of Ximena's protector, and he did not want the young girl near Gentleman should things get worse.

As they did.

Once settled in their room, Thumann finally shed his jacket and even loosened his tie. As he kicked off his shoes, he could smell the room fill with the odor of his own feet. *No matter,* he thought, lighting his pipe. *Latakia to the rescue.*

The ceiling fan above did little to lower the temperature of the room, and Thumann wondered how people survived living in this inferno. Momentarily falling back into his regular patter with his apprentice, Thumann said, "Lucifer's living room, eh, Gentleman? Hot as blazes here."

Gentleman grunted and did not reply. He appeared irked that Thumann had interrupted some inner monologue. That grunt reminded the Inspector that his relationship with his apprentice was very much different today than it was a week ago.

Thumann kept his thoughts well-hidden, however, and even as his eyes scanned Gentleman for additional signs of … well, *oddities*, his posture and lackadaisical smoking telegraphed an attitude of lowered defenses. *Let him think I'm not paying attention,* Thumann thought.

As he puffed, watching the palm-shaped wooden fan blades above him circle overhead, to little effect, Thumann ran the options. If Gentleman had been exposed to the gas, he would not be as lucid as he had been since his rescue by Ximena. No, the gas would have turned him into a somnambulist, not a grumpier-but-alert version of the same man.

Hypnosis, then? Indeed, the papers written by Milton Erickson were getting some attention at psychology conferences. But even Erickson would not have claimed hypnosis could hold its sway over a man for nine whole days. If Dr. Cuba had done something to Gentleman, it would have been at least a day before Ximena freed him. No, it was not hypnosis.

Trauma? This made the most sense, of course. Gentleman was a seasoned police functionary, if not a full officer, but had seen his share of badness, much of it at Thumann's side. But to be kidnapped, perhaps tortured? The poor man must be struggling with that deep inside. Shell shock would certainly manifest as a shift towards curt, even rude, dismissal of former friends.

Why, then, did Blavatsky insist it was drugs? What drugs? LSD would not produce effects of this sort. Nor cannabis. But Blavatsky was rarely wrong. When she was wrong, she was spectacularly so, but, in this case, she seemed so confident.

Thumann needed evidence, and there was one easy way to get it. He stood up. "I'm headed to the gift shop," he said. Usually, Gentleman would have done a double-take at the idea of the great Inspector Heiner Thumann perusing a Miami gift shop, buying alligator jerky and trying on a guayabera shirt, but this Gentleman hardly reacted. He may have grunted, but Thumann was not sure.

Thumann was not shopping for gator jerky or trying to dress like a banana republic bureaucrat. Well, that was a lie; he did buy the jerky and ate it on the spot. But his real reason was to buy something else entirely.

"I'd like to see your men's bathing suits, please," he told the young shopgirl. The poor thing could not control her eyebrows, which darted to the heavens as she thought of trying to find something to fit this six-foot-four German giant.

"I, I…" she stuttered.

"Not for me, young miss," he said, raising a hand to calm her. "For my assistant. He's about five-foot-eight, 140 pounds. Any color will do."

The shopgirl smiled, hoping the German would forget her reaction if she just prettied it away. "Of course, sir," she said, bringing him over to a selection of modern-style suits.

"Something more traditional," Thumann said. He was not sure what style Gentleman might like, but he knew he did not want to see his assistant in some god-awful Hollywood get-up. The shopgirl found a stylish two-piece—trunks and tank top—and Thumann purchased it. "And some more of that alligator jerky," he said.

The ruse was as apparent as it was ridiculous. Thumann would suggest he and Gentleman go down by the pool, all to get Gentleman into something that might expose his arms and legs. In that state, Thumann could check for recent needle marks commonly used by criminals when injecting their victims: arms, legs, feet, etc. Thumann hoped this might be enough. He returned to the room, store bag in hand.

If Gentleman had been somehow clued into Thumann's intent, he would have normally never agreed to it. But this Gentleman, in yet another uncharacteristic quirk, jumped at the chance.

"Yes, I need a swim!" Gentleman said, grabbing the bag and going into the bathroom to change. "I need to cool off."

Thumann had been ready to explain why he, himself, would not be swimming—he was not about to scare the locals by bathing in front of anyone—but Gentleman's nearly desperate agreeability wiped that obstacle off the board. This plan was working just fine.

As Thumann and Gentleman walked down the stairs towards the outside pool area, the Inspector fell two steps behind his assistant. No marks on the arms, no marks on the antecubital fossa where one might traditionally insert an intravenous tube. Nothing at the vaccination point near either shoulder. The legs, then? It was hard to see.

The two exited the hotel and spilled out to the pool, where a crowd of people were gathered. Photographers were taking photos of someone, and there was a loud buzz of activity. People wearing hot street clothes, as well as hotel staff, were gathered near the pool, mingling with hotel guests in swimwear.

"Bogie!" someone shouted. "This way, look this way!"

Thumann slowed down as they approached the crowd. There would be no getting near the pool with this many people here. But Thumann was not really interested in the pool anyway; he was trying to check Gentleman for puncture marks. "Let's head back to the room, Gentleman," Thumann said.

"No!" Gentleman shouted, "I'm hot, I need to cool off!" Gentleman pushed ahead, forcing himself through the crowd. People turned and scowled, and some swore as Gentleman shoved and pushed to reach the pool. He was manic, unhinged.

For a brief moment, Thumann saw what the fuss was about. Humphrey Bogart, the famous Hollywood actor, was sitting by the pool, being interviewed, and the crowd had gathered to take photos and get autographs. Gentleman—who was a Bogart fan—might have paused to enjoy the moment if he was not having a mental crisis. As he burst through the crowd and crashed across Bogart's pool chair, two giant bodyguards clotheslined him with their oak-like arms. Gentleman fell back, stunned, and the crowd turned their attention to him rather than Bogart.

Gentleman rose, however, and struck back. One swing landed a fist on the first bodyguard's jaw, sending the giant man reeling with a look of shock. The second guard grabbed Gentleman by the torso in a full bear hug, only to be beaten from above by Gentleman's raised arms and fists. Finally, the first guard recovered and landed a single blow on Gentleman's head, knocking him unconscious. He went limp.

An ambulance was called to take Gentleman away, and Thumann quickly intercepted the police to prevent an arrest. He explained the situation with only broad strokes—Gentleman had been kidnapped by a criminal gang only days ago and was believed to have been drugged—and the police agreed to let the medical doctors handle the matter. Bogie's henchman agreed not to press charges, and Bogart himself seemed amused by the entire spectacle. No doubt it was a story to tell at some future dinner party.

Thumann got what he wanted in the end: Gentleman in hospital for a complete medical evaluation. While he had been trying to plot some devious way to identify Gentleman's malady and trick him into a doctor's office. Thumann could not have known it would have all been much easier to simply get Gentleman to attack Humphrey Bogart at a swimming pool.

The shutting down of Dr. Cuba's operation had nothing to do with the threats presented by this "Homunculus" in Caracas, although it might have appeared that way to anyone watching events unfold. Instead, Dr. Cuba began halting operations because The Work was upon him.

The gold was pure. The quantity was sufficient. The airships and C54s were carrying their cargo to South Dakota as scheduled. The injector array was prepared. The Sunken Gods lay waiting. All was on track, all timelines synchronized, all milestones met. Nothing could stop him now.

Dr. Cuba made numerous radio transmissions and issued a range of new—and highly unusual—commands. He shut down the Berlin operation. The Chicago operation. Operations in Brazil, Paris, Ouagadougou. He ordered the dismantling of physical assets in key locations, the murder of witnesses, and the transfer of funds from one hundred or more accounts around the world. He ordered his most trusted men to kill his least trusted men, to leave fewer witnesses. He ordered the burning of warehouses, armories, and supply depots. He arranged the firebombing of evidence lockers in police stations, the bulldozing of bunkers, the toppling of entire buildings.

All of this was done in a single 48-hour period.

But Dr. Cuba knew not to be overconfident. He faced two adversaries now: the relentless Inspector Heiner Thumann and this unnamed Homunculus, alleging to be his "Father-Brother." For this reason, Dr. Cuba did not order a full-scale destruction of his entire network. Just in case, by some unforeseen calculation, either of these creatures managed to foil his plan at the last minute, Dr. Cuba left some aspects of his global machine in place, allowing for the ability to restart it if the need should arise.

As he turned off the radio, completing his final orders, his mind nevertheless calculated the possibility that what the Homunculus said might be true. Certainly, the mysterious man explained many things, and seemed to have answers for questions Dr. Cuba had roiling around his brainpan for decades. He knew that he was different from other people. Odd. Misplaced. He had attributed that to his incredible intelligence and lack of emotion, which made him a social outcast. Could it be more than that? Might he not be fully human at all? Might he, like the Homunculus, have been grown, not born, and lacking a soul?

The red finger. The need to drink gasoline and blood. His strength, his cleverness, his cruelty. The patches in his memory. The empanadas! Could all this have been imprinted in him, built into him, engineered?

If so, who was the Father-Father, the progenitor? How did an ordinary man create a set of super-men?

As he boarded the *Cassowary* for its final trip, Dr. Cuba allowed himself to yield for a moment; the great airship was one place he could allow himself this luxury. If he accepted that the Homunculus might be telling the truth, could this be connected to The Work? If the memories of the red bus and baked empanadas— *we're not savages, no matter what!*—had been embedded in him, then might not the awareness of King God Skyx and the Sunken Gods? How *did* he -- Dr. Cuba—come to know of these dead gods, and how to awaken them? The book by Jonathan Allan Godfrey only provided snippets of details, lacking major important information: the purity of the gold, the method of injection, and the precise depth required to reach the gods' circulatory system. And yet, Dr. Cuba knew these things instinctively.

How?

Suddenly, Dr. Cuba snapped out of it. This was a dangerous line of thinking. Distracting. None of this would matter when the Sunken Gods awoke. All of reality would be changed, and things such as where he came from and why would no longer be of any importance. Instead, he would be summoned before the King God Skyx, asked to climb the mountain of dead bodies to stand before the Great Monster, and be given his role in the new world, the new universe.

He was a super-man, and it was for this. No ordinary man could have completed The Work. Only a super-man.

Only Dr. Cuba.

The Homunculus had his own network of spies, of course. He had not lied to his Brother-Son: the homunculi were created to rule humanity, and were chemically programmed by the progenitor to use crime as the tool to achieve it. And whereas the criminal organization orchestrated by Dr. Cuba was monstrously large, this was only due to the number of henchmen and buildings it utilized; these were not always the most reliable types of resources. The homunculi had altered the planet's economy and set the world on fire with far fewer men, far less effort, and far more stealth.

Dr. Cuba's network was extensive, but clumsy; worse, it was forever leaking. Leaking rumors, leaking information, leaking details. Dr. Cuba used such leaks to maintain control and instill fear. But such things also increased risk; for sure, it was these leaks that the Homunculus had exploited to track Dr. Cuba's movements, for example, to learn about his plots and schemes.

Now, however, Dr. Cuba was dismantling it all; or nearly all of it, anyway. The sloppy, disorganized destruction of buildings and murder of associates was too obvious, too noisy. Newspapers were reporting on the wave of crimes, all occurring within a day or two of each other, clearly suggesting a pattern, a network, a single source of orders. It would only be a matter of time before Dr. Cuba would be identified as that source. Whereas Scotland Yard, through its inspector Thumann, was only just starting to realize Dr. Cuba was an actual man, this 48-hour spree would erase all doubt. There would simply be no other explanation for such an otherwise random set of catastrophes to occur, all over the globe, unless someone was directing them.

The Homunculus was pleased. In his mad dash to achieve The Work, Dr. Cuba had grown entirely careless, taking actions regarding people and buildings and equipment and relationships without thought of what would happen to them later. Unbeknownst to him, this played into the Homunculus's hand. With the war now ending, what would be coming next required a larger operation than the homunculi had at present. Nothing as flashy as what Dr. Cuba had built, but larger for sure.

And, so, as Dr. Cuba was taking down his operations, the Homunculus was relaying his own commands, to his own network via his own means, to recapture Dr. Cuba's discards.

The Homunculus knew that Dr. Cuba, distracted, had no clue. Dr. Cuba did not notice that some of his commands to kill contacts and associates had gone unfulfilled; the targets were quickly brought under the Homunculus' control instead. He did not realize that buildings he had ordered toppled remained standing, or that equipment he had ordered destroyed had instead been shipped to warehouses in New York, to be stored for later use.

Yes, many were killed at Dr Cuba's order. Much infrastructure was destroyed, and fires raged across Dr. Cuba's vast network. Newspapermen scrambled to cover it all, radio waves overflowed with news about the two-day devastation. But the Homunculus ensured that just enough was allowed to survive, just enough to help build a new network. Just enough that Dr. Cuba, with his eyes on some other goal, would not notice.

At the same time, the Homunculus advanced with his other, more immediate, plan: the inevitable, if regrettable, assassination of this Brother-Son. Because he was nearly identical, the Homunculus knew the strengths of his creation. Dr. Cuba was physically strong, resilient to most crude forms of attack, and bore incredible healing properties. He was also impossibly intelligent, no doubt able to calculate probabilities and likelihoods as quick as the Homunculus himself. This made it difficult to surprise him and even more difficult to kill him.

Instead, the Homunculus would have to rely on more obvious tactics: identify Dr. Cuba's weaknesses and use those against him. Here, the Homunculus had some advantages. Dr. Cuba was blinded by some obsessive quest.

"*I am affixed to a far greater purpose,*" Dr. Cuba had said in Caracas. "*This may be the one thing you do not understand of me.*"

The Homunculus recognized delusion. He and his Father-Father before him had, in fact, used such things to control people to their own ends. He now sensed that whatever defects plagued his Brother-Son, they had manifested in some delusion or other. The Homunculus and his two Brother-Brothers, the "Fantôme" in France and the "Doktor" in Germany, had developed under the guidance of the progenitor and thus lacked any such psychological defects. The discarded goo that grew to become Dr. Cuba could hardly have been expected to form perfectly, and mental and emotional flaws were all but inevitable.

But what was Dr. Cuba's delusion? What obsessed him? What ultimate plan did he have, and what did he think his "far greater purpose" actually was? These were the details that the Homunculus was missing, and which he had to uncover if he was to plot Dr. Cuba's end.

There was one man who likely knew these things, and the Homunculus smiled to himself. *Of course, it was always going to come to this,* he thought.

I must go meet Heiner Thumann.

Chapter 13: The Government Cut

Three days after their return from Madame Blavatsky's swamp, Ximena's brain was still wobbling long after her legs had regained their composure. Little Billy's manic swampboating aboard the *Beard* was frightening enough — although, having survived it, she was now of a mind that "thrilling" was a better word — but the entire experience in that murky shack had left Ximena questioning quite nearly everything.

Ximena sat in her hotel room, alone, as Thumann was off visiting Gentleman in the hospital. The fact that Gentleman's attack on a movie star was not the most bizarre thing that happened on this trip was, to say the least, troubling.

Blavatsky had terrified her; at least, at first. Ximena had never been in the same room with someone who so perfectly personified the image of a witch. Sharing the same space with such a woman, smelling her stink, hearing her voice, watching cigar smoke waft as she spoke… it was a very different experience from watching a movie. Eventually, over the course of the hour spent in that shack, she realized the Blavatsky really was Thumann and Gentleman had been accusing her of: part charlatan, part lunatic, part true mystic, and very much an intellectual powerhouse.

Blavatsky's occult leanings made Ximena very uncomfortable, and she ran to pray as soon as she had reached her hotel. Now, days later, Ximena prayed less, realizing that nothing bad had happened to her after all. *Sarañani,* she thought, in her native Aymara. *Come on, chica. You talked to a woman who wore rags and had roots sticking out of her hair. It wasn't much of anything.*

Ximena laughed to herself. With each quiet chortle, a bit of Andean Catholic superstition left her, and she felt lighter for it. Ximena began to realize she could still be Catholic, still be a good person, without succumbing to a preprogrammed dread of the unknown. The memory of what she had been forced to do in Lima was still sticking itself to the inner wall of her mind, but she was learning to ignore it, at least for now.

What was left were facts. *What did we learn?* she asked herself. *What did Blavatsky teach us?*

First, that Dr. Cuba was likely a real person, even if his name was not. Next, that this madman was probably pursuing a fanatical, profane quest based on books written by a discredited lunatic, with the intent of awakening a Dead God buried in the earth. And, finally, this may involve injecting massive quantities of gold into the earth to do so.

Insanity, Ximena thought. *But what I think is insane is irrelevant. If Dr. Cuba believes it, he will act on it.*

It was those actions that Thumann was tasked with stopping. Blavatsky's revelations were insightful, mainly as to the villain's possible motivations, but how could they be converted into facts that her German could investigate? Places, locations, people … these were the things that Thumann would need to probe.

Deep in her thoughts, Ximena was wholly unaware that her brain was reshaping itself by connecting neurons in entirely new ways, into that of a detective. Laying a thin towel across the tiny table of her room, she then plopped the mound of clay onto it, being careful not to make a mess that the hotel maids might later complain about. She tore off a small chunk of the clay, about four inches of it, and rolled it into a rough cigar shape. Wetting her hands in a small cup of water, Ximena began shaping.

Her mind was nearly unaware of what her hands were doing. *Dr. Cuba needs a hole. A mine, in fact,* she thought. *Where is the deepest mine in the world?*

It was now three days since Gentleman had been admitted to Jackson Memorial Hospital for tests and evaluations. The efforts were slowed by the hospital's overall priority: caring for wounded soldiers returning from both fronts. The war may have been winding down, Hitler might be dead, but the flood of injured soldiers had not yet stopped. Japan was still ensuring that.

It was an entire day before any doctor even reported anything back to Thumann, who had been camped out in the hospital waiting room for sixteen hours. The doctor who spoke to him did so only for a moment, and with little effort to appear concerned about his patient at all; he was simply overworked. "Your friend does have some drugs in his system. We have him sedated and are running tests. That's all I have for you, come back tomorrow," the doctor said.

Thumann stayed in the waiting room regardless, propping up his feet on a small table and caring less and less about what people thought of his increasingly disheveled appearance. Ximena visited every three hours or so, bringing Thumann newspapers, coffee, and whatever she thought might help him bide the time. Finally, the hospital threw him out at nine in the evening, and he returned to the Roney Plaza Hotel for a shave and hot shower. He also sent his socks, shirt, suit, and coat out for laundering, as he was starting to "smell like a bear," according to Ximena. For the next eight hours or so, he'd have to sit around his room in his underwear; he had no choice but to hand over more of the King's money to get overnight laundry service.

Remarkably, Thumann fell asleep. He had not thought it possible, given all the worries he had for his poor assistant, Gentleman, but his eyes closed and then opened a few moments later to the Miami sun blaring through his window. He had slept deeply for at least nine hours.

Thumann ordered room service for breakfast, a giant plate of eggs, bacon and sausages, and greeted the bellboy in the hotel's robe. He then ate his breakfast—also like a bear, Ximena might have noted—and burped loudly. He was alone and allowed himself this liberty.

By ten o'clock, his clothes arrived; he dressed to go back to the hospital and prepare himself for another sixteen-hour sitting in the waiting room. It was just before eleven-thirty when a different doctor approached him.

"Inspector Thumann?" he asked.

"That is me," Thumann said, standing. The doctor eyed him, likely hesitant after hearing Thumann's German accent.

"Come into my office, please," the doctor said.

They walked into the doctor's office, a tiny but nicely decorated affair, with a window facing a waving palm tree. The doctor sat, and Thumann did likewise.

"Your friend has a drug in his system that we cannot, frankly, identify. It's not lysergic acid diethylamide, nor opium, nor any form of heroin or something of that sort. It has caused him to be highly susceptible to suggestion, and, as it is wearing off, Mr. Gentleman is increasingly agitated. He has attacked a number of our staff, but we have him sedated, so he's not really able to hurt anyone. Just slaps and scrapes."

"How do you account for that?" Thumann asked.

"A psychiatrist has weighed in on this case as well. As near as we can surmise, the lack of suggestions is creating the agitation. It is as if he is waiting to be told what to do, but, because no one is doing so, he has fallen into a stress cycle."

"Can you give him orders? Simple commands, then, like telling him to brush his teeth? I mean, to alleviate the crisis?"

"We tried, but he is entirely unresponsive to us. I suspect these commands must come from someone else. I really don't know."

Thumann frowned. "This is troubling. If you don't know what the drug is, then you can't know a treatment… correct?"

"Exactly the case, Inspector. We don't know what to do, except to keep him sedated and hope the drug eventually works its way out of his system. We have him on an intravenous drip to try and hasten the process, but if the drug has affected his brain, that may not be of immediate help."

"I can call for medical help from England, if that would help," Thumann offered, "but I'm not sure they would arrive soon. It could be weeks."

"We have very skilled physicians here, Inspector. And by the time any overseas doctors arrived, we would hope Mr. Gentleman would have recovered."

"All we can do is wait, then," Thumann summarized. He stood to leave, thanking the doctor. "I will continue to wait in the waiting room if you have any news."

The doctor shook his hand, but then both men were drawn to a loud commotion outside. People yelling, running, something breaking. Thumann and the doctor rushed to the hallway.

"What is going on?" the doctor demanded, to no one in particular.

An orderly rushed past, shouting, "That drug addict patient has escaped!"

Thumann, through some intuition, knew immediately it was Gentleman. As the doctor ran down the hallway, Thumann followed. Due to the chaos, no one made an effort to stop him, even as he passed through a restricted area marked "hospital staff only." They came to a long hallway of patient rooms, and Thumann saw hospital beds and equipment scattered on the floor outside a room at the end of the hall. The doctor ran, with Thumann in tow, until they reached the room.

"Your man's gone crazy!" the doctor said. "He was sedated! How is this possible?"

The inside of the room looked as if rabid zoo animals had gotten loose. Everything was smashed, turned over, torn apart. A nurse lay unconscious on the floor, a small splash of blood on her forehead. Thumann instinctively knelt to check her pulse: unconscious, not dead. He scanned the room, but there was no sign of Gentleman.

Another orderly entered. "He got out the window, ran down the pathway outside, and was picked up by men in a truck. Craziest thing I've ever seen!"

"What?" Thuman boomed, standing again. He towered over the poor orderly. "Men in a truck? What truck? What men?"

"I... I dunno, sir," the orderly said, timidly. He assumed Thumann was some sort of hospital administrator. "It was a black truck, a small one, like a milkman's truck. But black and, I dunno, ... just black."

"How many men?" Thumann asked, looking out the window. He saw the path that Gentleman must have used.

"I dunno, I saw a driver and two guys in the back. That's it!"

"Did they take him? I mean, forcibly?" Thumann asked.

"No, he jumped in. They helped him."

"Damn!" Thumann grunted, storming out of the room.

"Dr. Cuba's men!" He stomped back down the hallway, through the various maze of hospital halls, and out to the front door. Ximena was there, on her way inside.

"Inspector!" she said, getting his attention. Ximena was dressed in something entirely different: a set of mannish cargo pants and a tan blouse. He hair was tied up in a ponytail, and she no longer looked like a simple Catholic girl from Chile. She was … contemporary?

"Gentleman was taken… again!" Thumann said, noting Ximena's clothes, but saying nothing. He scanned the area for signs of a black truck or any other suspicious signs. Nothing.

"Inspector, I received this," Ximena said, handing him a piece of paper. "A telegram, saying it was sent by Mr. Gentleman about a half hour ago. It's addressed to you. The hotel said you weren't in, so they gave it to me to bring to you."

Thumann snatched the paper. "A telegram? A half hour ago? That's not possible, Gentleman was here, sedated. Hooked up to an IV. How could he have sent a telegram?"

He opened it.

INSPECTOR H. THUMANN

= I WILL LEAVE HOSPITAL WITHIN THE HOUR. MEET ME ON ISLAND EAST OF GOVERNMENT CUT AT 1:30 EXACTLY. BRING XIMENA NO ONE ELSE. =

B. GENTLEMAN

"Government Cut? What is Government Cut?" Thumann asked. "And how… wait, we need answers!" Thumann stormed back into the hospital, Ximena hurrying behind him.

"Where's the telegraph office?" Thumann asked at the reception area. The girl behind the desk had barely finished pointing, and Thumann was off in that direction. A small office, with a window and desk, sat midway between the main waiting room and the patients' area. A skinny old man sat inside, listening to a Detroit Tigers baseball game on the radio.

Thumann banged on the glass. "When did you get this? Who sent this?" He slapped the telegram up against the glass.

The man squinted, looking at the note. He then went to a book and traced down entries with his finger.

"Come on, man, this was only a short while ago! You need the book to remember this?" Thumann barked.

The man looked up, over the top of his glasses. "A patient sent it. A Mister Gentleman."

"Impossible, he was in his room, hooked up to tubes in his arm."

The man sniffed. "The patient did have an IV but was walking with a portable rack. He was walking of his own accord. He came, picked up a telegram, sent that one, and returned back."

"Wait," Thumann said, with a growl. "You say he picked up a telegram? Before he sent this?"

The man nodded. "That's right." He ran his finger down the log sheet again. "Yes, that's correct. It's all here."

"Who sent the telegram?" Thumann demanded.

"Can't tell you that. Western Union don't allow me to reveal telegraph information to anyone but the recipient."

Thumann banged on the glass. "I am a police inspector! This is relevant to a crime. You have to answer me!"

Ximena watched with surprise as the telegraph operator

shrugged and began fumbling around his papers. Without questioning Thumann, he produced a copy of a telegram and handed it to him. Perhaps Thumann's official-sounding tone worked? Or was the telegraph operator just lackadaisical?

Thumann read it and handed it to Ximena. "Look at this," he said.

BERNARD GENTLEMAN

= RENDEZVOUS WITH EXTRACTION TRUCK AT 11:30 AM. SEND TELEGRAM TO INSPECTOR DIRECTING HIM TO MEET YOU AT STAGING POINT 89. BRING ONLY X TORRES. TODAS LAS COSAS NACEN =

DR. CUBA

"What's this last bit mean?" Thumann asked.

"*All things are born*," she said. "I don't understand the context, though. A code?"

"Likely so." Thumann shoved both telegrams in his pocket and turned to face Ximena. "This makes no sense. The orderlies say he went crazy. But just a few minutes prior, he was calmly strolling around the hospital hallway, sending telegrams?"

"Perhaps he is faking his breakdown?" Ximena offered. "To escape the hospital?"

Thumann nodded. "I wonder if it wouldn't have been easier to just walk out the front door."

Ximena pointed at the door. Two burly orderlies were there; they might have provided some resistance.

"Hmph," Thumann grunted, still not entirely convinced he

was wrong.

"Could the drug still be having effects on him?" Ximena asked. "Maybe he is fighting the effects? He was supposed to walk out, but in his attempt to resist the effects, he struggled instead?"

"You didn't see the mess he made in there. A poor nurse is unconscious with a head wound. It was as if he were rabid."

"This code, then. '*Todas las cosas nacen.*' Maybe it was a trigger of some sort?"

Thumann again nodded. "Again, you may be right. Nothing with this Dr. Cuba seems accidental. A violent breakout was probably part of his plan. Perhaps just to get our attention."

Thumann turned back to the disinterested telegraph operator. "What is the Government Cut?" he asked.

The man again barely looked up, only bothering to raise his eyes slightly above his glasses. "The feds dredged a strip of land out there, between the coast and Fisher Island, to make a shipping lane. They call it the 'Government Cut.'"

Thumann again turned, putting his back to the telegraph window; the operator inside went back to his baseball game.

"I need a map," Thumann said.

Ximena went to the front desk, and within a minute, she was unfolding a large map of Miami. She waved Thumann over to look at it. "We're here," she said, pointing to the hospital location. "We just have to drive to the coast, along these roads." She traced her finger rightward on the map, towards the coast. "It should be a quick trip. But look here," she said, pointing to an island just east of the coast.

"What's that? It doesn't have a name."

Ximena was pointing to a long, oblong-shaped mass between the Miami Beach coastline and Fisher Island. "It must be the meeting point. It's the island immediately east of Government Cut."

Thumann patted Ximena on the shoulders. "Well done. Let's see if we can get a cab, and then try to find a boat to take us across."

Thumann and Ximena headed outside and hailed a taxi. The ride to the coast would take about twenty minutes, and the taxi driver knew a place they could hire a boat to get over to what he called "Ugly Island."

"Still don't got a name, just a big ugly slab of dirt sitting out there," he said. "It'd be perfect for an airport, but nobody listens to me. I'm just a cabbie, nobody listens."

Thumann, watching as palm trees passed by and thinking about Gentleman, was not listening.

"This is a trap," he said. "You shouldn't have come."

Ximena sighed. "I am fine. I want to help. I care for Gentleman, I want to see him safe. I need to help."

Thumann nodded. "I know. You are braver than I was at your age. You constantly surprise me, and I am sorry for that."

"Sorry?" Ximena asked. "Why are you sorry?"

"I should not be surprised. It's not fair. You are a new generation. People your age are strong, and an old, smelly bear like me is still stuck thinking you're weak. Especially girls your age."

"I will be 26 in a month, remember. A woman," Ximena corrected, gently. "Not a girl."

"You see? I did it again. I look at you and I see a tiny, innocent Catholic girl, nearly fresh out of grade school. But you are a woman, a professional, whip-smart and unafraid. You helped solve a major element of our case, helped rescue our friend, and pushed yourself beyond your limits. And here I am, an old, smelly bear, still treating you like a child. I am sorry for that, young Miss. I am old and foolish."

Ximena smiled. "You are old and smelly, but you are not foolish," she said, holding his hand.

Thumann patted her hand. "No, I wasn't feeling sorry for myself. I wasn't seeking your approval. I just want you to know that you shouldn't listen to men like me. You are what comes next. I'm not a father, but I suspect that all fathers would want the next generation to be better than their own. If all the women of your age are like you, our planet will be a very good place."

Ximena smiled again but remained silent.

"Unless, of course, villains like this Dr. Cuba win the day," Thumann muttered, turning his head back towards the window. They were now approaching their destination. "If so, your generation will have a very hard time of it."

"Then it is our task today," Ximena said, "to make sure the villains lose."

———

The *Cassowary* was loaded with what would be its final load of gold. Dr. Cuba had the airship pause in Caracas to pick him up and then make the two-day journey to South Dakota.

Despite its name, South Dakota was very much in the northern part of the United States. At least it seemed as much, as the *Cassowary* flew over Mexico and into Texas, then over multiple other states—a bit of Oklahoma, all of Kansas, a clipping of Colorado, then through Nebraska—before continuing deep into South Dakota itself.

The Homestake Mine was located in a town called Lead, nearly exactly at the midway point between South Dakota's northern and southern borders and stuck far to the left near the state's western limit. It occupied a section of land on the northern edge of the Black Hills National Forest and was technically located in Bobtail Gulch. The size of the mine had grown beyond Bobtail Gulch, however, and now spanned nearly a mile across.

Dr. Cuba was not interested in the Homestake Mine's width, however. It was the depth that mattered. The mine was the deepest mine in human history, reaching depths of 5,000 feet through digging, with additional depths available by natural sinkholes and vents. His calculations put the Sunken Gods' circulatory system at between 4,250 and 5,500 feet, give or take a few dozen feet. Anywhere within that range would be sufficient to restart King God Skyx's dead heart.

The Homestake Mine was rich with gold, something which was very much not an accident, as Dr. Cuba alone knew. At this depth, the dead Skyx and his cohorts would have bled their last lifeblood into the area, naturally leaving gold splattered throughout the ground. This blood—this gold—would have become polluted over the millions of years that King God Skyx lay dead, no longer useful for revival without refining. But Dr. Cuba knew that the presence of this natural gold, at that exact depth, proved he was correct: this is where Skyx and Macapax and howling Aan and shuddering Fog'h lay in wait. An injection here would allow them to rise up, even if their bodies were physically much deeper, or even across the planet. The Sunken Gods' circulatory system ran through the entire world.

They would awaken.

Sitting in his private quarters on the *Cassowary*, Dr. Cuba meditated and trilled. For many hours. There were no more transmissions to be made, no more orders to be given. Only the injector array awaited now, and he would have to abide the time needed for travel, having patience, prohibiting anxiety to take hold.

He had not needed to alter his face in many days, and so was free from the influence of morphine. This also helped, as his mind would be clear for The Work. There existed the possibility that even if he was successful and the Sunken Gods arose, if he was deemed too clouded by impurities, Dr. Cuba might be denied his audience, denied his role in the new universe.

A knock on the door of the cabin.

"Come," Dr. Cuba said, his trilling stopped.

"Sir, we are over the mine now. Shall we descend?"

Dr. Cuba rose. "Hold position. I will come to the control gondola now." The operative left, as Dr. Cuba paused to gather his thoughts and his breath. He stood, adjusted his clothes, and put on a heavy overcoat. The control car would be cold.

He exited his cabin, which was contained within the "occupancy section" of the *Cassowary*'s huge envelope. The odd, flattened shape of the envelope allowed its designers to fit the lifting gas bags on both sides of the envelope, leaving room for an occupied section at the bottom; cargo could then be stored in the center of the envelope, on the two levels comprising the remaining two-thirds of the space.

The levels and rooms were all connected within the *Cassowary*'s belly through a system of metal platforms, pathways and ladders. Dr. Cuba made his way down a short metal stairway to a central walkway, which clanked as he walked across. He walked nearly half the *Cassowary*'s 800 feet in length until he was directly above the control car, mounted below the envelope. Now he descended various stairs and ladders until he reached the main vertical hatch, which allowed access to the control gondola.

Dropping down, Dr. Cuba had a 360-degree view of the world below him, with the giant envelope of the *Cassowary* blocking the sky above. Here, four copilots and navigators sat, along with the captain, at a set of seated positions circling the gondola's interior. From this position, the captain directed energy to the various propeller motors located all over the *Cassowary*'s exterior, pushing the great beast forward in the air. Other controls manipulated the various flight surfaces, such as rudders and ailerons, to provide steering and direction. From the gondola, the captain also controlled the helium gas, which kept the *Cassowary* aloft.

With an unobstructed view of everything below, Dr. Cuba could see the mine lying out, splayed, beneath them. "Bring us down to 350 feet and hold," Dr. Cuba ordered.

"Yes, sir," the captain said. "Drop to three-five-zero," he ordered.

"Three-five-zero, roger," another operative confirmed. Valves were switched and levers adjusted; pedals pushed. The great, laden ship began to descend. As it did, ever so slowly, the mine below came into better focus. The descent was slow, leisurely, but safe. Dr. Cuba did not rush it.

Finally: "Three-five-zero feet, Captain," the operative said.

"We're at position," the captain said to Dr. Cuba.

"There," Dr. Cuba pointed, indicating a visible construction near the front of the airship, slightly to the right. "That's it. Bring us to 75 feet, locate the mast, and get us moored."

As the Captain maneuvered the ship towards the mooring mast, Dr. Cuba ascended out of the control gondola and upwards towards an interior box-shaped room, high up inside the occupant area of the envelope. This was the hoist control room, where operators controlled the cargo bay doors, just fore and aft of the gondola, and used overhead hoists to lower the gold to the surface. "Prepare for unloading," Dr. Cuba said. "I want the gold placed directly near the feed end of the injector array."

There was no need for Dr. Cuba to personally oversee any of this. The crew of the *Cassowary* had made the trip before and were competent. But, for now, and given The Work was in its final stages, Dr. Cuba thought to occupy himself with details. No one would have noticed it, but there was an increasing mania in Dr. Cuba's actions, a detachment from his normal level of obsessive planning and preparation. Fewer calculations, and more raw, instinctive action.

But one calculation remained. Dr. Cuba went to one of the three radio shacks within the *Cassowary*'s vast belly and sent a message.

"Kill the brain," he said. "Leave no trace."

Chapter 14: The Vicious Knife

Thumann and Ximena disembarked the small boat they hired to bring them across the Government Cut to the as-yet-unnamed island. This oblong chunk of land was once part of the Florida peninsula but was now separated from the coast by the dredging operation of 1905. Ships floated through the Government Cut, lazily, ignoring the island where Thumann and his assistant now stood. Thumann told the boat's pilot to wait, but was not entirely sure he would.

The island itself was a flat slab of dirt and sand, uninhabited by either man or plants. Some of the island's cost was used, informally, for provisional anchoring of passing ships, or by local sailboat owners who wanted to spend the day at a private beach. It was not as pretty as the rest of Miami's shoreline, but it was certainly secluded.

For this reason, the island was used by various nefarious sorts, including smugglers and kidnappers. Despite its size—the island was two miles long and only about 2,000 feet across—its flatness allowed excellent visibility over distances. As they walked along the western shore, Thumann saw a set of trucks trundling towards them.

Thumann squinted. His eyes were still sharp enough to realize some of these trucks had armed gunmen atop them. "Get out of here, go, go!" he shouted, waving the boat pilot away. The pilot did not need any additional encouragement, seeing the danger himself; he frantically pulled the starter rope on his outboard motor and sped away.

Damn it, he thought. *I should have put Ximena on that boat.*

"Let me talk us out of this, if I can," he said, trying to reassure himself more than the young Ximena. They were on an uninhabited island facing a crew of armed enemies, without any guns, and without anyone even knowing where they were. Talk was all he could do.

Ximena saw Thumann fumbling inside his coat pocket. His right hand emerged; a glint revealed he had put on his polished, brass knuckles with the embossed Celtic knot pattern.

Ximena nudged him. Thumann looked down. She held open the pocket of her mannish pants and revealed a small pistol. This is why she had changed her clothes: she needed something with pockets.

"I don't like this," Thumann said, disapprovingly. He realized that Ximena's encounter with Dr. Cuba's men may still have left scars, and she might have been overcompensating. Was she now armed because she was afraid of a similar confrontation? Would she now live the rest of her life in armed fear?

Ximena said quietly, "Inspector, don't worry. I have permission."

Thumann had no inkling of what his assistant was referring to, but there was no more time to discuss it. He shook his head, setting it aside for now. "Anyway, we may need it," he admitted.

The trucks approached at an alarming pace. Six of them in total, three of them with gunmen atop, the others simply unmarked with God-knows-what inside. Each was about the size of a small delivery truck, but capable of holding additional men inside.

Would Dr. Cuba himself be one of them?

The trucks circled Thumann and Ximena, cutting off any escape route. The flat landscape left nowhere to hide, nothing to use as cover. They were entirely exposed!

A man emerged from the passenger side of one of the trucks; a thin, greasy man with thick glasses and a slimy combover atop his head. He bore a thin, wide smile that appeared to split his face from ear to ear. As he spoke, Thumann detected a Portuguese accent.

"Inspector Thumann!" the man said, arms out wide in welcome. "It is so good to finally meet you!"

"Dr. Cuba?" Thumann asked, fist clenched around his brass.

The man laughed. "Oh, no. No, no, no, but everyone assumes this! I am Dr. Vinhas, but everyone calls me 'Vines.' I work for our dear Dr. Cuba, however, and have his full authority to conduct this intervention, I assure you."

"Intervention?" Thumann asked. "Hmph. Where is my assistant, Gentleman?"

"He is here, with us! Have a look!" Vines waved a hand at someone, anyone, behind him. One of the trucks opened a side door, and Gentleman stepped out. His face was flushed and sweating, his eyes red, his hair matted. It looked like he was suffering from a fever. He stepped from the truck of his own accord, but he held his arms to his own body tightly, as if he were hugging himself. His posture was wrong, twisted, and he appeared to be in some physical distress.

"Gentleman!" Thumann said, stepping forward. A flood of armed men rushed forward, aiming their rifles at Thumann, stopping him. "Are you all right, man?"

Gentleman tried to speak, but choked, coughed, and clamped his mouth shut. Something was very wrong.

Ximena gripped the pistol in her pocket.

"Shall we picnic?" Vines asked, his broad smile splitting his face yet again.

Thumann refused to allow himself to react to the bizarre

request. He knew this was some form of dominance assertion. Vines waved his hand again, and more men emerged from more trucks. They carried a small duffle bag.

One of the operatives opened the bag and produced a red and white checkered blanket. The operative placed it on the ground in the space between Vines and Thumann. Vines tsked. "No, no, no. Let me." Vines then neatly and deliberately arranged the blanket so it was perfectly placed, without a single wrinkle, the edges lined up cleanly. Vines then reached into the duffle bag and produced a basket, and then a bottle of wine, and then two wine glasses.

He sat at one edge of the blanket, crossed his legs, and used a waiter's corkscrew to open the bottle. He indicated Thumann should sit across from him; Thumann did not.

"A red from Douro, Inspector. I think you will like it." Vines pulled the cork and poured two glasses. He gently set one in front of himself, and the other at Thumann's feet, being careful that it set sturdily on the uneven ground. Vines then reached into the basket and produced a set of plates, some cheeses, breads, and dried sausages. He retrieved a large cutting knife and some napkins.

He again indicated Thumann should sit, and Thumann again ignored him. Vines was asserting dominance in an unusual manner, by placing himself physically below Thumann; instead of making himself appear larger than Thumann, he was making himself much smaller, in a more vulnerable position. Except that Vines had thirteen armed men pointing rifles at Thumann, leveling things out a bit. It was all intended to disorient the German.

Vines continued to pretend he was at a Sunday picnic, as he tore off some bread, sliced a bit of sausage with the knife, and made an impromptu sandwich. He shoved it into his mouth. "Oh, good stuff, good stuff," he said, reveling both in the food and the little power play he was performing.

"Let me explain something to you, Inspector. May I do that?" Vines asked. He waited for an answer.

"Go," Thumann said, staring sternly. It was clear Vines was going to let the silence hang in the air until Thumann played along.

"The world, it rotates, yes? On its axis, spinning along, sending the sun moving through the sky. To us, of course, we cannot feel the spinning, so we think the sun is moving. But this is not the case. It is an optical illusion brought on by our own small stature amidst a much larger world. Such is Crime, Inspector. The average person sees a pickpocket, a bank heist, perhaps even a murder. He thinks these events are unique, happening in front of him, or even to him. But this is only because of his tiny stature in the giant world."

Thumann remained frozen in place, listening while trying to think of a way out of this predicament.

Vines continued on. "On the giant world, Crime is happening all at once, everywhere. Only to those specks on the street does it seem personal. If you were to, I don't know, hop on an airship and fly high up into the sky, to outer space, you might see the truth. Crime is not personal. It does not care for the tiny specks. It occurs. It simply *is*. And, more so, I say, if you were to hang yourself in space and look down at the Earth, you would see that Crime is the engine that spins the planet. It is what moves the sun in the sky. Without Crime, our society stops. Our Earth stops. The sun stops."

"If I kick you," Thumann said, with a low voice. "Your men would shoot me dead, but I would have had the benefit of shutting you up."

Vines smiled, sipping the Douro. He pursed his lips. "Oh,

this is not good. I am so sorry, Inspector. The wine is bad. Brettanomyces. An insidious little yeast that can ruin the best wines. I did try hard to ensure everything was in order. This," he said, holding up the bottle, "is undrinkable, I'm afraid." Vines stood, with the bottle in his hand. He held it up to the sun, looking at the wine in the bottle, searching for sediment. Then, with one movement, he swung the bottle towards the nearest gunman, striking him on the head. The gunman's head snapped to the right, blood pooled in his eyes, and he dropped, dead. His gun fell to the ground.

No one else moved. The other gunmen stayed in the same position, pointing their weapons at Thumann. Even Gentleman did not react. Vines had just killed one of their own, and they did not show any reaction at all.

Dr. Cuba's gas, Thumann thought to himself.

Vines saw the shocked expressions on Thumann's and Ximena's faces. He leaned closer, as if inspecting their faces. "Oh, what is this? Surprise? But let us think on this. What killed that man just now? Was it my hand swinging the bottle? Or was it the bottle striking his skull?"

Thumann and Ximena remained silent.

"Or—follow me now, Inspector—was it the wine? The Brettanomyces? If the wine had not been bad, would I have had need to discard it? And what made the wine bad? If it was heat, then blame the position of the sun, yes? The spinning of the Earth. So, which happened first? Crime spins the Earth, the spinning Earth creates more Crime. Like a combustion engine. Once it's started, it just keeps itself going. And men? They are the gasoline."

"Tell your men to put down their guns and let us leave. With Gentleman," Thumann said, ignoring Vines' strange rant.

Vines shook his head. "I think you will find that your friend Bernard Gentleman does not want to leave with you. He, like the others here, is happy to stay in my employ. In support of the great Dr. Cuba." Vines summoned Gentleman to his side. Gentleman shambled a bit, but came, as if following some silent orders. Vines handed him the large sausage knife.

"You've drugged him. Drugged all of them," Thumann barked. "Your control over them is artificial. These men don't have free will. You've taken it away through drugs and gas. You could not get their loyalty any other way."

Vines shrugged. "Perhaps," he said, smiling again. "But … it works." Then, turning to Gentleman, "Kill the girl."

Thumann's eyes widened to nearly all-white. Gentleman shambled behind Ximena, grabbed her, and held the knife to her neck. "Gentleman!" Thumann shouted.

Three men grabbed Thumann, holding him in place. Ximena struggled in terror, but to no avail. Gentleman was too strong. The drugs not only affected his mind but also made him physically stronger. She cried out, unable to escape.

Thumann, held back by three men, shouted again. "Gentleman! Stop this! You know her! You know me! Come to your senses! Think! Think!"

Vines sneered even more. "He cannot hear you, Inspector. He will only obey me or Dr. Cuba himself. No one else. But there is a way you can save the girl, Inspector."

"What is it?" Thumann demanded.

"Tell me everything that Scotland Yard knows about Dr. Cuba and his operation. And I mean everything. We have time and, as you can see," Vines waved his hand towards the picnic blanket, "I've brought food, in case it takes a while."

"You will only kill me afterward anyway," Thumann said.

Vines nodded. "This is true. But perhaps in these last few moments, you might think of some way out of this. Perhaps you can convince me to let you go. So long as you are alive, you can speak. So long as you are speaking, you have a chance to survive. Yes or no?"

Thumann needed the extra time, for sure.

Vines pushed further. "No one is coming to save you, Inspector Thumann. Only your great German Brain—isn't that what they call you at Scotland Yard, the 'German Brain'?—only that can save you. Perhaps."

Before much else could occur, however, a roar overhead was heard. Vines, Thumann and the others looked up. A massive C-54 Skymaster loomed above, appearing to hover in the air over the far eastern side of the island. Hovering, no… it was landing.

Vines held his finger up. "Hah! I can assure you, Inspector, that is not your savior coming. Far from it, I think our beloved Dr. Cuba has come to see you personally, to hear what you have learned about him," he said, smiling. "This is a great day, Inspector! You will finally meet your nemesis in the flesh!"

The group, still standing in place over the dead gunman, watched as the monstrously large aircraft used the entirety of the abandoned island as its landing strip. It lowered itself lazily from the sky to the earth, kicking up sand and dirt as its gear touched down. The monstrous roar of the four propeller engines filled the air and sent sand everywhere. The aeroplane taxied for just a bit, came to a stop, and the motors began to spin down.

Vines motioned for his men—and Gentleman—to hold their positions. "Stay here, don't move," he ordered. They obeyed, continuing to aim their guns at Thumann, while Gentleman still held the knife at Ximena's neck. Vines strode towards the plane, aiming himself towards the main door, about two-thirds of the way down from the nose and behind the wing. "I do hope you have much to tell Dr. Cuba. He is certainly very interested to hear your story, Inspector Thumann!" Vines shouted as he walked closer to the parked aeroplane.

The main cabin door opened, and a stairway swung down from inside. Out stepped a man wearing glasses, thin and tall, wearing black clothes and a black hat. From this distance, Thumann could not see his features well, but he appeared to be about 40 years old, stern-looking, with an entirely neutral expression. Glaringly white skin, like fine china.

"Dr. Cuba!" Vines said, arms spread in greeting. "It is so good to see you."

"And you, Dr. Vines," Dr. Cuba said.

This is Dr. Cuba! Thumann thought. *Just a man, after all!*

Vines and his superior walked over to Thumann and the gunmen. The strange Dr. Cuba raised a gloved hand in greeting. Thumann refused to take it. Vines moved to Thumann's side, grabbing the German's arm and yanking his giant hand out of his coat pocket, forcing it forward towards Dr. Cuba. Dr. Cuba grasped it, shook it. His grip was firm, cold, bloodless.

Thumann's brass knuckles were exposed now, but neither Dr. Cuba nor Vines seemed to care.

"We finally meet, Inspector. You've caused me some difficulty," Dr. Cuba said. His voice was like a ghost's violin.

"The entire world can say the same of you," Thumann responded. "I am placing you under arrest for terrorism, arson, murder, theft, and crimes we likely haven't words for."

Dr. Cuba smiled. "Admirable," he said, looking around.

The gunman continued to point their weapons at Thumann. It was an empty show of strength by Thumann, and everyone knew it. "But it won't be necessary."

Thumann plotted his next response, but it was interrupted when Vines' head exploded. The space where his head had been, directly above his shoulders, was now replaced with a sudden splash of red blood, pink brain matter, and white bone, haloed in a mist of red. Thumann, Dr. Cuba, Ximena, and the men were hit with flying bits of Vines.

Thumann's eyes widened. One of the round windows along the side of the C54 was missing its glass, and the barrel of a long-range rifle was visible sticking out. It smoked.

The gunmen surrounding Thumann remained frozen in place. For a moment, Thumann thought they might be under the influence of the same drug, stuck in place because of Vines' last order: *"Don't move."* Or, perhaps, they were merely shocked by the sight of Vines' headless body dropping to the ground.

No matter; Thumann jumped into action. Pulling out his giant, brass-knuckled fist, he swung hard at the closest gunman, knocking him down with one bloody blow. The man's head caved in from the punch, a visible embossed Celtic knot pattern left on the side of his cranium.

Thumann then went to grab Dr. Cuba, but he was no longer standing where he had been just a few seconds ago. Impossibly, Dr. Cuba was now behind two of the gunmen; how he moved so fast defied explanation. Using what appeared to be superhuman strength, Dr. Cuba's hands brought the two men's heads together into a single, mashed blob. More blood, more bone.

Thumann did not understand what was happening any more than anyone else. He continued to move, prioritizing taking out as many of the gunmen as he could. He could figure out Dr. Cuba's strange motivations later.

With surprising agility for such a giant, overweight beast, Thumann pushed Gentleman to the ground, temporarily separating him from Ximena. He then swung his fist at the second gunman, connecting directly with his nose, crushing it inward with an audible crunch. One of the men fired off a shot, grazing Thumann's shoulder. Grabbing the man with the crushed nose, Thumann swung the man's body around to use it as a shield. He maneuvered so he was in front of Ximena, offering her more protection from any stray bullets, which now would have to go through two bodies to get to her.

The other gunmen were not sure where to look. One of them fell dead, a bullet hole appearing in his head—sniped, as well, from the aeroplane window. Some began firing blindly at the C-54. They all avoided—or could not hit—the fast-moving shape of Dr. Cuba.

More gunmen fell, as Dr. Cuba leaped in the air, to a height of two meters or more, only to come crashing down on some of them with incredible force, using movements that Thumann had only seen in foreign wrestling films. Flying kicks, thrusting fists, jabbing elbows, within just a few minutes, the gunmen were all dead. Most were killed by Dr. Cuba himself, a few by Thumann, and the rest by the unseen sniper inside the C-54.

Except for one. Ximena stood over the body of one man, her small pistol smoking between her two raised hands. Her hands were shaking, but her face was not that of someone experiencing trauma. She was confident; there was anger, but also defiance. She was defending herself and her colleagues. Thumann saw no fear or hesitation in her face. Whatever ghosts had given Ximena permission to use her gun had also given her courage.

Gentleman was still alive, untouched by anyone in the melee. He remained half-hunched, clearly confused, disoriented, still holding the sausage knife. He appeared to be crying. The only figures left standing were Thumann, Ximena, Gentleman and Dr. Cuba.

Thumann wanted to go to Gentleman but was interrupted by Dr. Cuba. "I have a confession, Inspector Thumann," he said, removing his hat. "I have lied to you."

Thumann watched as Dr. Cuba raised his hands to his face and began pressing. Bones crunched, skin stretched, and blood appeared in the corners of his eyes. He was manipulating his own face, changing his appearance. Gone was the look of a 40-year-old bookish man, and in its place was a somewhat neutral blank slate. The black eyes were the same, but the nose and jawline had changed. Fuller, more uniform, more symmetrical. Younger? Older? It was not clear.

The figure lowered his hands and removed his gloves. Thumann saw a single red finger—the forefinger of the left hand—as the man extended his other hand once again. This time, Thumann took it. He had, after all, just saved their lives.

"I am not Dr. Cuba," he said.

"I assumed not," Thumann said. "Who are you, then? What is your name?"

"I don't have one. You can call me Dr. Cuba, if that's more convenient. The Dr. Cuba you were pursuing, well, he and I are brothers of a sort. But he's gone mad, and I am seeking to stop him. I've stolen his plane and a few of his men to get me here."

"Your face…," Thumann said. "You can alter it?"

"At great pain, but yes. Something I learned from my

brother, in fact. I admit he's better at it than I."

Monsters, Thumann thought. "Why don't you have a name?" Thumann asked.

"It's complicated. Very complicated. For now, we have more pressing matters." The Homunculus pointed at Gentleman, who was once again gripping Ximena and holding a knife to her throat.

Thumann's mouth fell open. "Gentleman! What are you doing?!"

Gentleman struggled, tears falling from his eyes. "I … I…"

Ximena looked terrified.

The Homunculus spoke, in a deep voice. "He's affected by my brother's drugs. He is following whatever last order was given to him. He cannot control himself."

Thumann knew this to be true. Vines' last order was, simply, "kill the girl." As hard as he might try, Gentleman was losing the battle to reassert his free will.

"Stop him, then!" Thumann barked at the Homunculus.

"I cannot. He will only respond to Dr. Cuba's voice. I have no more power over him than you do."

"Gentleman, breathe, man!" Thumann said, holding up his hands. "Try to breathe. Remember where you are. Who you are. Who I am! You don't want to do this. Ximena is your friend. We are your friends. We can help you!"

"I can't… I'm sorry… so… so… sorry," Gentleman said, choking back tears. The knife pushed into Ximena's neck; blood was beginning to show.

The Homunculus simply stood still, watching this drama unfold. It was as if he were watching a stage play, curious to see how it might end. "You will need to kill him," he said to Thumann.

"The drug is too powerful."

Thumann held out his hand to Ximena. "Give me the gun, young Miss," he said. Ximena's hand was shaking out of fear now. She slowly let the gun slip from her grip and fall into Thumann's bear-like paw.

Thumann, with his own eyes beginning to tear, slowly placed the gun in his right hand, and lifted it, aiming it at Gentleman. He aimed for his legs. "Please, Gentleman. Please... Bernard," he said. It was the first time Ximena ever heard him use Gentleman's first name.

The Homunculus reached over and raised Thumann's arm so the gun was pointed at Gentleman's head. He repeated, "You will need to kill him. He will never stop. He cannot. Even if you wound him, he will use every last bit of strength to kill the girl. He will live in an eternal agony, forever obsessed with the last order he received. So long as he has not killed her, he will go more and more mad. You know this, Thumann. You can see it in his eyes."

"I need you to put down the knife."

Gentleman shook, tears rolling down his cheeks, his entire body shaking. He was fighting the drug, and losing. "I can't, Thumann. Heiner. I can't. It's too strong. He's right... you need to fire. I can't live like this! You must fire!"

The Homunculus continued to watch, without emotion. Thumann's hand was steady, pointing the gun directly at Gentleman's head. "I don't want to hurt you, Bernard. But I have to stop this. I can't let you harm anyone. Not Ximena. Please, put down the knife."

"South Dakota," Gentleman said. "That... that's his plan. South Dakota. Homestake. Find him there. Kill him. Please. For me." The knife pressed further. One quarter inch more, and

261

Ximena's jugular would be penetrated. She gasped in pain.

"Gentleman," Thumann pleaded.

Gentleman sobbed now, the knife pressing further. "Homestake. Kill him. Kill me. Kill us both."

The shot fired, Gentleman fell, Ximena lunged forward, and Thumann's hand fell limp at his side. Ximena clutched Thumann, holding him as if her were a giant tree, sobbing. Gentleman lay bleeding, dead, on the ground.

Thumann turned to the Homunculus. "Take me to him," he said. Thumann's face was morphing from one of grief to one of fury.

"I will," the Homunculus said. "I did not know my brother's whereabouts. Your friend sacrificed himself to give us that information. I will take you there, and we can kill this Dr. Cuba together."

The three boarded the C-54. The stairway was retracted inward, the door closed, the engines started, the propellers brought to speed, and the great monster aeroplane again raced down the unnamed island to lift off and turn west, towards South Dakota.

Chapter 15: The King God

The injector array was a goliath of a thing. It looked as if someone had cut an oil refinery into pieces, discarded entire chunks, and then randomly reassembled the remains at the base of the Homestake mine. Its appearance actually pointed to its functionality: the array was a set of three separate systems, each of which had been transported just outside of Lead, South Dakota, separately, using the *Cassowary*'s sister airships long before they were recruited for the gold transfer flights. Then, with the help of Dr. Cuba's framing of Jacoby and dismantling of the labor union protests, the three units were moved via massive trucks down the mine's dirt roadway and assembled into a single gargantuan mass of metal tubes, spitting tanks and blinking control units.

The Homestake mine was characterized by, as all mines usually are, a descending set of concentric circles, providing a roadway down towards the center. The loops towards the outside of the mine were larger, much longer to traverse, but closed in as the road circled down towards the center. Dante would have been impressed.

At the center was the deepest part of the mine, a complex geological area with diverse terrain elements. There was a lake, of sorts, formed by dug-out sections of the region and filled with rainwater. Near this were the final spirals of the road, the final level of this man-made Hell, and at the very center, a deep pit. It was here, over this pit, that Dr. Cuba assembled the injector array. It sat on what appeared to be a set of steel frames, resembling a bug with odd, metal legs splaying out across the area. Some of the legs supported the array by sitting on solid ground, others extended down into the lake and, one presumes, rested on the lake bottom. The position allowed the center of Dr. Cuba's growling, smoking beast to be positioned directly over the maw of the Homestake pit.

Dr. Cuba kept a single gas truck on hand to use on any remaining security guards, local wanderers, or intransigent labor union gripers, ensuring that no word of the complex operation leaked prematurely. Dr. Cuba was not concerned about what might happen afterward, so his plan only accounted for keeping people silent during the preparation of The Work.

Now, the purified gold was unloaded from wooden crates by masked operatives onto a rattling conveyor that carried the metal up nearly 200 feet, towards the top of the injector array. The gold dropped, rudely, into an odd-looking, v-shaped hopper which acted as the mouth of a chute. Fed by nothing more than gravity, the gold would then pass down through the chute, subjected to a spray that cleansed any exterior dirt from each bar, and into the maw of the curious injector itself. Inside this, a set of molybdenum heating elements was powered by an exterior gasoline generator and brought to incredible temperatures. The inside of the furnace was filled with inert argon gas, supplied by two massive external tanks, to ensure the efficiency of the heating process and maintain the purity of the melted gold. The temperatures neared gold's evaporation point, turning the ingots into a pool of swirling, fuming metal.

This, then, fed into the injector apparatus itself. The liquid gold flowed, under vacuum pressure now, into a set of pumps that pushed the column of molten metal downward, into three long tubes. The insides of the tubes were lined with zirconia to withstand the temperature of the liquid gold as it traveled downward. The tubes extended into the lowest point of the mine, deeper and deeper into the belly of the earth. The tubes' diameters narrowed the closer they reached the injection point, with pumps attached at every 200 feet to ensure constant pressure. At the injection point, the final gold product was ejected at a pressure of at least 12,000 psi, capable of fracturing the rocks below. How far down the tubes went, only Dr. Cuba knew, based on his calculations of where the Sunken Gods' circulatory system may rest, waiting for the transfusion of new blood.

From a distance, the entire contraption appeared to make little noise, but up close it was a loud, howling banshee of a thing. The roar of the furnace met with the grumbling pumps and rattling conveyors, melding the sounds into what could only be described as an opera of devils. It was as if the machine were shouting into the earth, trying to wake the Gods by the sheer force of its voice, a mix of a continuous low growl with the occasional high-pitched scream of vents. While musical, there was nothing pleasant about the sound.

Dr. Cuba was immersed in it, however, bathing himself in the heat, the chorus of noise, the rising steam, the toxic gases that leaked from the pit itself. He had fashioned a metal platform near the base of the pit, at the point where the three tubes fed into the earth. Each tube was fitted with a thick diamond viewing port, so Dr. Cuba could see the flow of injected gold, under intense pressure, spewing downward at great speed. Now, the gold was being shoved into the earth, forcing aside any and all obstructions. Such was the quantity and pressure of the gold that rock formations simply gave way, yielding to the intentions of the madman and his brutal, howling machine above.

Dr. Cuba did not pray, of course. Neither the limited written works of Professor Godfrey nor Dr. Cuba's dream-fed information on The Work indicated the need for any ceremony during the process. There were no robes, no symbols, no incantations. This, Dr. Cuba understood, was science, not fantastical religion, and he was a simple scientist, not the Pope. The Sunken Gods lived during a time when the man-shaped creatures that roamed the earth could not have formed prayers or songs, and as a result, they had no need for such trappings. They needed gold and nothing more.

But Dr. Cuba's visual appearance did change, somewhat, indicating a level of mania that—at any other time—he might have otherwise controlled. His eyes were wide, his pupils dilated into tiny points, and his mannerisms jerky, uncontrolled. The gold was flowing, the veins and arteries of King God Skyx and grave Macapax were being revived with new blood, their hearts about to give twitch again for the first time in three million years.

This mania, coupled with the noise and spewing dust and gas, left Dr. Cuba entirely deaf and blinded from what was happening above him at the entrance of the Homestake mine. Five trucks rushed through the gates, with armed men hanging from the windows and shooting anyone and anything in their path. The Homunculus had landed the C-54 some miles away, in a rough landing that ended with the aeroplane's landing gear being hobbled. They would not be leaving the same way they came.

The Homunculus then used a team of fifteen men, previously recruited from Dr. Cuba's dismantled organization, upon the promise of continued wealth and opportunity, to act as his invasion force. This team of fifteen, along with the Homunculus, Thumann, and Ximena, was as much as they'd need. Thanks to Dr. Cuba's prior manipulations, the mine was largely abandoned, and the raiding party would only need to take down the remaining men, who were scattered across the circling, oval road leading down to the steaming, glistening injector array.

Thumann and Ximena were in the back of the rear truck and were not happy. "They are killing innocent men!" Ximena declared, trying to sneak a peek from a separation in the heavy denim material that covered the rear of the truck.

"I know, young Miss," Thumann said. "This is not how I wanted this to occur. But I simply don't have a better plan. We must stop this devil." Ximena did not sense it, but Thumann's voice was still filled with rage at the death of his friend, Gentleman, at his own hand. As blind as Dr. Cuba was with his manic desire to raise the King God, Thumann was now blinded by his emotions from the events of the past day. The C-54 flight from Miami had taken eight hours, and that time had not been sufficient to calm Thumann's racing mind and broken heart.

"If it's a consolation," Thumann offered, his teeth gritting from the raucous, bumpy ride as well as his own buried rage, "they may be in the same state as Gentleman. Stuck in a command loop, unable to break free, forced to obey until death. We can only hope that there won't be many lost today." Thumann held a hand to his shoulder, which was now bandaged, albeit roughly. The bullet had only broken through the meat of his fatty upper arm, and fortunately had not pierced bone. But it still hurt.

Ximena looked at Thumann with a mix of surprise and confusion. "This other man," she said, pointing a finger to the front of the caravan, "he may not be better than the first."

Thumann nodded. "We may be trading one devil for another, I know. But we must focus on the moment, right now. We must stop Dr. Cuba."

More gunshots echoed through the valley, sending chills up Ximena's spine as the truck pushed forward.

The Homunculus drove the lead truck. Unlike his Brother-

Son, he did not merely issue commands to subordinates, but instead led the action personally. Derek Fell, now finding himself working for this new ivory-skinned man, sat next to him in the passenger seat, firing an automatic rifle at anything that moved. Fell could not have known that his efforts to help kidnap Gentleman contributed to the rage of Thumann, sitting just a few trucks back in the very same convoy. If his head had not been blown to bits, Dr. Vines might have mused, with his greasy sneer, that Crime was spinning the world.

They met little resistance, but as they neared the belching injector array, the Homunculus saw a group of about eight armed men standing in a phalanx, automatic weapons aimed at them. They were still out of range, however. The Homunculus stopped his truck, and the other vehicles came to rest, their engines still running, however. He stepped out, went to the back, and produced a matte-painted M9 bazooka. This, too, had been liberated from Dr. Cuba's operation, specifically for this contingency.

The Homunculus loaded the massive M6 rocket-propelled grenade into the rear of the bazooka, snapped up the metal sight, and threw it effortlessly up on his shoulder. He walked around to the front of the lead truck, aimed the bazooka, and fired. The RPG shot forward, a stream of smoke trailing behind it, traveling the distance between the convoy and the phalanx of Dr. Cuba's operatives. With a violent blast, the men were cleared, sent flying in a ball of fire and burnt flesh, leaving behind a small crater and plume of black smoke. The Homunculus tossed the bazooka aside, no longer needing it, and climbed back into the truck. They advanced.

From his platform, Dr. Cuba heard nothing of the explosion above. He gripped the metal rail and darted his eyes from the diamond portholes, down to the pit, and back again. He was constantly seeking assurance that the gold was flowing. He monitored a pressure gauge, which showed that the injection was maintaining a steady 11,500 pounds per square inch, well within the tolerances. A rumbling was beginning, the result of the intense pressure at which the gold was forced into the earth, fracturing the structures below.

Then, suddenly, a great silent eruption. The ground beneath the entire mine shook, for just one moment, a single contraction that Dr. Cuba and even his adversaries above could feel. The entire Homestake area shook, for just two seconds, and then fell to rest again. There was no sound, just a single geological twitch.

Dr. Cuba knew immediately what this meant: the heart of dead King God Skyx had restarted. This was the first beat of a giant heart left dead for over 3,000,000 years.

The Sunken Gods were awakening.

And then, a voice. Not inside his head, no, but from below. Was it a voice? Yes, … but perhaps not. It was more like a growl, but one of a giant beast. Something nearly the size of a mountain, below the earth. The size of a valley, the size of a country. Perhaps larger. A moan, the guttural sound of a waking God, feeling energy returning to his body, waking after thousands of millennia. Sad, angry, desperate, and lonely—all at once. Then another sound, this one clearly a voice, now angry more than anything. The words it spoke were unknown to Dr. Cuba, as the language predated language itself. But these *were* words. The first words spoken by the dead Sunken Gods since before humans walked the earth.

The Work was successful. The Sunken Gods' hearts were beating, their eyes opening, their muscles twitching.

Homestake was only the injection point into their vast circulatory system. The Gods themselves might not be positioned below but might instead raise themselves anywhere on the planet. Dr. Cuba did not trick himself into thinking he would see the Great Monster, King God Skyx, arise before him. He might climb up from the depths of the earth in China, or in Central Europe, or even smash his way upward from beneath New York City. None of this mattered; only waking them was important. What they did once they arose was their will alone. Dr. Cuba would, at that time, present himself before the mountain of the dead and receive his Godhead.

And then, another voice. This one of a man, barely heard over the roar of the injector's furnaces and pumps and generators.

"I've come to kill you," the voice said.

Dr. Cuba turned. There, below him on the lower section of the platform, stood this strange creature who had insisted he was Dr. Cuba's "Father-Brother": the tall, black-haired creature with ivory skin and one red finger.

"The Gods awake! You are too late!" Dr. Cuba shouted, his voice carrying over the noise of the great machine. "King God Skyx is speaking. Breathing. The Earth will be shattered. Their golden blood is restored!"

The Homunculus climbed ever closer. Behind him on the metal walkway followed Thumann and Ximena, along with a handful of armed men. Thumann held the pistol he had taken from Ximena on the island off Miami.

"You're mad, Brother-Son. Come down from there! I will take you to our progenitor's laboratory. I am sure you can be corrected, your chemistry repaired. I do not want to kill you. There are only four of us!"

Four of them? Thumann thought. *There are two more of these devils?*

The great voice below spoke again, the earth shook. "The

Great Monster speaks. You cannot deny it. He rises!" Dr. Cuba shouted.

The Homunculus crept ever closer, now within fifteen feet of his creation. "There is no voice, Brother-Son. It is in your head. You are mad," he said.

Thumann gripped his gun — the one Ximena had used previously — waiting for his opportunity. *Should I kill them both?* he wondered.

The earth shook again, a violent contraction that shook the flimsy metal walkway, sending vibrations rattling through everyone on it. "You feel that? The Sunken Gods are sunken no more! They rise!" Dr. Cuba shouted, his face contorting with mania.

"You are fracturing the earth below, Brother-Son. The pressure of the injector is affecting the plates below us, nothing more. You are forcing an earthquake with your machines. There are no Sunken Gods, brother! Your belief in them is a result of your insanity. I can fix this, *we* can fix this, together! Come with me!" The Homunculus held out a hand to his creation, a look of desperation and sadness on his face. It was the first time in decades that this face, poreless and ivory, had shown any such intense emotion.

The Homunculus now stood within a few feet of his Brother-Son. Dr. Cuba did not move away nor recoil. If anything, he seemed happy to have someone at his side to share the moment. "On the contrary," Dr. Cuba said, still struggling to be heard over the howling chorus of the injector array, "I will fix you. I will present to you Skyx and Macapax. I will convince them to grant you Godhead as well! If you are correct, and we are not human, then our soulless nature makes us perfect for the world that comes. We will be gods, together!"

Thumann had also advanced, the pistol raised at Dr. Cuba's

head. But he was still too far away, and the gun was small, its bullets weak. He moved closer.

Finally, Thumann spoke. "Dr. Cuba, you are under arrest! Come down, the both of you, now!"

The Homunculus and Dr. Cuba looked down at Thumann, both sharing an expression of surprise at the audacity of this inferior creature interrupting their conversation. They promptly ignored him.

Dr. Cuba reached out, grabbing the arms of the Homunculus to focus his attention. "If you are my brother, then listen. Hear it. The voices are loud, growling, angry. Listen, brother… you can hear it, I know it!"

The Homunculus' face returned to its normal stoic state. "That is just the sound of the machines, Brother-Son. Nothing more. There are no gods. None in the sky, none on the earth. None in the churches, none in the plants, none anywhere. None in anything that is born, and certainly none in things that are not. Such as us."

"All things are born!" Dr. Cuba insisted. "And all things have Gods. It is just a matter of becoming them. The Sunken Gods created themselves, and then created their religion, before man could even speak, before they could barely think! Even you cannot deny this."

"I can, and I do. All things are not born, brother. Look at us! Created, not born. But all things die. Todas las cosas mueren."

Now the Homunculus grasped his counterpart, holding him in place.

Thumann was close now. He knew speaking to the mad Dr. Cuba would do no good. There was only one action to take now, but unlike when he shot poor Gentleman, this time he would aim

272

to kill. He would kill Dr. Cuba, he would!

The shot fired, but the pistol was too unreliable and again proved inaccurate. Now the bullet pierced the injector tube next to Dr. Cuba, venting it with great steam and violence. A spray of high-pressure molten gold was ejected sideways, shooting outward across the pit, onto the ground below. The hissing sound was a high-pitched scream, as if the injector array were writhing in pain. Dr. Cuba's eyes widened, a sudden sense of disaster upon him. But it was too late.

The Homunculus pushed. Dr. Cuba fell backwards, into the pressurized spray of molten gold. His body was immediately thrust sideways from the incredible pressure, sent flying off the platform and across the pit, and down, down. The body of Dr. Cuba, covered in gold, fell into the lake below, which screamed and hissed with steam as it met the hot metal. The gold solidified, encasing the melted corpse of Dr. Cuba within it. The golden statue of the God of Crime sank to the bottom, spewing vapor as it did.

Thuman and Ximena stared in shock. The Homunculus turned and began to descend down the platform, towards them. Thumann aimed his gun at the great man pacing towards them.

"Stop there. You're under arrest. I'll figure out why later," Thumann boomed.

The Homunculus ignored his threat, raising a single hand—the one with the red finger—to calm the big German. "You've won, Inspector Thumann. There's no need for this."

With a single rapid movement, the Homunculus' hand struck out, like a viper, grabbing the pistol and tossing it over the side of the railing. Thumann was now unarmed. Again, with a calm voice, the Homunculus repeated, "You've won."

Thumann stood firm, turning his right hand into a mighty,

hammer-like fist, but holding in reserve at his side.

The Homunculus continued. "Your investigation is complete. The heists have stopped. Your friend is avenged. The great Dr. Cuba is dead. His organization is in shambles, his crimes ended. Why, look," he said, waving his hand over the pit and the surrounding area, "much of the gold can even be recovered. Not all, but most."

Thumann's fist relaxed. "I've lost," he said, recalling Gentleman.

The Homunculus remained stoic. "Every great victory has losses. You know this. The War is ending, and your side has won that, too. But you suffered losses to achieve this. Nothing is different here. Your investigation is complete, the villain dead, the loot recovered. You will return to Scotland Yard a hero."

"No one will believe this," Thumann said. "They will think I am mad."

"Just bring them to the gold. That is all your people care about. They will promote you, hold parades for you. Don't tell them anything about soulless monsters with sunken gods and vast conspiracies. This is a simple tale of a powerful criminal brought to justice by the great German Brain, Heiner Thumann. With the help of his loyal assistant," the Homunculus nodded towards Ximena, "and the late Bernard Gentleman, who died in the line of duty."

The Homunculus grasped Thumann now by the upper arms. Thumann winced from his injury, but the Homunculus maintained his grip. Thumann knew instantly this creature was much stronger than he was. "Go home, Inspector. You have won."

The Homunculus then released Thumann and strode past him. He descended down the walkway, past Ximena, to the ground below.

"What are you?" Thumann asked, shouting over the continued noise of the injector.

The Homunculus did not answer and continued to walk towards his convoy. He entered the lead truck and drove away. One truck remained; the Homunculus' gift to Thumann, to allow him a way out of Homestake.

The vented tube lowered the pressure of the entire injector system, causing sputtering and spitting. The gold continued to spray out across the valley below, and into the pit, but with less pressure now. The generators began to fail, and the entire injector array succumbed to a slow, weakening death.

"Todas las cosas mueron," Ximena said to no one in particular.

As Thumann and Ximena reached the bottom of the walkway, the injector behind them fell silent. Rumblings and vibrations still rattled the ground above, to some degree, but the pressure below was stabilizing. No Sunken Gods would arise today.

Chapter 16: The German Brain

From his Father-Father's laboratory on Monito Island, the Homunculus rested within the copper iron maiden, using the time to meditate. His Brother-Son was dead, and word had come through his own network that his Brother-Brothers in Germany and France were either captured or killed, as well. A brief sense of loneliness entered him, but he committed himself to finding out what had happened. If they were indeed alive, he would find his brothers and free them.

Should that fail, the Homunculus reminded himself that he still could create new Brother-Sons, this time under improved conditions. The new laboratory equipment sitting in Leonard Port's warehouse on 110th Street would be shipped to a larger hidden location, even more remote than tiny Monito Island, allowing him greater chances at continuing the line with less risk of exposure.

The situation with Dr. Cuba was unfortunate. The Homunculus could not have imagined that his Brother-Son was on a religious quest, a notion that the Homunculus found absurd on its face. None of his Brother-Brothers had suffered such delusions. They used religion to obtain power and change the course of earthly events, but never with the misbelief that this would give them some supernatural reward in a mystical afterlife.

And yet.

As he stepped out of the maiden and slipped on a robe, he remained troubled. At the injector site, he *had* heard a voice, a low rumbling he could not translate. He had dismissed it as the sound of the machines, but intuitively, he knew it was something more. He felt a presence unlike anything he had ever experienced. A greatness. A great menace. A great power.

He climbed the ladder to the upper level of the chamber,

into the dingy and dark area holding the rusted tank of his blood/gasoline mixture. Standing at a small wooden table, he opened a drawer and produced a small oblong box. Inside was a hypodermic.

The Homunculus rolled up his sleeve and prepared the mixture. One part gasoline, one part human blood, and a third ingredient: purified gold in suspension. He filled the hypodermic, injected the solution into his arm, sat, and waited.

Inspector Thumann sat in his office in Scotland Yard, smoking a pipe with a fresh mix of Latakia and Burley. The smoke filled the room, but it actually smelled pleasant. He had just finished speaking with yet another reporter on the end of the investigation into what the papers were calling the "Insidious Dr. Cuba Gang." One headline read, "The Invisible Devil is Dead." It was as the Homunculus had predicted: the banks were happy to know that most of their gold could be recaptured, the public was happy that a villain was caught and killed, and governments were happy to hear that the wave of crimes had stopped.

Thumann had gotten some of the credit, but by reducing the scale of the story—just a madman criminal with a mafia-like network, brought to justice in the end—he wasn't granted parades nor invited to the opera. A few parties were held in his honor inside Scotland Yard, and he was given a slight promotion and a bit of money. He was happy with this, however, as he was never the sort of man seeking fame.

As expected, some of Thumann's superiors at the Yard were happy to step in and take a portion of the credit for themselves, and they received far greater promotions and raises. A few now eyeballed positions in Parliament, or the War Department, and were likely to get them. "Good for them," Thumann thought, puffing calmly.

Thumann's friend and superior, Dr. Brühl, was rumored to have a plan to improve his station at the International Criminal Police Commission and had left a message that he wanted to talk to Thumann about it. Thumann decided that Brühl could wait.

Bernard Gentleman now had a picture, framed in black, hanging in the hallway of Scotland Yard, alongside police officers who had died in the line of duty. Gentleman was the only non-officer to be included in this distinguished array, and this made Thumann happy. He hoped the Flywheel's Apprentice was sitting in heaven, relaxed and at peace, with Thumann's beloved Hilda.

Then, a knock on the door. "Come," Thumann belted, feeling content. Ximena walked in, bringing a stack of papers.

"They say we can choose what case we want," she said, smiling. "They're giving you your pick. There is an interesting one here, a giant madman in Prague causing terror. They call him 'The Golem.'"

"Hah! Nonsense, of course, but all of this is a nice prize, I dare say. At least, nice enough for me." Thumann leaned forward and opened his desk drawer. Inside were boxes and boxes of alfajores, shipped from South America. He took out a box, opened it, and held it in front of Ximena. She took one; Thumann took three. "And, I hope, nice enough for you, dear miss."

Ximena had agreed to come with Thumann to Scotland Yard, upon the promise of training her to become a detective inspector. The Yard put up a bit of resistance, claiming it was "unusual" to hire a civilian, and more so a girl from Chile whose first language was Spanish. Thumann won the argument by reminding the Yard's leadership that Europe had a Spain, too, and

Ximena's skills were sorely lacking in their building.

Ximena had no family left in Chile, other than distant aunts and uncles, and so had little to lose by moving to the United Kingdom. She genuinely enjoyed the company of Thumann, her great, smelly bear, and had found a greater sense of duty and personal reward with this new career. She was studying, on her own time, to become a full police officer, but the classes were not nearly as interesting as the work alongside the German Brain.

She played the role of his caretaker at times, such as now when she brushed powdered sugar off his vest, but it was done mainly out of affection for Thumann and, strategically, to telegraph that she was not an upstart. The men and women within Scotland Yard appeared more suspicious of this olive-skinned, black-haired young woman with a strange accent than they did of Germans or Japanese, and Ximena was no fool. So, yes, she would allow herself to be seen as an innocent, helpless third-world assistant for the great German Brain while she learned. And, because she knew Thumann loved her like a daughter-figure as much as she loved him as a father-figure, she knew he'd forgive her if she maintained this image... for now.

And, in fact, Thumann did know this, even if he never admitted it. He saw in Ximena Alejandra Torres Orellana a bright future, not only for herself, but also for Scotland Yard and every stuffy, pipe-smoke-filled police agency around the world. And, to be frank, he needed someone to brush the powdered sugar from his vest.

I am an old, smelly bear, he admitted to himself.

———

In November of 1945, just about six months after Dr. Cuba was transformed into a golden statue at the bottom of a lake, an

8.1-magnitude earthquake shook the Makran coast of Balochistan. The quake, along with a resulting massive tsunami, brought a final death toll of over 4,000 souls.

Geologists had little explanation for the quake, saying that there had been no activity of that sort in the region for decades.

The villainy continues in

The Three Heads of Dr. Cuba

www.drcuba.world

Author's Notes

DR. CUBA is the product of my desire to play inside the world of old cinema classics and serials. As a child in New York, I would occasionally get a chance to watch old silent films, usually on PBS, which required us to clunk-clunk the TV dial all the way around to channel 13. There I discovered F. W. Murnau's 1922 *Nosferatu*, Fritz Lang's 1921 *Metropolis*, and Robert Weine's 1920 *The Cabinet of Dr. Caligari*.

I went on to study film at university and found that being drawn to the "German expressionist movement" in cinema was not a taste, but a prerequisite. You are not allowed to *be* a film student if you're not enthralled by them. Such disobedience was no more tolerated than if you had suggested *Citizen Kane* was anything less than peak cinema.

Whereas most people were happy to settle on *Nosferatu*, *Metropolis*, *Caligari*, and Lang's *M* from 1931, I wanted more. In an old book on horror films—whose title I cannot remember—I found a blurry image of a man in black hugging a small child. The accompanying text said the still frame was from a 1916 serial called *Homunculus*, starring Olaf Fönss. The serial told the story of a scientist who created an artificial man, whose soulless nature drove him berserk. I read this in the 1970s, long before the internet, and the serial had been lost at that time; now, a portion of the serial is available online.

I then came across the 1947 book *From Caligari to Hitler: A Psychological History of German Film* by Siegfried Kracauer. The book remains mandatory reading for anyone interested in the subject, and it features even more photos from the films of the era. (You can still find it available on Amazon, with the latest republication date of 2019.) It was here that I learned of Paul Wegener's 1915 *The*

Golem and its 1920 sequel, *The Golem: How He Came into the World*. Once again, the theme of man creating artificial, soulless things caught my attention. The book also gave ample coverage of the elusive *Homunculus* serial. It hinted at something even more fantastic: the massive four-and-a-half hour epic by Fritz Lang, *Dr. Mabuse, the Gambler* from 1922. It would be a decade later when I was able to get a grainy, bootleg VHS tape of *Mabuse* at a film convention in New York City.

Once again, I began to understand that not only were there a great deal of "lost" films from this era, but they also featured themes I was personally interested in: the creation of monstrous life, soulless and tortured beasts, and ties to ancient mysticism. The fact that the images I saw were faded, black and white, vignetted, and blurry only made them seem even more mystical, as if the photos were never intended to exist in our reality at all.

More fantastic works found their way to me: Henrik Galeen's *Alraune*, which told the Homunculus tale from the point of view of an artificially created woman; Paul Leni's 1924 *Waxworks*; Murnau's *The Last Laugh*.

Soon, I found similar works from Germany's neighbor, France. *Les Vampires* was a serial that told the story of a ring of cat burglars. *Fantômas* serial appeared to mimic Lang's *Dr. Mabuse,* but in fact predated it, having been released in 1915 and based on books published two years earlier.

These properties occupied my brain and cultural interests for many decades. My attempt at comic book publishing resulted in the self-published series *Reverend Ablack: Adventures of the Antichrist*, created in the late 1980s and then given a run in the professional comics industry in the mid-1990s, published by the late Joe Monks under his Cry for Dawn imprint. (Whereas I drew the self-published version, the Marvel Comics artist Michael Lilly did the art for the commercial run.) *Reverend Ablack* was very much informed by the imagery of *Homunculus, Nosferatu* and *Caligari.*

As my career shifted away from filmmaking and into aerospace consulting, I stopped much of my creative writing. To keep myself sane while doing aerospace work, I kept my hand in writing but constrained it largely to whistleblower reporting and industry news. And, to keep my sense of humor well-exercised, I began drawing and writing *The Auditor* comic script for my company's website.

By 2024, the comic strip had become my only creative outlet, and it wasn't enough. I wanted to write something and get back into fiction. Then I saw *The Testament of Dr. Mabuse,* Fritz Lang's sequel to his original *Mabuse* serial. This remains one of the best films ever made; its sound design incredible despite having been made in 1933 … not a time when cinema sound was particularly advanced. Fans of that film will recognize some inspirations for *Dr. Cuba.*

I connected some dots: the worlds of *Mabuse* and the French *Fantômas* could well have been a shared universe. Both told the story of powerful criminal overlords who spread terror through their cities through an organized army of subordinates and complex plots. Both had quasi-supernatural powers, both were masters of disguise, and both were pursued by dogged, scruffy inspectors who were always one step behind. Both were roughly operating in the same period, in the same geographical location. Mabuse and Fantômas might well have been brothers. I toyed with the idea of intruding in this universe.

In March of 2024, I grabbed my tablet and scrawled out the entire plot for a book I would call *"Dr. Cuba."* I had created the character's name as far back as 2012, for an art project I was working on at the time. That never turned into anything, but the name stuck with me. It fit perfectly in this context.

In plotting *Dr. Cuba*, I concocted a way to create a universe where the villains Mabuse and Fantômas might exist (although they are never named outright), and where my own criminal mastermind might run amok, chased by his own dogged, scruffy inspector. The connective tissue would come from that elusive source, *Homunculus*, as well as *Alraune*. These creatures were not human, thus explaining not only their evil and intelligence, but also their superhuman abilities. Bringing together all the elements gave me a way to not only explain these villains but build a new canon around them. Dr. Cuba would not have been born; he would have been *grown*.

Thumann was a hybrid of various characters: Inspector Lohmann from Lang's *M* and *Testament of Dr. Mabuse* (Lang had already begun flirting with a shared universe for his films), Inspector Juve from *Fantômas,* and my own Father Frederico from *Reverend Ablack*. The name "Thumann" actually came from a character in an unpublished book I had written in my twenties, titled *GEV*, which also had a character named "Mister Vines."

I then surprised myself. Having not written prose fiction in decades, *Dr. Cuba* was finished only two-and-a-half months later. As you can see, it isn't particularly long, but that level of output was surprising even for me. I didn't stop. Three months later, the sequel was also done. As I write this, the third book is underway.

A few random notes:

- Each of the books contains a chapter named after a pipe tobacco blend from Cornell and Diehl. I'm a fan.
- The entire homunculus biology and birth cycle is fully mapped out. It's wilder than it even appears in this first

book.

- Tarot and mysticism will play a larger role in the future books. This world is Crowley-adjacent.

- Humphrey Bogart really did frequent the Roney Plaza Hotel in Miami.

- Empanadas *should* be baked, not fried. We're not savages.

About the Author

CHRISTOPHER PARIS is an aerospace consultant, author, satirist, and cartoonist. He previously wrote the comic book *Reverend Ablack: Adventures of the Antichrist* and led the comic book self-publishing Small Press Syndicate in the 1990s. His business management books include *Surviving ISO 9001* and *Surviving AS9100*. He created and starred in the satirical political podcast *The Mark Spittle Show* and writes and illustrates *The Auditor* comic strip for his company Oxebridge Quality Resources. His aerospace clients have included SpaceX, Starlink, Piper Aircraft, JetZero, and NASA.

Born in New York, he lived in Florida until moving to Lima, Peru, in 2011.

Visit the Oxebridge website at www.oxebridge.com.

www.ingramcontent.com/pod-product-compliance
Lightning Source LLC
Chambersburg PA
CBHW020416260626
47156CB00007B/2422